By T.A. Venedicktov

CHRYSALIS CORPORATION
Chrysalis Corporation
The Titan

Published by DSP Publications
www.dsppublications.com

D1737266

T.A. VENEDICKTOV

THE
TITAN

DSP PUBLICATIONS

Published by
DSP PUBLICATIONS

5032 Capital Circle SW, Suite 2, PMB# 279, Tallahassee, FL 32305-7886 USA
www.dsppublications.com

The Titan
© 2020 T.A. Venedicktov

Cover Art
© 2020 Tiferet Design
http://www.tiferetdesign.com/
Cover content is for illustrative purposes only and any person depicted on the cover is a model.

Trade Paperback ISBN: 978-1-64405-627-1
Digital ISBN: 978-1-64405-626-4
Library of Congress Control Number: 2019952429
Trade Paperback published April 2020
v. 1.0

Printed in the United States of America
∞
This paper meets the requirements of
ANSI/NISO Z39.48-1992 (Permanence of Paper).

Dedicated to B.L., a Knight, & S.C., a Vet and a Brother.

Both were taken too soon, too young, too unexpectedly—all those things and more. They are loved and missed every hour of every day.

If you need help, get it! Fight for yourself, because YOU are worth it. You are loved.

Narcotics Anonymous Hotline is 888-653-0269.

National Suicide Prevention Lifeline (1-800-273-TALK [8255])

Prologue

Saturday October 22, 455 MC
Zodiac Hermes, 1001 GMT
Juni

JUNI MATHIS yawned as he circled the *Hermes* back toward the *Zeus,* letting the *Ares* take point on leading the *Olympus* toward its security ships. He rested his head back and took in the vessel they all lived within. The *Zeus* was the largest battleship in the Chrysalis Corporation military fleet. The Corporation controlled everything from Earthside—research satellites, Pluto—and the *Zeus* was the flagship and symbol of their complete power. It also housed more than one thousand people, military employees and their families.

"*Hermes?*" Qyuin called over the comm. Along with being a fellow Alpha, Qyuin was a friend, although not as close a friend as Damion.

"Yeah, *Jupiter?*"

"We have twelve hours until our next Sims."

Juni chuckled, having a good idea where Qyuin was going with this line of conversation.

"Oh, whatever shall we do with all that down time?" he drawled, tossing a look over his shoulder to his Core. The dark-skinned man had his eyes closed and looked damn near dead, but Juni knew better. 108 was lost in the miasma of information known as the system. He would love to have some alone time with 108, but he couldn't voice that particular thought out loud.

Except for Damion and his Core, 47, aka Requiem, no one knew that Juni and 108 were in a sexual relationship beyond what a Fighter should have with a Core. The Corporation didn't care if you used your Core for sexual release; that was one of a Core's many purposes. However, to have feelings for the human beings that some viewed as nothing more than a screwdriver could get you in trouble. It could even lead to a court martial. Tampering with a Core's primary programming was not allowed, because the temptation to take them off their supplements and encourage freedom and emotions was dangerous. Juni had done some reading. Research showed that in the rare cases when a Core had been taken off their supplements and then put back on them, sociopathic tendencies had resulted.

Within the Corporation, hurting a Core incurred a slap on the wrist compared to the punishment you could receive for allowing a Core to *feel.* So they kept their secrets, and 108 and 47 could only be their true selves behind the doors of their quarters.

"I'm thinking we meet up in my quarters with Shamey and Rogers," Qyuin said, shaking Juni out of his thoughts and back to reality.

"Give me two hours to catch a nap and I'll bring the bottle my dad just sent me." Juni's father was a high-ranking businessman for the Corporation, stationed out of Juni's home, Lunar. The alcohol there was high-end—as was everything Father sent, for that matter.

"I'll try not to take all your money." Qyuin's laugh came through the comm. "Actually, it's usually Damion."

"He'll be back soon and take all our money, unless we get him really drunk first."

JUNI HEARD the comm click off and chuckled as the *Jupiter* buzzed close by them. Patrol was pointless since the Betas were always eager to get out. But Juni knew it was an excuse for the Alphas to put their personal Zodiacs through their paces and have a bit of fun. Alphas were the only pilots chosen by a Core. The choice was rumored to be made on strictly performance and scores, not personality. Cores and pilots had to work in sync to be able to pilot one of the ships built for them—elite killing machines when the right pilot and Core were paired. Juni had helped Damion rescue 108, and then in a day, he was chosen to be an Alpha.

Juni hadn't expected to hit Alpha status for years after arriving on the *Zeus,* but when 108 fell into his lap—almost literally—he was immediately promoted. Only Alphas flew with Cores. The Betas had Cores that were stationed on the bridge of the *Zeus* and only communicated through relays.

"Hey, 108." Juni turned again to look at his Core. His flight chair was back-to-back with 108's control chair, so he could really only see the top of 108's head, but he'd take what he could get. "We're supposed to be docking here damn soon. Anything you want to run through?"

"Negative. I have no experiments to commence at this time." 108's voice was soft, barely audible, and husky as if he rarely used it. And he pretty much never did. He always spoke with as few words as possible to relay information.

"Anything you want to do before the guys steal all my money?" Juni knew he treated his Core with a bit more appreciation than most Alphas did, and the change was because of how Damion treated 47, how he was beginning to see a bit more human behind 108's eyes. Damion had a dangerous protective streak when it came to 47. Hell, Damion had even named the Core, because he thought calling his lover by his designation number was too impersonal.

Juni had pulled back 108's supplemental meals, and so far, this had escaped notice of the other Alphas and Creators. Creators were the curators and monitors of the Cores. The Cores were fed meals meant to keep them emotionally stagnant. The idea was that the less the Cores felt, the more they could integrate, control, and manipulate the systems within the Zodiacs and other computers. Technology was cold and analytical; therefore Cores had to be as well. Juni didn't understand how it worked—hell, no one really did. Nor did they question it. All Juni knew was that in his experience with 108, having emotions hadn't affected his Core's relationship with the system in the least.

108 was silent for a few minutes, concentrating on the scans and all the intricate systems in the *Hermes a*s they made their way back to the *Zeus.* "As I will not be accompanying you to Fighter Qyuin's quarters, I am planning to… take a shower and go over a few simulations that 47 has assigned to me."

While 108 had come a long way since he bonded with Juni, he was still very shy, especially when it came to intimacy between them. It was as if he was constantly waiting for the floor in the Zodiac to fall out from below him, expelling him into the cold vacuum of space. Of course, so was Juni. The sudden sexual relationship between them had come as just as much of a surprise to Juni as it had to 108. And while he had developed feelings for the Core, it only made things even more confusing. So as with most things that Juni didn't understand, he ignored it and simply enjoyed whatever it was they had at the moment.

"Unless you have other orders, of course," 108 carefully added.

"You in the mood for some food?" Juni asked as they looped around to the open docking door. "We clear to pull in?"

"We are authorized to dock in slot thirty-six," 108 reported, and then added softly, "and yes, I should consume sustenance."

Juni ducked under another Zodiac and then dropped down to access their docking slip. "Want to finish off those sweet-and-sour treats Mom sent?"

A twitch of a smile flickered over 108's lips. It was easier for him to accept emotion than 47, for some unknown reason, but there was still a learning curve. "While the confections cannot be perceived as sustenance, they would be agreeable."

Juni remained quiet as the *Hermes* completed the docking process and his Core finished the sequences for shutdown. He pulled his helmet off and placed it on the control panel before running his fingers through his blond hair, pushing the sweat-dampened strands out of his blue eyes. When the ship's canopy opened, he reached out to begin his short climb up to the walkway via the ladder within the Zodiac. As his gloved hand touched metal, he pulled himself onto the platform. "Hurry up in there," he called to 108, stretching to relieve himself of the kinks in his body that came from sitting too long. "You would sleep in the damned ship if I let you."

"It would be sufficient," the Core replied as he appeared at the top hatch of the *Hermes,* soon joining Juni on the catwalk. He looked at Juni out of the corner of his slate-gray eyes, the smile twitching at his lips again. "But not as warm."

"I'm not sure what they do to make you guys like the computers so much, and I don't think I want to know." Juni waved a hand, motioning for them to start moving.

108 followed with his head bowed. "I believe you already have the answer to that particular question."

Juni only nodded in reply as they started the long walk out of the docks and toward their room. He remembered Damion talking about how Requiem was bred in the tanks. His friend even mentioned kids being taken from pleasure colonies at infancy to be made into Cores. Cores were apparently the Corporation's solution to poverty and maintaining population control. Instead of an overabundance of people, there were now less people and more slaves. Although the Cores weren't outright called such, that was how the general population thought of them. *Slaves* was actually one of the kinder terms used.

Juni's stomach knotted up tight as his thoughts wandered. He had grown up in the best area of Lunar, in the heart of the Corporation world, and had only seen the good. The Corporation gave them all structure. It kept balance.

It also made humans into Cores. Living machines. Emotionless, perfect slaves.

He let out a weary sigh as he walked into their room, wondering when he'd changed from an oblivious rich boy to a man who hated the very system that had given his family all that wealth he used to take for granted.

108 didn't speak until the door was closed. "You are thinking of something serious."

Their quarters were identical to Damion and 47's. One full-size bed with a bookshelf embedded in the wall at the head of it, a two-sided closet, bathroom, small two-seater table, a couch, vid wall, and of course, 108's capsule. But their room was much messier than Damion's. 108 attempted to pick up after Juni, but that had proven early on to be a fairly useless endeavor. Juni was used to having a maid who did nothing but clean, and despite his years in the military, that part of him hadn't changed. 108 had other duties to attend to and couldn't devote as much time to cleaning as the space really needed. Despite the futility, 108 attempted to tidy up now anyway, removing a few items of clothing thrown haphazardly on the small couch and taking them to the laundry chute.

Juni sank into the empty space 108 had cleared and began to remove his boots, shaking his head. "The more I think about all this damn drama with 47 and Damion, the more I hate myself."

"I do not understand. Why would you be displeased with yourself?" 108 questioned, walking back to the couch.

"It all felt normal. Seeing Cores pick Fighters, but the Fighters are the ones who call the shots. I grew up thinking everything was done to help. I never questioned where Cores came from or what you had to go through to be created. I was told at one point that Cores were people who had volunteered to become what you are. Another time I was told that it was a type of punishment chosen by criminals to avoid the death penalty or being shipped off to a penal colony." Juni paused and reached for his Core's wrist. "I didn't know what *you* had to go through."

The more Juni thought about the abuse the majority of Cores had to live with, the worse he felt. His father had believed Cores were soulless bodies with no emotions or desires of their own. He'd said they should be treated as the empty vessels they were, and not to think any further on the matter. Juni had done just that, and his dreams of flying had come true. But it had taken Damion saving 108 from a physically and sexually abusive sadist and then dropping him into Juni's lap for Juni to get what he'd wanted.

Juni had only needed to be the right friend at the right time, and now he was an Alpha.

"Sit next to me," he asked his Core softly, tugging gently at 108's wrist.

108 kept his gaze directly on the floor as he slowly lowered himself onto the couch to comply. "My previous... *history* was not any fault of your own. Additionally, it has been proven that an offspring's views are affected by his upbringing and the influence of his guardians."

"Don't say that around my dad. He thinks I'm too soft." Juni chuckled as he moved his hand from 108's wrist to the top of the Core's thigh. "I just wanted to say thanks."

108 raised his eyes to meet his Fighter's before placing his hand on top of Juni's. "What is your gratitude for?"

His previous dark thoughts dissipated. "I'm not sure. Surviving? Giving me the *Hermes?* Fuck if I know."

He was still confused about what was going on with him and 108. He had gotten plastered and slept with the dark-skinned Core one time. But then it happened again a few days after that, and now it was a semiregular occurrence. Juni came from a nice upper-class Corporation-loyal family. A proper spouse and kids were just expected. He had grown up thinking about grabbing that perfect girl and showing her off to his stuck-up cousins.

Now here he was, sitting in a Fighter's uniform instead of a tux and leaning forward to kiss 108 without even hesitating. He might still be confused about the nature of their relationship, but it wasn't going to keep Juni or 108 from enjoying it.

108's fingers twitched on top of Juni's as he leaned into the kiss, his body immediately relaxing against his Fighter's. In the beginning, on Lunar, he had been pliable to Juni's inebriated, fumbling hands because it had been what was expected of him. But then Juni, even in his drunken stupor, had informed him if he didn't wish to be touched, he could go free and Juni would never touch 108 again. It was the first decision, besides picking his own Fighter, he had ever been given the opportunity to make on his own. He had a *choice,* and giving in to Juni was a huge step that had not only gotten them to where they were now, but had started a positive change within him that benefited Juni as well.

And 108 had come a long way from that first night. He now knew without a shadow of a doubt that Juni would never harm him, would never abuse him, and never, ever rape him. Additionally, Juni would not make him do anything he did not want to do. He listened to what 108 had to say and made his own suggestions and observations. However, that's all they were, suggestions. 108 was his own person now, a odd yet familiar concept to him.

And he knew 108 cared for him too, as much as a Core could care while still on a small dose of the supplements the Creators had made to suppress Cores' emotions.

108 let out a long sigh as their lips parted, tongues sliding along each other's in a slow dance. Juni slowly stood up, pulling 108 against him for a full-body caress. The bed was only a few paces away, and they had enough time before he was supposed to meet the others for poker.

"Alphas, report to your ships immediately. Code 258. Repeat: Code 258!"

The loud announcement boomed through the room, rattling Juni's bones and making him jump straight up in the air like a startled cat before releasing a slew of curses. "What the hell is that?"

"The *Olympus is* under attack. Code 258 stands for Presidential Distress." 108 turned to Juni, a tightening around his eyes the only sign of his own worry. "The *Ares is* accompanying the *Olympus* to its security ships. It is the only Alpha Zodiac to do so, per the president's orders."

"Shit." Juni's heart leaped into his throat at the realization. "*Shit!*"

He slipped his boots back on with practiced speed before grabbing 108's hand. He ran toward the lift as fast as his legs could carry him, with 108 easily keeping pace. Five of the ten remaining male Alphas on the *Zeus w*ere already in the lift, each with his own Core. It was a tight fit, but Juni pressed 108 to his chest as the doors closed in front of them.

"Who the fuck would attack the president's ship?" Qyuin sounded annoyed, and his own Core was pushed into a back corner, keeping quiet.

"Don't know, but we're a good twenty minutes away from their location, and even if we push it, ya know it'll take at least fucking fifteen to reach them," said Juni after quickly doing the math.

"Even at maximum output on all thrusters, it will take seventeen minutes and fourteen seconds," Alan's Core informed the group in a low tone. He obviously did not want to upset the Fighter by correcting him, but knew the information was important enough to be announced.

Alan snorted, even as he patted his meek Core on the shoulder to let him know the update was appreciated. "What the fuck are we going to do?"

108 remained silent, his back plastered to Juni's front in the cramped lift, eyes directed toward the floor. "Rebels," he finally whispered. "47 stated that they have seen traces of an anomaly on the outside of their sensor range for several days now."

Juni's hands tightened on 108's biceps for a moment before the doors opened. He didn't even have to push; 108 was out and running, Juni running alongside him toward the large hangar bay. If the other Alpha Fighters were doing the same, he wasn't aware, nor did he care. "Damion and 47 wouldn't go down without a fight," he commented as they raced for the *Hermes.*

"If there is a danger to the *Olympus,* it is large. The *Olympus* has fairly substantial weaponry. To attack it would mean a carefully planned assault utilizing a much larger vessel. I agree that they will not go down without a fight, however…." 108 didn't have to complete the sentence as he led the way up the *Hermes* ladder to the top hatch, his fingers flying as he input the unlock code.

"47 installed that Impulse thing into the *Ares.*" Juni followed 108 into their ship. He slammed on his helmet and zipped up his flight suit, locking the air seal from suit to helmet with practiced ease. "108, that seventeen minutes was with all the safeties on the thrusters, right? Take them off. Get us there without getting spaced, but get us there quick."

"Removing the safeties from the thrusters will result in an overload of the engines. We would risk an imminent shutdown of the thrusters."

"I trust you to figure it out." Juni flipped on all the comms. "Are we ready to take off?"

"Affirmative. Thrusters are unlocked."

Juni reported to Control. "Alpha *Hermes* undocking and heading out to *Olympus's* last coordinates." He navigated his Zodiac away from the metal dock and then pulled up and raced through the shield toward open space. He flipped his thumbs over the speed controls, and the craft made a hard pull back before launching ahead at maximum burn, jerking the occupants with a whiplash whirl. "What's gonna be our ETA?"

"Approximately 9.8 minutes," 108 intoned as they pulled out into open space, thruster wake burning bright as a comet behind them. "We will be leaving the rest of the Fighters behind. This is not advisable."

"What? No faith in my awesome skills?" Juni could hear how flat his joke sounded, but he didn't care. He wasn't willing to wait for the other Alphas or his Beta team. "They'd do the same for us. Just tell the Commander it was my idea."

"There are numerous transmissions coming in from the other Alphas, in addition to an order from Control to pull back into formation. Should I terminate transmissions?"

"No. When we get there, I want to be able to report everything that we see quickly. Let them bitch. Have your scanners fully open."

"Acknowledged. Scanners on." 108 went silent for a few minutes as they sped through space, leaving their compatriots far behind them. Saving Damion and Requiem was worth any possible reprimand from the *Zeus.* "There was just a burst from the supposed battle site. I hypothesize it is from the Impulse Barrier."

"Next fucking seven minutes are going to feel like eternity." Juni's hands clenched tighter around the controls. He knew they couldn't move any faster, but tried to make it happen through pure force of will. "Will our thrusters be okay for evasive maneuvers, at least, when we get there?"

"I would not advise it. It would only increase the chance of a burnout." 108 continued to monitor everything around them from his deep dive into the *Hermes* system. From there, he was connected to all of the alerts and sensors that made the Zodiacs, and the Core and Fighter bond, an efficient and deadly combination. "There has been another burst...."

"Two? So close?" Juni frowned as he tried to think of the implications of two emissions of the *Ares*'s Impulse Barrier, one after the other. "Can you pick up how many enemies are out there yet?"

"There are two large ships, one approximately similar in mass to the *Zeus* and the other matching the specs of the *Olympus.* Although the larger battle cruiser seems to be absorbing the *Olympus.* As for smaller ships... because of the space over which they are expanding, I cannot make an accurate count at this time."

Juni looked at the screens in front of him, stars blurring as they raced to his best friend. His heart was beating so hard he could hear it thumping like a war drum in his ears, and he knew adrenaline was taking over.

"Five more minutes, guys. Just hold on," he whispered into empty space, praying the Gods carried his words. Their Zodiac was the *Hermes*—the fastest of the Gods, the Messenger. Hopefully the ship would live up to its name.

"Juni... the Impulse Barrier...."

"Yeah, what about it?" Juni turned in his seat. 108 sounded worried. His Core sounding worried scared the piss out of him.

108 continued. "There was another Pulse. Even with the modifications that 47 implemented within the *Ares's p*ower boosters...."

"Fuck." Juni turned back around and leaned forward until his helmet hit the navigation screen. "They'll hold on. We're almost there."

"I hypothesize that 47 took the risk of using the Impulse Barrier beyond what it was specified for to give Fighter Hawk an avenue of escape. While 47 is an exceptional Core, even Cores have limits. We are, after all, only human," 108 pointed out, though it sounded difficult for him to admit this. His businesslike manner quickly returned. "We are approaching the outer edge of the battle zone. Visual should be coming online."

Juni squinted into the darkness. "I don't see anything." He frowned, checking the buttons he pushed. "Dammit, 108! Shit. Motherfuckers, all I see is space! Why haven't we heard any communications from them? Open me up to the *Jupiter.*"

"I believe all players have left the field of battle. Communications to the *Jupiter* Zodiac have been opened."

Qyuin's voice suddenly boomed through the speaker. "Juni, you stupid fuck, what the hell!"

"Shut up!" Juni yelled, not having time to explain himself. "I don't see anything! I need you to double-check the scan area."

"Your own Core too fucking busy, or what?" Qyuin asked.

"108 needs to adjust my thrusters and look for 47's ping. 108, patch me to the Commander."

Qyuin growled over the comm. "Who fucking died and made you head of the Alphas?"

Juni pulled his Zodiac into a tight loop as they entered the area where the president and Damion should have been. "My best friend, jackass."

For a few minutes, there was nothing to see, but then they bumped into several pieces of debris. Debris that had the Corporation's logo on it and half of Damion's Zodiac's name—*Ares.* But all the debris was not enough to be an entire Zodiac.

"Patch complete. Commander Sandrite is online," 108 informed.

"Commander. The *Ares* is gone. The *Olympus* is also gone. No hostiles in the area." Juni took a deep breath. "Request permission to continue to look further?"

"Request denied. Get your ass back here, Fighter Mathias! You're lucky you're not going to be thrown in the brig for going off all half-assed like you did. You endangered your Zodiac, your Core, and yourself. The *Zeus* as a whole will continue to look for the *Olympus,* with help from the Presidential Security Team. Fighter Damion Hawk and Core 47 are MIA. And good fucking riddance." The last sentence was mumbled right before Sandrite clicked off.

Juni slammed his fists into his controls, and the hot sting behind his eyelids made him grow even angrier. "Damn him!"

Qyuin sighed over the comm, his Zodiac flying next to Juni's now. "Juni. There is nothing out there."

"Never thought Damion and his fucking weird Core would go out like that," Alan said through the Alpha channel.

"Just shut the fuck up, man," Rogers cut in as he pulled his Zodiac on the other side of the *Hermes.*

The comm went quiet as the nine Fighters stayed there to await the *Zeus's* arrival.

"108," Juni called out, only loud enough for his Core to hear. "Anything?"

"Negative" was the soft reply. "Juni… 47 would not have survived activating the Impulse Barrier three times. As we have not found any significant wreckage from the *Ares,* I would hypothesize that Fighter Hawk was captured by whoever took control of the *Olympus.* More than likely, rebels are responsible."

Juni's hands rose, but stopped halfway to the controls. Instead he pulled off his helmet, finding it suddenly hard to breathe and needing to rub his eyes clear. Then he turned off all outgoing comms. "Dammit."

He tugged at his hair with both hands. "We need to get to their quarters before the Creators do, just in case. Get me his mom's location. I'm not going to let her get a piss-poor sorry wave from the Commander and nothing else."

"Affirmative. Once we dock on the *Zeus,* I will start all sequences to initiate your orders." 108's voice was smaller than usual. "I am sorry."

"Thanks." Juni managed a half smile, but he kept his eyes focused ahead on empty space. What was life going to be like without Damion and 47?

Chapter One

DAMION COULD hear screaming outside the Zodiac's hull. He figured someone had noticed the countdown. The shrill klaxon of the one-minute warning was distant as he tried to focus on his breathing, on Requiem not breathing, the idea of dying coursing like cold water through his veins.

And then… nothing. Complete silence.

Damion raised his head and saw that the inside of the Zodiac had completely died, screens black, the countdown shut off by outside controls. He screamed in animalistic rage, his heart racing and all that controlled fear roaring through his body. He punched the back of his seat hard, and he would have tried to rip out the computer panel, but there just wasn't any room inside the vessel.

"What the fuck?" He looked out the front window and saw the president and others approaching with guns. Damion tried to remain in control as he looked away from the window and down at the unresponsive Requiem.

"I am not particularly excited about the welcoming committee," Damion muttered, still confused and pissed. He wasn't sure if they were going to shoot them now and drag them off, or just take Requiem to dissect him like some science project. Perhaps, along with high treason, the president got a kick out of that sort of thing. All Damion really cared about as he opened the hood of his Zodiac was if there was a chance to save Requiem.

As the top hatch of the *Ares* opened from the outside, Damion moved, not even stopping when he heard guns being cocked. He crawled farther into Requiem's space and pulled the cold man carefully forward, looking for a pulse or sign of life. Cables stretched taut from Requiem's limp body as Damion pulled him into his arms. The Core's head fell back and slid along the headrest. Damion couldn't feel him breathing, and his skin was cold and clammy. He had drained all of his energy, every last drop, into the Impulse Barrier to protect him. Damion felt a cold rush of anger and sadness. He should have done more or told Requiem how much better he was than Damion.

Then Jasper, who was the President of the Planets and the man Damion and Requiem were attempting to rescue, appeared above the hatch, his normally composed features scowling at the guards around him, getting them to back off, before he finally focused on Damion and then Requiem.

"Damn. A little too late. Well, there may still be hope if we move fast enough." His words were mumbled at first, but then he addressed Damion. "Hawk, I know you're angry and confused, and I promise I'll explain everything, but right now we need to figure out a way to unhook your Core from the locking mechanism of the cables and get him into Medical's hands."

"Give me a reason why I should trust you," Damion growled, not afraid to point a gun at the president as he held Requiem close to his chest with his other arm.

In response, seven guns were pointed at Damion's head, held by men with cold faces. "Because your Core is dead, and if you don't, he won't come back to you," the president told him, a pleading tone to his words.

"The ship needs power or else the cables won't detach from him, or you have to cut the lines." Damion didn't lower his gun. "And I stay with him the entire time, or I make sure the first round goes in his brain to scramble it before the next goes in me." He wouldn't let anyone use Requiem like a computer or worse.

"They won't detach from him without a code, so you'll have to cut them." Jasper nodded to the security man beside him, who reached down, his gun keeping aim at Damion's head as he retrieved a knife from his boot and handed it down to Damion, hilt first. Then Jasper waved his hand and the guards reluctantly lowered their guns, backing up only to be immediately replaced with medical personnel.

"Hurry, Hawk," Jasper urged. "You know if he remains that way much longer, we're risking brain damage."

After lowering his own gun to use both hands, Damion began to cut away the lines, but he found it difficult to get to the lower ones since Requiem was a cold, dead weight in his arms. He wasn't so heavy, though, that Damion couldn't lift the pale man up and out to the waiting medics when he was finally cut free.

Damion hopped out of the Zodiac after Requiem. He watched the medics begin their work on his lover, injecting medications into Requiem's heart, most likely stimulants to urge it to beat again.

"Tell me, Mr. President," Damion said, spitting the last word with obvious distaste. "What do you get for betraying the Corporation?"

"Betraying? No. Leading these people, yes," President Barlett replied as the medics rolled the Core away on a gurney. One man rode on it with Requiem, a paddle in each hand that he placed to Requiem's chest, pushing down repeatedly to try to reboot his heart and lungs. "It is the Chrysalis Corporation who is the real betrayer of mankind. Or at least a few key players have twisted the Corporation."

"Twisted is such a nice word, Jasper," a woman's voice purred. The redhead appeared at Damion's other side, and they followed the gurney. "Manipulated, murdered, connived are all other words that work as well. Along with kidnapping, drug dealing, and annihilation of innocents. I also do not know why you insist on trying to save the doll, Jasper. He's as good as dead anyway."

"Don't doubt Requiem, and he's not a doll," Damion growled. "And it won't be long until they look for us."

"Mmm, so the doll's string puller has bite," the woman mused. "Yes, well, they can look, but they won't be able to track the *Titan* moving away from them so swiftly. However, they will be able to track the doll's control device, so if the medics can revive him, they're going to have to remove that." She flashed Damion a toothy white grin. "Try to, anyway. Those chips have a tendency to blow up if you're not too careful, and getting them out is pretty difficult since they'll have to dig in his brain."

"Athena, be nice," Jasper said with a hint of warning. Eerily familiar eyes flicked to Damion's face. "I thought you'd be a little more upset, Hawk. You're taking this all pretty calmly."

"Calm?" Damion turned to glare at the president again. "Requiem and I just fought the last half hour under the presumption that we were trying to save your ass. We were ready to die for you, because that was our duty. But you sucked us in here, and this bitch keeps tossing insults around about us just because she's pissed off that we kicked the majority of her shitty pirate lackeys' asses."

Damion paused to take a deep breath. "At this point I don't care what your reasons are for betraying the Corporation, and I really don't give a shit about her opinion of us. Requiem is going to live. Until I see him open his eyes, I'd prefer that you both just leave me the fuck alone."

Jasper blinked as he looked at Damion. Athena was scowling and opened her mouth to say something, but Jasper raised his hand for silence. "You gave him a name. You named your Core," he said quietly as they turned a corner in the hallway, the gurney long out of sight. "Why do you care genuinely for your Core?"

Damion let out a sigh. "They're not numbers. I understand why they were raised the way they were, but they're still people. They're individuals. Requiem is very different from Juni's 108, just like I'm different from you. Besides, saying 47 all the time was annoying me."

"I don't think that fully answers my question, but I believe it will be all you tell me," Jasper said as they stopped in front of the medical facility doors. "I'm sorry if this is all very confusing to you, but I promise it will all be explained once you're more receptive to the truth. Our medics will try their best to save your Core's life. However, as for now, I must leave for a few days."

"The *Theia* is ready for you in bay three," Athena stated. "I will warn you again that it's bad, so don't come whining to me saying I didn't."

"I will keep that in mind," Jasper told her before turning back to Damion. "Captain Athena will be watching you from now on, and I'm sure she'll explain everything. I'll keep your Requiem in my prayers to the Gods. Let me know the outcome, Athena." And with that, he turned on his heel and left.

Damion watched the medics work through the large windows in the upper half of the doors. It was all he could do. He was helpless; he was useless. He was deeply afraid and still really pissed. It would be so much easier if he could just shoot someone. "Did you name yourself after a Goddess?"

"No, my mother did," the captain replied, looking at the medics through the window. Then her blue-green gaze slowly lowered to the gun clutched in Damion's hand. "You might want to stop doing that. You're making my security detail nervous." And it was true. Two men and one woman still stood behind them, eyeing Damion with suspicion.

Beyond the window, the medic eased Requiem off the gurney with help from his comrades. The holo-screen above Requiem's head showed an erratic, but definitely present, heartbeat. The severed cords still draped from the Core's body. Damion was reminded of the old dolls his mother had that dangled from strings. Marionettes. Marionette strings hung from Requiem's unconscious form even as a nurse plucked the jacks from him. They no longer gripped to his input ports, since there was no power sustaining them. The medics had cut away Requiem's flight suit, so Damion could see the patches they had stuck to his lover's ribs to encourage his lungs to function. The technology forced Requiem to continue breathing, even if his body tried to shut down again.

"I told you that everything hinges on if he lives or dies," Damion said, even as he frowned at the people crawling all over his lover. It didn't matter that they were trying to save his life. He hated it when anyone besides himself touched Requiem. "We don't have to fucking like each other, but right now, you should know that I keep my word."

"And what do you think you'll be able to do if he does die?" Athena let out a small laugh, crossing her arms over her chest. "This ship is nearly as big as the *Zeus*. There's no way you'd make it out alive. I doubt you'd make it five feet even, despite your impressive record."

Both stopped talking when Requiem began to convulse, his body arching off the table and against the onslaught of personnel trying to hold him down. Doctors yelled, nurses scrambled, a needle was inserted into his arm. As soon as whatever they gave him hit his system, Requiem's eyes shot open wide. He took one look around him, inhaled deeply, and then screamed. It was awful for Damion to hear his Core's voice—which was always so soft—become a guttural noise that echoed throughout the medical facility.

Damion pushed past Athena and rushed into the room as Requiem tried to free himself from the hands holding him down. "Get off him!" He knocked the men away before he pulled Requiem toward him and off the table, keeping his gun out while hugging his Core tight to his chest. "I'm here. I'm here," he assured Requiem, rocking him back and forth as they slid to the floor, Requiem eventually landing in Damion's lap.

Requiem thrashed for a few moments, then went quiet. Without looking up, he curled his trembling body around Damion, his arms around Damion's waist and his legs splayed along the cold floor.

"Damion?" Requiem's voice was soft, barely a raw whisper. "Damion, it hurts. My body burns." The fact that he would admit to anything hurting only told Damion that he was in agony. Requiem clung to his pilot like one would a lifeline.

Guns were still aimed at the two of them. "Mr. Hawk, I suggest that you lower your weapon immediately before I have to order my guards to take action," Athena advised through clenched teeth. "You're making my medics nervous. Currently, we do not wish to kill you; however, you are testing my patience."

"Funny, you seem to have a lot of nervous people around here, yet you want me to trust *your* men by putting *my* gun down first?" Damion let out a bark of laughter. "Your men first, then I'll lower mine. Then someone get Requiem something for his pain. After that, I'll give you the gun."

"We don't understand why he's in pain, fact number one," one of the doctors commented with a scowl, her hands opening and closing as they formed fists. It was obvious she wanted to help Requiem but had to get through Damion first. "All we gave him in the first place was something to calm him down. But if he had a reaction to it, then I wouldn't want to risk giving him something else in case he has the same reaction. We only just got his heart beating again."

When Damion nodded his understanding to the doctor, Athena signaled her guards to stand down. They looked at her for a moment, just to make sure, and then lowered their weapons.

Requiem continued to cling to Damion, his face buried in Damion's chest as he trembled and panted. "Drug. What drug?" he whispered. "React... stimulants... react, too many."

Damion locked the safety on his gun, then tossed it to the side. He stood up and lifted Requiem back on the table. "On the *Zeus,* they use immersion tanks. He hates them, but it's something he's used to."

The medics immediately swarmed the table again, the doctor barking orders. Athena knelt down to pick up Damion's weapon. Requiem stayed curled on his side, his arms in a death grip around Damion's waist.

"We wanted to get him stable first before putting him in the tank," the doctor said as she shooed one of the technicians off to prepare the tank in the next room. "He's going to have to let you go. His heartbeat is still erratic, and I'm worried that if he overloads too much, it may stop again. I'm guessing, from what he said, that whatever we gave him reacted with the stimulants and mind control drugs they would have put in his food. I'm sorry about that. I should have done more research. I haven't experienced this before."

"He's alive," Damion conceded. "As long as he stays that way, I'll forgive you." Then he turned his attention to his Core, petting the top of Requiem's sweat-dampened head. "I am not going to leave your side. I know you must be in a lot of fucking pain, but you need to go into the tank. You know it's the only way for them to fix you up." He didn't want to tell Requiem they were also planning to do brain surgery on him.

"He's not going to stay alive," the doctor growled, "unless he lets go of you now." Her gloved fingers appeared to itch with the need to tear the Core away from Damion.

"As you order," Requiem finally replied softly, giving one last quick squeeze to Damion's waist before easing away. As soon as he showed signs of releasing Damion, the doctor and the nurses grabbed him and pulled him away abruptly. He let out a small whimper, his eyes flying open to meet Damion's as they stripped him of everything but his undershorts. He flailed, trying to grab Damion's arm, clothes, anything, but he couldn't reach as they carried him away to the tank. "Damion," he pleaded. He seemed to want to scream, however his voice wouldn't respond with the level he wanted it to.

"I've never seen a Core fresh from the Corp show so much emotion," Athena said as she stepped up beside Damion, her eyes sliding from Requiem to watch Damion's face. "He seems scared, even."

"You'll never find a Core like him." Damion walked up to the tank and put his hand out to the glass, letting Requiem see he was really going to stay with him as the techs lowered the Core into the thick fluid. "He's the best."

Requiem reached out frantically inside the tank, his eyes so wide they were almost more white than blue as he placed his hand on the glass to mirror Damion. His nose was plugged with an air ventilator so he could breathe in the liquid around him. As soon as their hands met with the glass between them, Requiem's heart rate slowed to normal, steady. Requiem's eyes followed him, focusing on him for a few minutes until they fluttered closed, almost reluctantly. The tension in his body seemed to leave him, and his head fell forward as exhaustion dragged him down to sleep.

"Mmm, so we've heard and read. He definitely has some interesting abilities," Athena mused, her attention more on Damion's face than on

Requiem. "Like that damn weapon he created that stops our pilots in their tracks. I'm not sure how it happened, especially with your skills, but none of my people were killed. Severely injured, yes, but no deaths. Excellent, considering that you were shooting to kill and they were only shooting to disable. I've never seen a Chrysalis Corporation Fighter who cared about their Core so much that they were willing to die for them."

"He's *my* Core, not the Corp's." Damion turned and sat down on the floor, his back resting against the cold glass tube containing his lover.

"Mm-hmm," Athena intoned again, her arms still crossed over her chest, leaning to one side as she followed Damion's movements. "That doesn't explain your actions. I've seen Fighters throw away Cores like yesterday's trash, and others give them up in a heartbeat if it'll save their own skin."

Chapter Two

THE DOCTOR walked over with a thin screen, her eyes flicking back and forth over it before they rose to look at Athena. "We're not going to be able to extract the chip. Not right now and not without killing him. I have to admit, it's amazing how he used his own energy, the electrical impulses within his own body, to power the device. But right now he's too weak, too unstable to perform that type of extraction." She turned her head to look at Requiem, clinical in her observation of the nearly naked form.

"He calls it the Impulse Barrier." Damion ignored the doctor as he looked right back at Athena in a challenge. "And I'm not like other Fighters. I know he's human."

"The Impulse Barrier, interesting." Athena's eyes glazed over as she thought. "I haven't seen it from any other vessel beside the *Ares*. Why hasn't he shared it with the rest of the fleet? You would think it would be taken from him to save lives from us horrible, vicious rebels."

"And do you know how he feeds his energy to the system? That shouldn't be possible," the doctor added, her attention not wavering from Requiem's unconscious form, obviously thinking of possibilities and tests. "Is it something all Cores can do? I've never seen anything like it."

Damion shrugged. "I knew he was using his body somehow, yeah, and he was supposed to turn over the plans tomorrow. You try telling him not to do something when he wakes up. I dare you."

"Tomorrow? Really? How interesting, and also how fortunate." Athena's lips curled into a catlike grin. "And no, I do not believe he will listen to anyone but you, and I will not attempt to take away that security." Her gaze turned to the doctor. "Down, girl. I don't think looking at Hawk's Core like a pretty new toy to play with is going to get you any points with him, nor will you have any chance at all of studying him if you continue on your path, Lizzy."

The doctor looked at Athena, shaking her head slightly as if coming out of a daze. She gave a sheepish grin. "Sorry, Captain." Lizzy turned her attention toward Damion. "He should wake up in about an hour. We've programmed an accelerated resting process into the liquid, along with supplying his body with the energy it needs to continue on its path to recovery. I figured out that the serum we gave him definitely reacted to the supplements, causing his nerves to inflame badly. I do apologize for the misjudgment in treating him and causing him pain."

"Just get him fixed and awake." Damion ran his fingers through his hair, frowning. "But once he's awake it will just be hours until they track him through that chip, or worse."

The doctor opened her mouth to answer but was interrupted by the lights flickering. She frowned, looking up at the ceiling as if the lights themselves could explain what was going on. "That shouldn't happen."

"Lizzy, did you plug the Core into the system?" Athena asked with a long sigh, closing her eyes and raising a hand to rub at her face.

"Of course I did. It was the only way…." The doctor paused, and her attention fell upon Requiem. "Shit. Jonas, release the attachments!" she yelled, running toward her technician, who was near one of the control docks next to the tube.

Requiem's eyes were open and he was fully awake, looking around the room as he started to drain the energy from the Med Bay. He was also rapidly downloading the information from the main system of the ship through the cables connecting him to the medical terminals.

Damion didn't move, but now he was the one with the smug smile on his face. "He's in charge now, I believe."

Athena's eyes widened as Requiem raised his arms and grabbed the retracting cable that had just unplugged from the back of his head, letting it pull him out of the tank. Once above the liquid, he used the cable to swing and jump down to land in front of the console on the platform near the top of the tank. He placed his hand on the screen before the technician could do anything but stare in disbelief at the dripping man. The lights flickered again as Requiem pulled off the access panel on the side of the terminal with his other hand and buried his fingers in the wires, pulling knowledge from the system, along with bringing down all the lights except for the emergency ones.

"Stop him!" Athena demanded of Damion. "What the fuck is he doing? Does he think he can take over the ship from a mere medical console?"

"I will if my Fighter orders me to do so," Requiem replied, voice gravelly from misuse but steady.

"You okay, Requiem?" Damion asked. "You in the system all right?"

"I am below acceptable, but functional," the Core replied, his eyes now focusing on Damion. "Affirmative. I have activated the system. It is… intriguing."

"Captain! He's in the communication system! He's dialing the frequency for the *Zeus!*" the technician next to Requiem shouted. Then he pulled out a pistol and put it to Requiem's temple. The cold steel didn't seem to faze the Core, but his eyes shifted sideways to look at the man. He lifted his hand from the console so fast it was a blur, his other hand still buried in wires, and grabbed the technician's wrist. The man gasped as electricity ran through him, and then he fell to the platform unconscious, the gun falling to the floor below.

Athena raised the gun she had confiscated from Damion to aim at Requiem. "You stop him, Hawk, or I will." Three other guards brought rifles to attention, two on Requiem and one on Damion himself.

"Requiem, stop contacting the *Zeus*. Right now we're in a less than ideal situation. But do me a favor and download all personnel files." Damion gave Athena another carefree grin.

"Download already complete," Requiem reported. "Awaiting further orders."

"Dammit, Hawk. I mean it, get him out of the system or I will take him out," Athena hissed. "I don't know how the fuck he's doing it, but get him to stop. We brought you onto the *Titan* to show you the truth, but I will not hesitate again if he does not pull out of the fucking system."

"I'll order him to go to sleep and let your medics fix him, but he will also have your life-support systems in the back of his mind. But I'll only give him the order if you agree to tell me what is going on." Damion made a weary sound, the grin slipping from his face. "No more games."

"We were planning to anyway," Athena spat, her finger tightening on the trigger for a moment before easing off it. "Your little Requiem just had to jump the fucking gun."

Requiem's eyes were steady on Damion, but it was obvious to anyone who knew him as well as Damion did that his strength was fading quickly. He had taken what he could from the system to keep him awake and functional, but it was still too soon after his figurative heart attack.

"I guess we're just going to have to trust each other." Damion turned and gave his Core a warm smile. "Requiem, let them heal you. Don't fight them, but don't let them access your memories either. You did good; now rest up. They won't hurt me. If you wake up and I'm not here, then you can blow up the ship. Okay?"

"Affirmative," Requiem replied as he pulled burned and bleeding fingers from the cables. Lizzy came out of the shadows of the platform as soon as he did. She immediately slid a needle into the skin of his neck and pushed the plunger. The Core didn't have any time to react, his eyes rolling up into his head as he crumpled to the floor, guided carefully by the doctor so he wouldn't hurt himself.

"Well, that takes care of that," Athena stated, tucking the pistol back to its temporary spot in the back of her tight black pants. "I assure you, she didn't harm him, merely gave him a sedative. Now...." She paused, giving Damion a charming smile that didn't quite reach her calculating eyes. "I am sure you are hungry, and you really need to get looked at by medical yourself. I don't think you've noticed it, but you have quite a number of bruises from being bashed about in your vessel."

"If this is where I'm supposed to trust you and leave this room and Requiem unattended, I am letting you know now that if he does wake up and I'm not here, Requiem will scuttle your ship," Damion said. "But with the promise of a cold beer and a lit cigarette, I might be a bit more tempted to follow you."

The captain gave a small laugh, humor finally reaching her eyes. "You're asking me to risk my ship for a beer and a cigarette?" She shook her head before looking around for the doctor. "Lizzy, how long until he wakes up?"

"About two hours. I'm still trying to figure out if we can pull out the chip," the doctor yelled back.

"Well then, I guess we have two hours to get you a beer and a cigarette," Athena said.

"Great." Damion winced as he stood up. Some of his adrenaline had worn off, so the little aches and pains were coming to the forefront. He turned to look at his lover in the tank. A throb of pain and a bit of fear overtook him for a moment because Damion couldn't help Requiem at this point. The most he could do was find out what the fuck was going on and why they were here. "Let's start with that beer."

"Very well. Follow me. I have something a little better than beer, and I think we both need it," Athena replied. "You are released," she told the three guards. "Go get some rest and check in with your team leader. Thank you for your assistance." Immediately the rifles dropped and the men snapped to attention, saluting her. Then their cold expressions melted into warm smiles as the three comrades started ribbing each other and joking around as they exited the med bay.

Damion followed the captain—he really had no other choice. "How are you keeping a ship this big hidden?"

"By being very, very careful. Hiding behind dust clouds, moons, and also by avoiding the Chrysalis Corp fleet as much as possible. Plus our spies, of course." Athena took him down a long corridor to an lift. Once they were inside, she vocally directed it to go up.

Damion leaned against the lift wall with arms crossed over his chest. "Why did you bring us here? What is the president's part in this pirate ship?"

"The president is the leader of the rebels, of the revolution, really, against key figures in the Chrysalis Corporation. You're here because Jasper respects you, respects your and your Core's skills, and also saw your malice toward the commander of the *Zeus*. He wanted to see if you would join our cause, and I think you will once you learn the truth about who and what you've enlisted for."

"Last I heard and saw, you pirates like to set Corporation property ablaze, if not blow it to small bits. I am not going to support high-tech vandals," Damion growled as he trailed Athena out of the lift.

"Yet currently you're supporting murderers, kidnappers, and dealers in black market slavery rings. Not to mention helping the people who annihilate whole colonies who want to be self-governed instead of under the Corporation's rule."

"You have proof?" Damion was sure the Corporation did dirty deeds, but he wouldn't believe they were the worse devil to follow just yet.

"Hundreds of vids are available for you to view. Plus you can ask anyone onboard the *Titan*. Every single one of us has either been a victim of the Corporation or has lost a loved one to their atrocities. I'm not saying everyone in Chrysalis is bad. Look at the Cores. They're merely victims." She opened a door to a room and waved Damion in. "But a few very evil seeds direct the movements of the people involved with Chrysalis, all in the supposed name of peace."

"And so you want me to believe you're in some war for the small man?" Damion shook his head. "I know you've killed pilots and we've killed pirates."

"We *are* the small man," Athena insisted, closing the door behind him. "And while we try to avoid killing your pilots, we will also do what we have to in order to survive and make our point. And we'll protect our larger vessels at all costs." She motioned to a table by a window showing the black space outside.

The room was large and luxurious, but not overly so. There was a four-poster bed to the right, the red comforter looking warm and inviting. To the left was a couch and a vid screen, but on the walls were pictures—many, many pictures of many, many faces.

"Have a thing for people?" Damion sat down where she offered and hoped the promised drink was soon coming.

"You could say that," Athena told him, glancing at the wall of photos before she moved toward a cooling unit in the corner of the room. She pulled a bottle from a cabinet beside it and filled glasses with ice before moving back to the table. "Those are the people that have been lost while under my command, or people whom I've lost personally."

"You really remember all their names?" Damion sipped at the liquor, testing it before tossing more back.

She nodded. "Every single one of them." Athena took her own sip and then grinned at Damion as she slid into a chair close to him. "Does your sensitive palate approve?"

Damion shrugged. "It's good, but I've had stronger. Of course it was barely distilled and could clean an engine."

Athena took one small sip, swallowed, and set the glass down, leaving much more liquid than Damion had. "I assure you, this liquor is strong enough. It just hasn't hit you yet," she said with a mischievous glimmer in her eye. "You'll feel it in a minute."

"And the smoke?" Damion asked as he looked around the room again.

"Ah, my apologies." Athena reached down and took a metal case from a cargo pocket in her black pants. Thumbing the latch, she opened the case, revealed the cigs it contained, and held it out to him. She took a lighter from another pocket and placed it on the table. Her smile was soft, almost sultry, as she looked at him with appraising eyes.

As Damion reached for the lighter, his vision blurred. "Thanks. Now what?"

"What do you mean?" Athena replied smoothly, the coquettish smile still in place as she took another sip. The smile looked more natural than a scowl on her attractive features. Tendrils of red curls framed her pale face. She didn't appear like a woman who was the captain of a rebel ship, nor like the woman with such a severe expression who would have shot Requiem without hesitation earlier. She licked a drop of the liquor from her full lips, taking the lighter from Damion's fingers and lighting the stim cig gracefully.

Damion blinked again and took a long puff of the cigarette. "Well, aren't you going to try and sell me on this becoming a pirate thing?"

"There's time," she purred, keeping her eyes on Damion over her glass as she took another sip. She reached over, plucked the cig from Damion's fingers, and took a drag. "I must say, though, your record is quite impressive. Your scores are amazingly high, you have a Core that's quite intriguing, and on top of that, you're sexy as hell. Quite a combination."

"Are you trying to hit on me?" Damion pinched the bridge of his nose and sighed. "You were just threatening to kill me."

"Just because I was threatening to kill you due to circumstance, that doesn't mean I find you any less attractive." Athena laughed, refilling his glass with a clink of the bottle against the tumbler. "And in my defense, I was threatening to kill Requiem, not you." She handed him back his cig. "And just for curiosity's sake, when was the last time you were with a woman? I know there aren't many on the *Zeus* and that they keep you separated."

"A few years." Damion happily smoked the rest of the cigarette but eyed the glass of liquor a bit more closely this time. "Why are you asking?"

"Really? A few years?" Athena mused, the grin still apparent on her face. She reached over and took a sip of liquor out of Damion's glass, as if to prove it was safe. "And like I said, mere curiosity." She casually slipped out of her jacket, tossed it over on the bed, and leaned back in her chair so her black zip-up vest showed off her ample assets.

"Right." Damion sipped at the liquor this time instead of tossing it back. He lit another cigarette and tried not to stare, since this wouldn't lead anywhere. The woman was dangerous, and Damion knew better than to trust a pretty face.

Athena topped off his glass again before sipping from her own. She reached over, took a cig out of the metal case, and lit it herself. "So what made you join the Chrysalis Corporation?" she inquired, watching him.

"I didn't want to die working in the mines like my family." Damion shrugged, knowing it was the truth, and he wasn't ashamed of it at all. "Why did you become a pirate?"

"I prefer the term *revolutionist*," Athena replied slowly, rolling her tongue around the word. She shifted, her leg sliding in between Damion's seemingly casually, her knee resting against his groin. "And because the Corporation killed my whole family. My parents, two younger sisters, and older brother in a purging because we wanted to be independent." Her eyes darkened in memory. "I was sixteen at the time."

"How do you know it was the Corporation?" Damion smoked this cigarette much slower. He was still nervous, but the alcohol had kicked in and he was a bit more relaxed.

Athena reached over, grasped Damion's arm in one hand, and ripped a patch off his flight suit with the other, then tossed it on the table. It was the Chrysalis Corporation's logo. She continued to hold his arm as she looked him in the eyes. "They didn't exactly try to hide it. Starting with their uniforms and continuing all the way to their ships. Plus we have documentation, vid, audio, all from Corporation higher-ups." She squeezed his arm. "I know you have your questions, but please don't act like we're stupid people who've been duped."

"You captured us, so you are far from stupid." Damion met her gaze. "But the problem with wars like yours is there are always a lot of innocents killed on both sides of the fence."

"Capturing you was not easy in the least, but luckily no one was killed. We do attempt to disable vessels rather than kill people. Not something I can say of the Corporation." The captain took a long drag of her cig and blew out the smoke slowly. "But that is the nature of the beast called war." Athena squeezed his arm again. She smelled of amber and the sweet tang of the liquor they had been drinking. Leaning forward as she was, every time she moved, her knee rubbed teasingly over Damion's groin, but she didn't seem to notice the action.

Damion's brain began to function after a long moment, despite the tightening of his pants. "You know, I think you have a very interesting recruitment technique."

Athena's lips eased into a sultry grin, and she stubbed out her cig without looking at the ashtray. "Really now? I must admit, it's not my usual plan of action. But you inspire me to try a new tactic, and I have some other ideas. Perhaps you can advise me on whether or not they will work for special cases such as yourself. For example, I was thinking *this* might be a good plan of action."

Before Damion could move his alcohol-sluggish body, Athena had climbed onto his lap, her legs straddling his. Her arms wrapped around his neck, and her soft, full lips pressed against Damion's insistently. Damion dropped both his cigarette and his glass as he tried to push the woman's soft, supple hips away. How the hell did he get himself into this situation? Feeling good wasn't the issue. Damion just had this cold fear that afterward she'd behead him like some sort of praying mantis.

The captain ignored his strong hands, her booted feet hooking around the legs of the chair. She kept one arm wrapped around Damion's neck, her fingers tight in his hair. The other hand slid over his chest, unzipping his flight suit quickly and efficiently. Before Damion could react, it was opened down to his waist and Athena's hand had slipped into it, rubbing Damion between his suit and his undershorts, long fingers caressing him with skill.

Damion was stunned. He had been with women before, a lot of them, but none could pin him down like this. His body was instantly hard. He was also concerned.

"Mmm, so you do fancy women. I was starting to wonder," Athena purred. Her lips smiled against his as she took possession of his mouth again, her tongue effectively coaxing his in a battle for supremacy. While one hand continued to stroke him through the fabric, the other wrapped around one of his hands and moved it to her breast, where he could feel her hard nipple through the thin satin cloth of her vest. "Come on. I know you haven't felt one of these in a long time." She drew out the word *long,* slipping her hand to a much more opportune position against his bare skin, gripping his hard length in long, calloused fingers.

"I haven't, and it feels good, but I... I need to get back to... um... that... the room." Damion shook his head, trying to clear the haze of lust that was clouding his mind. "My Core might need me." He tried to stand up, but it wasn't as simple as that, since Athena was really flexible and his hands were being quite traitorous.

"Your Core is fine. He'll be asleep for at least another hour. I'm sure he'd appreciate you getting out some tension after such a rough day." Athena spoke against his lips, and before Damion could do anything, she used his attempts to get out of the chair against him. She quickly slid off his lap, grabbed him his suit, and threw him on the bed.

Athena was strong. Stronger than him at the moment, at least. Damion landed in the center of bed with Athena straddling him not a second later. She pulled his uniform off his shoulders so that it gathered a little below his hips. Unzipping her own vest, she revealed her ample breasts through the black lace of her bra and grabbed Damion's hands to place them where she wanted them before she moved her own hand to slide tantalizingly up and down his confined length. "My, my, how this escaped attention for so long, I'll never know. Your balls must be blue after so much inactivity."

The soft yet firm suppleness of a woman, of this woman, was intoxicating and a feeling he had not had in over a year and… and fucking Gods, there was a reason for that, a very good reason.

It was right there on the tip of his tongue why this would be very bad. A loud moan escaped his mouth as he had a sudden surge of brave stupidity. He sat up and flipped the woman over onto her back, shivering at the look in her eyes.

"I… him…." Dammit, he had to stop babbling like a fool! "Requiem wouldn't understand. I'm sorry."

Athena grinned, her hands sliding up his arms slowly, her nails caressing him. "You're right. He wouldn't understand because he doesn't feel the way we do." Turning the tables on him, she grabbed his wrists and used a leg and the power of her hips to flip Damion on his back again. "But there's no need to worry because he'll never know, and even if he did, he'd probably just blink as if he's disturbing us and leave. Waiting for you to give him orders once you're done."

The sound of chain and the soft snick of metal might have alerted Damion to something if he had been paying attention to more than his cock. The cold feel of steel wrapping around his wrists did. "Now stop worrying about your Core and let's take care of your needs." Athena toed off his shoes with the tips of her boots and dragged his uniform the rest of the way off. "My goodness, you're a fine specimen of the male species," she purred, her eyes hooded with lust as they roamed over his body.

Damion barely registered he was bound until he tried one last time to fight against his lust and common sense. "Not that I don't like to be flattered or—dearfuckinggods." His eyes rolled back when her extremely warm, wet body met his own. "I... his feelings could be hurt 'cause he... uh... he...."

While Damion was fumbling, Athena had rid herself of her own encumbering clothes and, just for fun, sliced through Damion's last remaining bastion of hope with a knife concealed in her boot.

"Stop worrying about your Core. He doesn't have any feelings. The Corporation made sure of that. I seriously doubt he'll give a shit. One would think you don't find me attractive, Hawk. Nor would one think you had the reputation that you do for wooing women. Now shut up and kiss me."

Damion looked up at her, baffled, and pulled at the handcuff again. "If you do that, I won't want to stop. And you're wrong about him and his feelings."

Letting out a purring laugh, Athena pressed her soft lips against Damion's, teasing him again by rubbing against him. "That's the idea," she whispered. Then the hiss of the door opening caused her to turn her head quickly, surprise lighting her face. "What the fuck? I locked it!"

Chapter Three

Damion

REQUIEM LET the door slide closed behind him, his hand on the panel beside it. Icy eyes took in the situation quickly, flicking from Athena to Damion, his expression not changing. He stood in the doorway in just the boxer shorts he had been wearing in the tank; now they were wet and clinging close to his pale skin. His white hair was plastered to his face and neck. His eyes settled on Damion, ignoring Athena. "You were not there," he stated in a raspy voice. "Although I did wake ahead of schedule." He paused, tilting his head in the birdlike motion he was known for. "Do you wish for me to leave?"

"He can break into anything," Damion whined. Now he was faced with his conscience—or the small part that was impressively still there. "I'm sorry, Requiem, but I seem to be handcuffed, and then… you see… we were drinking and…."

He never had to explain himself. This fucking sucked. Did he just pass up sex? With a *woman?* Was he feeling guilty? Dear Gods, why was she still on him? He let out another moan, this time in frustration.

"I thought you were told to blow up the ship if Hawk wasn't there when you woke up?" Athena nearly growled, angry that her good time was ruined. But she clearly intended to make Damion suffer for it, as she continued to rub her wetness against him.

"It was illogical to destroy this vessel if Damion was still present and not terminated. When I observed that he was not where he said he would be, I disabled communications, confined the medical staff in one of the quarantine bays, and used the comm video system to search for him. That is how I came to be here." Requiem's eyes never left Damion's tortured form. "I do not see the logic in apologizing to me. I am the one who follows your orders. I do not have any control over you. What are your orders at this time?"

"Oh fuck." Damion tried to rub his eyes, but the tug at his wrist stopped him. Now it was becoming annoying. Requiem just had to prove the sexy naked woman writhing on top of him right. Now she looked like she would fuck him and kill Requiem right afterward. He was sure she was capable too. "Look, I'm gonna need to get uncuffed from this bed. Now. Then we, I mean me and my Core, need a room." He wasn't even sure he'd be able to walk straight, he was so hard, but he couldn't fuck Athena with Requiem watching.

Athena scowled at him for a moment, her eyes near murderous. "Fine," she finally spat out, rolling off him and then opening up a bedside table. She took out a key and unlocked the cuffs from the bed. She did not undo them from Damion's wrist. She tossed the key to Requiem, who caught it deftly with a look of minor confusion. "Take your little doll and go. Your room is down the right side of the hall. The third door on the left. I will have my guards on the door." She said all this as she pulled on her clothes with angry, jerky movements. "Now get the fuck out of here before I decide to slit your precious Core's throat. And if you decide to come to your senses, you know where to find me."

She whirled around and grabbed Damion by the throat before kissing him senseless. "But I promise you, I'll do a lot worse than cuffing you to the bed next time. You'll enjoy it." She released him. "Now get the hell out of my sight."

"Out, yeah, great idea." Damion got up, feeling utterly disoriented as he tried to find his clothing. Deciding it wasn't worth his manhood or more of the captain's wrath, he grabbed what he saw, covering himself as much as possible before walking toward Requiem.

Requiem blinked at him, keying the door open again. "As you order." Taking the unsteady arm, Requiem led him out the door without a second glance at Athena. As soon as the door closed behind them, a growling scream of frustration could be heard through it. Requiem led Damion down the hall to the room assigned them, ignoring the guards and Damion's rumpled form as the door opened and he led the inebriated Damion inside.

Requiem

INTERNALLY, REQUIEM was studying his own reaction to the scene he'd walked in on. When he first saw Damion through the observation systems, a feeling of… pain went through his chest. He had attributed it logically to his recent heart attack. But then he actually saw Athena on top of Damion and his partner's obvious reactions to her. He saw the hardness of Damion's cock and heard his moans and the pain arrived again, along with a burning in his eyes. The burning was accompanied by a watery appearance in front of them, distorting his vision, and there was a feeling of… betrayal. Luckily he had acted as he should and pushed all of these odd feelings aside to go over later.

Requiem realized that the door had locked behind them, but it did not concern him. He could hack it later. "If you wish to, I am here now, and Captain Athena's want for your company was quite obvious. I will be fine here."

"Go back? I just fucking escaped! If I go back, I know what will happen!" Damion tossed his stuff on the ground violently. "I know you're a bit slow on the uptake, but didn't you care just a small fucking bit that she… well we… because of the shit she gave me to drink and… fuck! At least try to pretend you don't want me fucking around with other people!"

Requiem's eyes were on the ground, his brow furrowed in obvious confusion as he opened his mouth to reply to Damion's questions but couldn't.

Damion rushed over and slammed his mouth against his Core's, so hard that their teeth clacked as he began kissing Requiem with a passion he'd never felt before. He stumbled back as Damion knocked him off balance, and Requiem found himself slammed against the door, Damion's mouth still devouring his own.

The kiss caught Requiem by surprise, his body stiffening momentarily as Damion's tongue dominated his mouth when Requiem's lips parted in shock.

There was something different about this kiss. Yes, there was anger involved in it, and desperation, but also more warmth, more heat than Requiem had ever felt before. There were many other things that he just didn't understand. He gently cupped Damion's face with his fingers, the key to the cuffs still held within Requiem's hand, and idly thought that this was going to be a test on his newly healed heart.

Damion grabbed Requiem's hair. "Last year, fuck, six months ago, I would have had wild, messy, fantastic sex with that woman, to hell with loyalty." He kissed Requiem again, this time cutting a lip with his teeth. "You almost died, you son of a bitch."

After getting no response, he slammed Requiem against the door, harder this time. "Say something."

He winced as his head hit the metal of the door, his still tender body flaring with mild pain, the type he could deal with. He curled his hands against Damion's chest as he stared at the Fighter with wide eyes, blood from his cut lip dripping down his chin. He had seen Damion angry like this before, yes, but never directed at him. And what he said made no sense. First he lamented the fact that he hadn't had sex with Athena; then he was pissed that Requiem almost died, and then he wanted Requiem to respond. Requiem had no idea what Damion wanted him to say. And he was so stunned by Damion's violent actions that his brain couldn't piece together a sentence.

"I apologize," he finally replied in a voice that was barely above a whisper, ragged from misuse. "But I honestly do not know what you wish me to say. I do not know if you want me to apologize for disturbing you or apologize for my actions on the *Ares* that resulted in my near fatality."

He paused for a moment, but then quickly spoke up again when it looked as if Damion was merely becoming angrier. "And while it is your prerogative as to whom you have intercourse with, I did... *do* feel what I believe is called... hurt... by the events I witnessed. I have always believed that your actions with me were perhaps a matter of convenience, due to there being no available females present. I do not blame you for participating with the captain in sex of a type that you prefer. But I cannot lie to you... it did feel... odd."

"Odd?" Damion let out a loud bark of a laugh that sounded a bit unhinged. "Odd? It's something, I suppose, but not enough to make this mess seem any better."

He looked at his wrist and the dangling cuff. "I am losing my fucking mind, but I know what I want. Give me the key to the cuff."

Slowly, not wanting to make any sudden movements, Requiem held up the key. His eyes didn't leave Damion's face. He didn't quite understand what Damion had planned, and he was actually a little afraid of him at the moment.

Damion unlocked the cuff connected to his wrist. "You always muddle things up. My damn life was on fucking schedule, and then *you!*"

He flung the handcuffs against the wall above the bed and then grabbed Requiem's shoulders and kissed him.

He dragged Requiem over to the bed and pushed him down roughly on the queen-size mattress. "I hope you're feeling well enough for happy-we're-both-not-dead sex."

Requiem flipped over on his back as soon as his body finished bouncing on the large bed. His eyes were wide as he scrambled backward. He wasn't really trying to get away from the angry man, but he was definitely frightened now. And hurt. Damion's words caused pain in his chest. Caused his eyes to blur with that strange water again. "I… apologize. I did not mean to disturb your life."

"I was scared. I'm glad you stopped us." He bent down to resume kissing Requiem.

Requiem's eyes stayed open, a bit of fear still in him as he kissed him back. He was pushed up against the headboard and didn't move so as not to make the man angrier. He just didn't know what Damion wanted from him.

Damion pulled the damp boxers off Requiem's hips and then legs, then tossed them to the floor. He pulled away when Requiem kept lying there like a cold, broken doll. "What is it?" he growled.

Licking his split lip and effectively smearing blood along it, Requiem hesitated for a moment before replying. "You are angry, and I do not know what I have done to upset you. I have tried to answer your inquiries, but this only seems to make you angrier."

"See, this is what I mean." Damion punched the bed, causing them both to bounce. "I am trying to get out this frustration. Do you know how long I've had this hard-on?" A flash of sanity appeared in his eyes. "Wait, you're not still going to die, are you?"

"Approximately thirty-three minutes," Requiem replied automatically, and then frowned slightly at Damion's change of subject. "There is still a possibility of death if the chip is not removed. But at this time, there is no danger."

"I really want to throttle you, but I'm too happy you're not going to die on me…." Damion opened the built-in drawers by the bed to find some lotion. "You're taking responsibility!"

"But I do not know what I have done," Requiem said, confused and still frightened by Damion. He swallowed the lump in his throat. "If you wish to… throttle me, I will not stop you."

"What the hell are you going on about?" Damion spat. "When have I ever hit you?"

"You have never hit me. Oddly, you have caused me pain in other ways. But you stated 'throttle,' which is a synonym of strangulation. Nothing about hitting me," Requiem replied honestly, the movement of his lips causing another trickle of blood to drip down his chin. "I am merely saying you have the right to do with me as you wish."

"Look, Requiem. I am in no mood or state of mind to be having a conversation like this. I don't know what the hell is going on anymore! Unless you want me to go back to her, you need to start showing me that you want me here!"

"Why would I want you to go away?" Requiem inquired quietly. "I am merely saying that I am yours to do with as you wish. If you need to use me to get out your frustration, do so."

"You know, for this once, I don't care if you don't mean that." Damion found the handcuffs he had thrown earlier and used them to bind Requiem to the headboard as Athena had done to him. He leaned down and kissed Requiem again, grinding their hips together.

Requiem looked at the cold steel around his wrists in surprise, but Damion's kiss forced his head to turn. His hands fisted and pulled against the cuffs, and he gasped against Damion's mouth at the burning contact of Damion's groin pressing against his own, sending sparks of pleasure through his body.

Damion kissed and bit his way down Requiem's neck, leaving a trail of bruises. Requiem let out a whimpering gasp before biting his abused lip to prevent even more noises from escaping. His body was tense, trembling from the effort of trying not to squirm and the pleasure/pain of Damion's mouth on his cold skin.

Damion moved back up to kiss Requiem with ravenous desire.

Forgetting about the cuffs, Requiem attempted to bring his hands down to touch Damion's face, but he was thwarted by the cold bite of metal into his skin. Instead, he merely raised his head so he could battle with Damion's tongue properly, taking pleasure in the hot wetness. He still didn't know what Damion wanted from him besides sex, but if that was what it took to calm the man down, Requiem was happy to oblige.

Damion grabbed the lotion he had found on the bedside table and sat back on his heels. He poured a generous amount into his palm and pressed two fingers against Requiem's tight entrance. "Try and bear with it. I'll do my best not to hurt you."

Nodding, Requiem idly thought that it was a little too late for that. Damion's earlier words were still sitting like a weight in his chest, and his lip and head still throbbed slightly. But he would comply with whatever Damion wanted. And *this* was something Requiem had no problem agreeing to, because he wanted it just as badly. His fingers unclenched and wrapped around the chains of the handcuffs, gripping tightly.

Damion pushed his fingers inside, quickly stretching him without his normal finesse. "How's this?"

Requiem bit down harder on his lip, his eyes squeezing shut from the burning pain. Whatever Damion was using did not help much in the way of making the stretch easier. But he had dealt with much worse in the past, like no lubrication at all. "Acceptable," he finally replied softly, his tone tense.

"I like it better when you just moan, so I guess it still hurts." Damion didn't stop scissoring his fingers.

"This is not about my release. It is about you relieving your frustrations. Do not worry about me," Requiem replied after a while, once he thought he could do so without inflection in his voice. The pain had lessened, and Damion's ministrations were becoming pleasurable. His head fell back on the pillow, his sore, abused lungs working rapidly to bring in air while Damion's fingers were inside of him.

"See, when you say shit like that it can really ruin my mood." Damion pulled Requiem's cut lip into his mouth and sucked on the mostly closed wound for a few seconds. "I was ready to die with you, and you were going to leave me behind."

Damion's actions caused the cut to start throbbing again, and Requiem opened his eyes to look at him. "I did not, and do not, want you to die. Why did you not retreat while there was an opening?" This was the question that had been bothering him. "And I would never leave you behind. I do not understand what you mean."

"Why didn't I retreat? Do I seem like the retreating kind?" Damion pushed his fingers deeper, trying to find that firm bud of nerves that he knew would make his Core shut up. "If you don't want me to die, does that mean you're finally feeling something for me that is more than just blind loyalty?"

Requiem let out a loud gasp that fell into a low moan as Damion found what he was searching for, sending heat zipping through his nerves. Requiem pulled against his bindings, not even feeling the metal bite into his skin because of the hot pleasure that wrapped around his spine. "My feelings?"

He didn't know how to respond to Damion's question. He honestly didn't know what he was feeling, so he didn't have the ability to explain it. "I no longer feel loyal to you merely because of programming. I have never wanted you to be terminated, and I did what I had to do in order for you to survive. Not just to report what had happened to the Chrysalis Corporation, but because I needed you to live even if I perished."

"That's the only reason I tried to hold her off." Damion gave him another searing, demanding kiss as he removed his fingers from Requiem's body so he could slick his very hard cock with the insubstantial lotion.

Gasping against Damion's mouth, Requiem arched his sensitive body at the loss of those stimulating digits. "I do not understand. What reason?"

"You keep getting under my fucking skin and driving me insane." Damion chuckled darkly as he pulled Requiem's left leg up and over his shoulder so he could finally press inside his tight body.

Requiem let out a soft scream as Damion slid inside him. While Damion had attempted to prepare him thoroughly, his fingers just didn't match the width of Damion himself, and the lotion he was using to slick his way wasn't meant to be used in this capacity. Burning pain flared up his spine, making him almost oblivious to how he was cutting his own wrists by pulling too hard on the cuffs. He knew it would get better, it always did with Damion, but for now, his body clenched down tightly on the Fighter.

As soon as he'd quieted, there was a knock on their locked door, loud and demanding. "Everything all right in there?" one of the guards questioned.

"We'll be fine," Damion growled. "Requiem... breathe."

"Any more screams and we're coming in," the guard grumbled, and then there was silence from the other side of the door once again. It was amazing that when Requiem was being slammed into the portal they hadn't come to check, but one quiet scream and these guys were bothering them.

"I... apologize," Requiem said, trying to take deep breaths and relax. His whole form trembled from the tension and the slowly disappearing burn. He focused on Damion's eyes, trying to ground himself.

"That's better." Damion slowly pulled out just a few inches before pushing his body forward again. "Gods yes, that feels good."

Moving his right leg, Requiem wrapped it around Damion's waist, raising his hips farther off the bed so it would be easier for Damion. With his other leg over Damion's shoulder, he was practically folded in half, but he didn't mind in the least. He gasped in pleasure this time as Damion found that spot inside him that made him tremble. Requiem moved his hips slightly, meeting Damion's thrusts as best he could.

He began to move a bit faster and harder. The sound of skin slapping against skin and the smell of sex filled the room, creating harmony with Requiem's muffled pants and Damion's moans. Requiem's eyes were only half open, but he wondered at Damion's expression, which looked feral as he continued to release his anger and prove that Requiem was still alive underneath him. It was a punishment, in that Requiem couldn't wrap his arms around the Fighter and in the ferocity with which Damion was taking him. And it was also a proving of ownership.

Requiem whimpered, his body straining against the cuffs as heat started in his groin and began to blaze its way through his body, promising him oncoming ecstasy. His icy eyes squeezed closed and his head tipped back as his pants increased.

Damion surged forward so his tongue could reach the trails of blood on Requiem's arms and wrists. Something about Damion lapping up his blood—perhaps the warmth of his mouth, the scrape of his teeth, or just the fact that Damion was taking a part of him inside his own body— stirred something within Requiem. A gasp strangled his throat and his body stiffened, his back arching as white sparked across his vision and he came onto both their stomachs and chests.

Damion chuckled as he looked down into Requiem's pleasure-filled, flushed face. "That was fast, but I hope you know I'm not done yet."

All Requiem could do was swallow, trying to get moisture in his dry mouth as he nodded. It wasn't like he could ignore the still hard, throbbing length inside his sensitive body. It intrigued some part of Requiem to see his blood smeared on Damion's mouth and the near-mad gleam in the dark eyes looking down on him. He didn't dwell on it, but instead tried to steel himself against his lover's next onslaught to his twitching and trembling body, now hypersensitive from his recent orgasm.

Damion's hips continued their brutal pace as he swooped down to ravish Requiem's panting mouth.

Requiem let out a brief, soft scream as Damion's assault continued, his body flaring with additional pleasure. Luckily Damion's mouth muffled the noise so that it wouldn't alert the guards at the door. He continued to struggle against his bonds, trying unsuccessfully to force his hands down to grab Damion's shoulders, but only causing the metal to bite deeper into his ravaged skin. He didn't even feel it, couldn't feel anything beyond the ecstasy that Damion was inspiring in his body, pushing him past a threshold he didn't know he had.

Damion reached out and grabbed the headboard for leverage. Requiem could hear how lewd their bodies sounded, the sounds of pure enjoyment escaping Damion's lips, then a roar of ecstasy as he came.

Biting his lip against his own whimpers of pleasure, Requiem felt the hot come fill him, connecting them just as his blood in Damion's body did. Unexpectedly, that feeling caused another hot wash of pleasure to pulse through his body as he came again. His eyes squeezed shut, tears leaking down his face as he let out his own muffled scream. His lip split open again as he bit down on it hard to stifle his own surprised, bliss-filled outburst.

Chapter Four

Damion

DAMION WAS a shivering, sweaty mass of skin. He licked his lips as he looked at the mess between them. Damion grabbed the small key and freed one of Requiem's hands, but he was too fucking tired to undo the other. He fell to his side, wincing as his cock slipped out of Requiem's warm body at an odd angle. "Fuck."

Damion was a bit saddened by the marks left by the medics. Requiem's chest was mottled with bruises from the contraptions on his chest and red burn marks from the adhesive devices used to restart his heart and lungs. It had been one hell of a day. He wanted to hold his lover and feel everything in the world was right for a few damn hours.

Seconding the wince and punctuating it with a gasp, Requiem continued to tremble with aftershocks. His eyes were glazed and looking at the ceiling as he panted, not even noticing when his hand fell free above his head. He licked his crimson-stained lips, swallowing thickly. "May I assume that your frustrations are thoroughly appeased at this time?" he whispered, his voice even raspier now from the abuse his throat took. If Cores had a sense of humor, this might have been considered a joke.

Damion chuckled, wiping his sweaty brow with the back of his hand. "Yeah, for the moment."

Requiem let out a whoosh of air, his eyes fluttering closed. "That is good. I do not believe I could handle your frustrations again, not for a little while." He turned his head away from Damion as he sat up, trying to hide the wince as his arm lifted from its position to fall at his side. A pop from the abused joint was audible.

Damion sat up and rolled his neck, sighing in relief as he felt a sudden release, which allowed it to move with more ease. "I guess we should worry about them sneaking in and killing us in our sleep, but that can wait until we get a shower."

"I have already keyed the lock so they will not be able to enter unauthorized," Requiem replied, the cuff still around his one wrist clanking as he moved to the edge of the rumpled bed and threw his legs over the side.

"Good." Damion stood and turned to crack his back, then looked over at Requiem. "You going to be able to make it to the shower?"

"That is unknown at this time." The Core attempted to stand, but slid to the floor rubbing his unfocused eyes. "Unfortunately, I believe the answer at this time is negative. If you wish to partake of a shower, I will wait here for now."

"Right," Damion slurred, voice thick with sarcasm as he walked over to pick Requiem up. "This is becoming a habit."

"Only because you made it so," Requiem said, wincing. "And I do believe I am not fully recovered from my temporary termination."

"If you mean nearly fucking dying, I understand that." Damion walked them easily to the bathroom that was connected to their room. In the back of his mind he was glad that the *Titan* didn't have communal bathrooms. The bathroom was cramped for space, and Requiem was able to press close.

Requiem closed his eyes and turned his face into Damion's neck, taking deep breaths. He was silent for a few minutes before speaking in a soft voice. "I apologize for 'muddling' up your life. It was not my intention to do so."

"Neither one of us planned this." Damion reached in and turned on the water, managing to balance his lover in his arms as he did so.

Requiem didn't respond.

"Here, this should be warm enough now." Damion slowly let Requiem's feet touch the floor while still holding the pale man's upper body for support.

Requiem hissed through his teeth as the hot water ran over his wounds. "Thank you," he said in a voice that could barely be heard over the hiss of the shower.

"Not a problem." Damion smiled and held Requiem close, glad to feel his lover's body warming in his arms. "What a fucking day."

Requiem wrapped his trembling arms around Damion's waist, the dangling cuff still attached to his wrist clanking dully against the tile as he laid his head on Damion's shoulder.

Damion chuckled, but his amusement was cut short when he saw the raw marks on Requiem's wrists left from his struggle against the cuffs. He had taken it a step too far. He should have stopped himself even if Requiem had pissed him off. He needed to control all of these highs and lows. He was getting whiplash from his own emotional responses. He cared for Requiem, but was this caring the love Requiem deserved? He had never been in a relationship long enough to know if he was a complete asshole all the time or only now. How could he say he wanted to save Requiem, then become no better than the ones who abused him on the *Zeus?* How had his life become so damn complicated?

Requiem lifted his head, opening bleary eyes to look at Damion. "What is wrong?" he asked.

"You're scared?" Damion asked with a frown. "Why?"

"You are angry again," the Core explained. "I still do not know why you became angry in the first place, and I do not want to risk angering you further."

Damion rubbed his forehead with the heel of his hand. "I don't want you to act like a battered woman. But this is my fault, again. Always my fault."

Requiem tilted his head slightly, obviously not understanding. He eased himself to a straighter position, nearly falling as his weak legs caused his feet to slip on the tile underneath. He caught himself by grabbing a bar in the tiled wall, the metal of the handcuff clanking against it loudly. "I apologize."

"Stop fucking apologizing if you don't mean it," Damion growled in frustration, pulling Requiem close again. "Here, let me wash your hair."

"But I do," Requiem stated as he fell against Damion's slick body. "I cannot lie to you."

"You can damn well try to die on me!" Damion snapped as he lathered up the man's pale hair a little more violently than he meant to. "Seriously, Requiem, never do that again. If the ship is going down, we're both going with it."

Requiem bowed his head. "Word needed to get back to the *Zeus,* and it was the only way to open a window in order for that to be conceivable. Besides, you have already said that I have disturbed your life, that everything would have been better if I did not have a hand in it. My death would make that possible for you." His words were quiet but had a touch of his normal unemotional coldness—as if protecting himself from a hurtful or disappointing response from Damion.

"You are the stupidest man I know some days." Damion urged the Core under the spray to remove the lather before continuing. "Yes, you really make my life more difficult on days, but I never remember saying I minded so much that I wanted you to die. Fuck *Zeus*. They could have figured out we were under attack and the president was taken, don't you think? You would have left me alone. I know you're pretty hollow when it comes to feelings, but if you keep saying this 'you're better off without me' bullshit, I might lose it. I want you in my life, and that's my decision."

"Why?" Requiem questioned. "I acknowledge why I want you in my life. But I do not understand why you are adamant about having me in yours. And while I do not have feelings the same way you do, I am beginning to notice… that I am not as emotionally detached as I used to be. From that, I have learned the meaning of fear."

"Because you're Requiem. Because I act cold, but when you're around I feel so much. Because for some reason when she was on me, I knew I'd feel guilty because you'd be hurt." Damion sighed. "Is that enough?"

"I think perhaps I was hurt," Requiem replied. He stepped out of the way so Damion could get under the spray, keeping one hand on Damion's arm for balance. "I do not know what the emotions are that I believe I am starting to feel. It is very… disconcerting."

Damion quickly washed his own body and hair. "Well, you'll feel more now that you can't have your gruel."

"Mmm." Requiem's gaze slid to the bottom of the tiled shower. Not only did he have to concern himself with blocking the signal of the chip in his brain, he also had to monitor his reaction to not having the stimulants in his system anymore. There hadn't been a chance for him to wean himself off them.

Damion frowned, his brow furrowing in concern. "I'm done rinsing off. You okay? Are you going to pass out? Hey?"

"I am merely weary," the Core replied quietly, raising his still-bound wrist to rub his face.

"Need to get the cuff off so you can wrap those cuts." Damon wasn't regretful about cuffing the man; he'd found it rather hot. He stepped out and wrapped Requiem up in a towel. "Here, sit down and I'll go get the key."

Requiem nodded and did as he was ordered, sitting on the countertop, watching Damion. When he returned, Requiem was sluggishly drying himself off with the towel.

Damion came back and released the cuff, then tossed the metal object to the side to clatter on the counter. "Let's see if they have anything we can wrap those wrists with in here. Hmm."

Requiem leaned back against the mirror and closed his eyes. "May I suggest checking in the cabinets below?"

"I don't mind you suggesting anything. You're right often." Damion found some med tape and gauze. "Hand over those wrists."

Opening his eyes to a slit, Requiem placed his arms in Damion's care. His wrists were no longer leaking like a sieve, but they still looked bright red. He watched Damion's face from hooded eyes as Damion inspected his handiwork before quickly bandaging his raw wrists.

Damion smirked, picking up his lover again and carrying Requiem into the other room. "I think it's time to get you to bed. I'll try and hold back my ravenous self until morning."

"I do not mind," Requiem replied as he wrapped his arm over Damion's shoulders, burying his face in Damion's neck. "We are going to require clothing. And a plan on what to do from here."

"I'm sure they'll wake us up when they want to tinker with your brain some more." Damion sighed, resigned to the idea of his lover being poked and prodded. "I think a creep is a creep no matter the ship."

"I do not understand what you mean." The Core wrapped his other arm around Damion's neck and shoulders like he didn't want to let go. "And I am suppressing the chip right now, blocking the signal, but I do not know how long I will be able to keep this up. It is a risk we have to take unless you decide that you wish to attempt to return to the *Zeus* and report."

"I don't know what we should do, Requiem," Damion said honestly as he laid them down on the messy bed. "I'm not really one to go traitor, but they could also kill us if we don't plan things right."

The Core was quiet for a few minutes, as if trying to decide what to say and fighting off exhaustion. Coming back from the dead was surely tiring. "If we go back to the *Zeus,* they will more than likely wipe me and either terminate or discharge you. Additionally... Athena was not lying when she explained the *Titan* and the rebels' reasons."

"You knew about them?" Damion frowned at his Core before shaking his head. "You know, just wait until we get some sleep."

"I found the evidence when I connected with the *Titan's* system." Requiem's words were interrupted by a yawn, and he wrapped his body around Damion's warmth. "Should talk now. Important," he continued, but it was obvious the Core was losing the battle against sleep.

"Right, and you'd end up falling asleep anyway." Damion pulled the covers up around them, then let out another sigh and said, "One hell of a day."

Requiem murmured in agreement, twining his legs with Damion's as he used Damion's chest as a pillow, his arm wrapped around the larger man's bare waist. Sleep pulled him down as soon as he was settled into Damion's warmth. The stress of the day also weighed Damion down, and he quickly joined Requiem in sleep.

Chapter Five

EARLY THE next morning, Damion woke up with a full bladder and a growling stomach. He was confused and disoriented, but he quickly remembered where he was. After prying himself free of Requiem's viselike grip around his waist, he fumbled his way to the bathroom. Requiem didn't move, so deep in sleep that the ship could have exploded and he wouldn't have noticed. His limbs flopped down where Damion moved them and stayed there.

A polite knock on the door greeted Damion as he emerged from the bathroom. "I know you're awake, Hawk, so you might as well answer," Athena's voice came through the metal.

"Fuck, do you have x-ray vision?" Damion grumbled, wrapping an errant towel around his waist before opening the door. Then he realized Requiem had locked it. "Crap, one moment."

He quickly turned back to the bed and crawled on top of Requiem, then put his lips to his lover's ear. "What is the code to open up the damn door?"

"I'm getting impatient, Hawk," Athena chirped, not actually sounding impatient at all.

Requiem's eyes barely cracked open. They closed again as he mumbled, "Four-three-six-three-seven-four-seven," and then he was asleep again.

"Thanks." Damion placed a quick kiss to Requiem's earlobe before going over to the door and pushing in the code. He stepped into the doorway, not letting Athena pass. "If you're here for a three-way, I must say that I haven't discussed that with my Core yet."

"Mmm, yes, well. I'll just leave it to my imagination, then," she purred, looking over Damion's shoulder at the comatose Core. Then she raised her hand, revealing the holo-cube held in between her thumb and forefinger. "It's not like I don't have enough material to stimulate the mental images." She grinned almost evilly, her jewellike eyes moving back to Damion's face. "You should have told me you already had a lover in your little doll. I might have gone easier on you. I thought I had lost my touch."

"Trust me. Your touch is quite… skilled. Damn near inhuman. I have no doubt you'd make the most celibate man beg at your feet." Damion cleared his throat, trying not to remember the previous night. "But as much as that would have been… it would have been really… I can't betray him."

"A Fighter in love with his Core. How interesting." Athena pocketed the holo-cube, putting her hand on her hip and shifting to one side, looking at Requiem around Damion's shoulder. "He's not waking for anything, is he? That's too bad. Lizzy was really hoping to get some brain scans to see what the safest way to remove the chip would be. We wait much longer and they may just fry him to keep their toy out of our grubby hands."

"One, I never said anything about being in love, and second…." Damion paused to look back at his Core. "I'm still not comfortable with someone fucking with his brain if you're not even sure it will work. I mean, has that woman even done this before?"

"Wow you're dense. I wonder how often you lie to yourself." Athena shook her head. "As for Lizzy," she continued, "yes, she has. We have quite a few liberated Cores on the *Titan.* Most of them were rescued from black market rings where they were being sold as sex slaves. A human body that can't protest and follows every order is a hot commodity. It doesn't matter that they don't show any pleasurable emotions and repress even the impulse to express pain."

She frowned, her eyes slipping back to Requiem's sleeping body. "Usually those Cores on the stimulant can't feel pleasure, but I'm suspecting that he took a full dose before you guys set out on patrol yesterday." Her eyes moved back to Damion's face. "How does he show and feel so much?"

Damion shrugged, unconcerned. "I've been able to get that response since we came back from leave and we started to have sex. I thought all Cores would respond that way if they were treated well."

"You really don't know much about Cores. Typical of the Corporation to hand out lives and know pilots won't ask questions and men do not change their ilk," Athena replied blandly. "And if you got him to start emitting emotion just by fucking him, then I must have missed out on a hell of a good time."

Shaking her head, she crouched down and picked up two bundles of clothing from the ground before handing them to Damion. "As much as I, and plenty of other people on this ship, would appreciate you walking around in your skivvies, it might create a disturbance, and I don't want the *Titan* crashing into a moon. Get dressed, and I'll take you somewhere to get some food and we can talk more."

Athena stepped into the room and walked to the bed. Requiem was sprawled on the mattress, the sheets covering him from the waist down. The numerous bruises and bite marks were stark against his pale skin. She looked at his wrists, noticing they were carefully wrapped, covering the painful wounds that she had seen on the vid.

"And leave him?" Damion frowned, considering her offer for a minute before deciding. "Only twenty minutes." He took the offered clothing and went to his bathroom to change.

"You were a bit rough on him, huh?" she called out to the closed bathroom door. "You'd think you would have taken it easier on the poor guy after he nearly died on you."

"Maybe," Damion answered truthfully. "But since he tried to kill himself...."

"So you punished him for saving your ass?" Athena replied with venom. As Damion reentered the room, he saw her touch Requiem's wrist, and bleary ice blue eyes looked straight into her own. The Core shook his head, silently disagreeing with her before dropping his hand and closing his eyes again. "Stupid doll," she mumbled under her breath.

"I punished him because he thought his life was worth less than mine," Damion yelled as he pulled the shirt roughly over his head. The fabric stretched wide but clung close once it touched his skin. "Me and him are a unit. If one goes, we both go. There is no exception. He can't leave me behind."

Athena gently ran her hand over Requiem's soft white hair. "Too many Cores are treated like slaves, sold and bartered for because they were born unwanted. I don't like seeing them hurt. You don't want to be left without him. And you say you're not in love?"

"Why do women always want to say 'love love love'?" Damion grumbled. "He's mine and I'm going to protect him, even if it's from himself."

"Because men are too stupid to notice love even when it smacks them upside the head." Athena crossed her legs on the bed, her hand casually resting on the back of Requiem's neck, on top of the port slightly protruding from his skin. "But perhaps I'm mistaking love for ownership. Maybe it's simply, 'I don't want to lose my play toy, because who else can I chain to the bed, abuse, and fuck without a protest?'" Athena quirked an eyebrow at Damion.

"All right, let's get one thing figured out here before you really start pissing me off." Damion gave her a truly annoyed look. "He's not a toy or a thing. He's a person. He made his choice and he chose me; it wasn't the other way around, lady. And anything else is between he and I."

Athena grinned. "I know what he is and isn't. It's just so much fun to piss you off. You're mighty testy when it comes to him. Let's just call it revenge for leaving me all hot and bothered last night."

Requiem slowly moved out from under Athena's hand, looking at her with wide eyes. She lifted her hand immediately. "Don't like to be touched? Sorry about that, meant no harm."

"He's a bit nervous about other people, yeah." Damion went over and wrapped Requiem tightly in the sheets. "I'm going to eat. Lock the door behind us."

Requiem quickly took Damion's wrist with a light touch. His eyes focused on Damion's face before flicking to Athena and back to Damion, silently asking Damion if he was sure it was safe to go by himself with the captain. "As long as you do not require my presence," he finally said.

"Yeah, I'll be fine." Damion gave his Core a tender smile. "It's me who's supposed to protect you, remember?"

"I am discovering that sometimes it needs to go both ways," Requiem replied, his fingers sliding slowly from Damion's skin as if reluctant to let go. His hand was shaking as he reached for a terminal near the bed, his cold eyes looking at Athena again. His eyes glazed over as his fingertips rested on the terminal. There were several pops and the smell of electrical components frying as he short-circuited devices in several hidden corners of the room.

Life came back into Requiem's eyes when he let his hand drop, and he stared at Athena for another moment before he looked away, turning his back to her. "She is not lying about the rebels' purpose. However, she will be very determined to persuade you to their cause. I request that you be cautious."

Athena's eyes traveled to where all the cameras had been, and she swallowed nervously at the display of the exhausted man's abilities.

"You just don't want her to sweep me off my feet and take me away." Damion ruffled his lover's soft hair with a smirk. "I'll see if they have any ice cream."

Requiem opened his eyes again long enough to look over his shoulder and give Damion the briefest of smiles. His cold eyes warmed slightly before he rolled back over to return to sleep.

The captain stood silently and led Damion out of the room. The door closed behind them with the sound of the lock activating. "That will teach me not to underestimate a Core."

"Not that Core at least. I told you he was the best," Damion said with pride. "He also has a bad temper."

"I'll admit, I have heard about his abilities, but I suppose seeing is believing." She shook her head, moving off down the corridor. "I didn't think that Cores felt anger, so I still don't understand how he could lose his temper when he's not supposed to have one. And the last time he had his supplement was yesterday? And you said he was already feeling emotions before that? It's amazing that he was able to while on them. That's some vicious shit. I'm also surprised the Creators let him get away with it."

Pain filled Damion's chest, and his heart clenched in fear of the Creators. "They did wipe him once. They want his plans and his abilities." He looked at Athena and squeezed his hands into fists. His confusion was easy to forget when he knew he did need to protect Requiem. "Like you."

Athena only held his eye contact for a moment before looking down the corridor. "I'm not going to lie—which is completely against my character, mind you—I am interested in what both Requiem *and you* can do. We grabbed your ship partially because of your Core's abilities, but also because of yours. And your animosity for the Commander of the *Zeus* was just the icing on the cake. However, we never imagined that Requiem would be as talented as he is. Lizzy is growing increasingly impatient to get her hands on him, but we won't force him to do anything he doesn't want to do." She paused, wrinkling her nose. "Not much, anyway. We need to get the upper hand over the Corporation, and he could get us there if his brain doesn't explode. And I would do anything to get that leg up."

She took a deep breath, letting it out slowly as they turned a corner. "But I won't abuse him the way the Creators did. I'll let him experiment to his heart's content—as much as he has one—as long as it benefits us and doesn't harm my people."

"You want us to help you take down a billion-man corporation?" Damion said incredulously.

"You make it sound so impossible," Athena said with a wave of her hand as they walked into the mess hall. "No, the Chrysalis Corporation has done a lot of good, and the galaxy needs them. If we take them away completely, many more would suffer. In the beginning, their goals were honorable and they helped many. But power corrupts. We just need to take out some of the main players and keep that power out of destructive hands."

"Like the Commander?" Damion chuckled. "And who decides who and where and when?"

Athena showed no humor on her face. "Exactly like the Commander. Commander Sandrite is the head supplier for Cores on the black market. Any Core that has been wiped, has no more use, or has been deemed as too much trouble ends up in the hands of a twisted sex ring or plugged into the ship itself. But most end up as supplies." She took a tray and placed a plate of real food on it, not military rations. The plate contained a slab of meat, which smelled amazing, potatoes, and a salad. "As for giving you specific details of our plan, that depends on how much you want to cooperate and how deeply you want to get involved."

"Where do you get this food?" The bounty placed before Damion distracted him from the serious conversation. Food on Mars was a basic fare of potatoes and what little else would grow in the soil. The *Zeus* was protein and vitamin supplement foods, which at times was more like the gruel Requiem ate than not. This food smelled fresh, not processed.

Athena grinned at Damion's worship of the meal on his tray. "Donations mostly. A lot of our people, and also the people attacked by the Corporation, are simple folk. Farmers and the like who support our cause by supplying us with a treat every now and again. We just got in a shipment yesterday, so we'll have real food for a few days and then we're back to rations."

"I only saw food like this Lunar-side." Damion remained incredulous. "You don't really have ice cream."

"Not real ice cream, but we do have a nice imitation," Athena said with a grin as she sat down at a nearby table. She waved to a few people who shouted greetings at her, smiling warmly at them. They seemed to come from all over the room. She sent greetings back, asking about a few of the people and their families before they left her alone long enough to tuck into her meal. "I'm not going to be able to speak with you for long. I have to get back on deck or my second-in-command is going to string me up."

"Not a problem." Damion began to eat. He was fighting a battle between sating his hunger and trying to savor the flavors of real, hot food.

"You should probably pick up a tray for your lover boy. I don't know how he'll react without the supplements, but I don't think it'll be good, especially because he can't be weaned off them," Athena pointed out. "We don't have any on the ship to even attempt to do that. But he's going to need some real food soon. If you're hungry, he probably is too. If he wakes up long enough to realize it, that is. Anyway, I know you have questions, so go ahead and ask while we have time."

"I can ask again and again *why us* and you'll still give me the same answer, but I am still not sure why we should join you." Damion really had no qualms about killing the Commander—no more than he had with Arkin—whatever that said about him personally. "I would be an outlaw."

"Ah, but that's the beauty of the plan. In actuality, you will be a hero. You will be the one to save the president and return him to the safety of the Chrysalis Corporation's waiting arms and control." There was a calculating gleam in Athena's eyes before she leaned back in her chair and shrugged. "Of course you would have to leave the Core here and be working as our spy, but those are minor details."

Damion finished chewing the steak, not wanting to waste one bite. "Wait." He put his fork down and folded his hands on the table. "You want to send me back as a spy and make me leave my Core here, alone, unguarded?"

"He would hardly be unguarded. The *Titan* is as fortified as the *Zeus*. He would be perfectly safe here." Athena stabbed a piece of lettuce and chewed on it. "As long as I can keep Lizzy away from him and keep him from hacking into my ship."

"Yeah, you're forgetting one big point here." Damion raised his hands, then let them slap against his legs. "We're a team, a unit; he won't be able to tolerate it."

Athena sighed and put her fork down, bracing her elbows on the table and cupping her chin. "*He* won't or *you* won't? And it's not like you won't still be working together. He'll be your contact with us."

"Look, he doesn't trust anyone besides me, and there is a reason for that." Damion shook his head. "Even if I go back, they're going to think something suspicious is up."

"Call it broadening his horizons. He's going to have to learn to trust other people, and if you tell him to trust us, then he will," Athena pointed out with a small, patient smile. "And they won't think anything is suspicious, because once your Core's chip is out of his head and destroyed, they'll believe that he is dead. They'll never dream that we removed it. Besides, you'll be a hero, with the president's blessing and a promotion."

Damion was sure he was going crazy, or at least was sure this plan was definitely a long shot. "Requiem needs me. He isn't as docile and well-behaved as you believe Cores should be. He's a royal pain in the ass. He won't eat if he's not watched closely; he won't even sleep; he'll just be jacked in for hours. He's too naive to leave by himself."

"You mean he's like a stubborn pet," Athena drawled, shaking her head and leaning back in her chair. "I'll make sure that he eats and at least attempts to sleep. We don't have many capsules here, and they're locked down for safety, so he won't be able to jack in like he's used to, and I'll make sure it's regulated if he does. I'll make sure he has a caretaker that you approve of. What promises and assurances can I give you for you to agree with this?" She paused for a moment, tapping a finger to her lips. "You claim that he needs you, but I think it's you who needs him. Perhaps he isn't as naive as you believe him to be. He survived fine before he met you, didn't he?"

"He killed three Alpha Fighters and was raped repeatedly by one of them while another group hazed him every moment they were able to get away with it." Damion stabbed the meat with his fork, devouring what was left in only two more bites. "I'm not agreeing to anything without Requiem's approval."

Athena's eyes widened slightly, her hand falling back down to her lap as she shook her head. "Cores do not lead an easy life, I know that, but it seems that he suffered more than most. I knew that he had killed other Fighters, but I was never able to get the intel as to why. If you want to talk to your Core first, that's completely acceptable and understandable."

"One other thing: What does the president have to gain in all of this?" Damion wondered what would make the leader of the known worlds turn on his biggest cash cow.

"He's looking for his son, for one. He's as much a victim of the Corporation as the rest of us." Athena dug into her potatoes. "That's how they've kept the presidents under their control for the last 142 years. If their own pick isn't elected into office, the one who is elected is blackmailed or threatened to keep him under their thumb. With Jasper, they took his son, Jaz. That was ten years ago. Jaz was eight, and Jasper was still a senator but quickly on his way to becoming President."

Damion wasn't surprised by the information since he had heard and seen unlawful political procedures before, all done in the name of the greater good. He cleaned his plate, feeling more full than he had since he'd left Juni's family home on Lunar. "They're just keeping his son locked up in a cell somewhere? If that's the case, why haven't you staged a rescue mission by now?"

"Because we don't know where he is or what they've done with him. They keep claiming he's still alive, but we don't have any evidence either way." Athena shrugged, finishing off her own meal.

"This is all so much like one of the bad novels I read from the digital library on the *Zeus*." Damion couldn't believe his luck in life.

"Welcome to the glory that is our lives. It's more common than you think," she said.

The communicator on her wrist beeped, and her expression turned serious as she sat up. "Athena here."

"Captain, we need you back on the bridge. We are approaching Io," a male voice reported.

"Acknowledged. On my way." She pushed a button on the side of the watch-like object. "Duty calls. If I don't get my ass back up there, Wolfe will drag it back kicking and screaming." Athena stood and stretched. "We'll talk again later. Get some rest and speak with your Core. Don't think about doing anything you shouldn't. I'll still have people watching you. But other than that, you have full range of this corridor, and when he's up to it, take your pet to see Lizzy. She needs to do a checkup. Take as much food as you need back to Requiem. I'm sure he needs it." With that, she picked up her tray and walked away, waving over her shoulder.

Chapter Six

Damion

AFTER ATHENA left, Damion continued to sit at the table in the mess alone for a long while, just thinking. He didn't know what he had gotten Requiem and himself into here, but he still couldn't think of a way out of this either. He wanted to get Requiem free, but not by becoming a traitor himself. Yet this seemed the closest to freedom he could offer his lover. With a deep sigh, he finally got up and returned his tray before grabbing a fresh one and piling on the sweetest things he could find, along with another slab of meat. Once he was done, he left the mess hall, sucking on a cigarette all the way back to his room.

Requiem was still asleep when Damion returned, wrapped up in a cocoon of blankets and sheets, his face buried in the pillow. He didn't even move as Damion keyed in the privacy code Requiem had set.

"Requiem." Damion put the tray of food on the four-person table that was near a small kitchenette in the corner before kicking off his boots so he could crawl into bed. He hugged his Core's thin body close and kissed an exposed piece of neck. "Wake up. I brought a horrible amount of fattening food."

Requiem's eyes opened slowly. Damion could see Requiem struggling to stay awake. He snuggled further into Damion's arms. "Was the conversation with Captain Athena acceptable?" he asked, his voice cracking a little.

"She wants us to kill people and save the universe." Damion would explain this in more depth once he was sure Requiem was fully awake. "How are you feeling?"

"I will admit to my head aching slightly and feeling chilled. I believe it is from the effort of suppressing the signal in the chip. However, the pain is currently at an acceptable level," he replied, turning so he could bury his face in Damion's neck.

"What is acceptable to you is usually very bad for others." Damion brushed back the hair that was tickling his nose before hugging Requiem again. "Let's sit you up and let me force-feed you."

"I am capable of feeding myself," Requiem said as he unburied his arms from the blankets, his body immediately breaking out in goose bumps. He set his feet on the floor, and his eyes lit up at the sight of the food. "You were able to obtain some ice cream."

Damion got off the bed and brought the tray back over to Requiem. "Well, it's a simulated product, but it might be better than what they have on the way stations. It's actually real meat too."

Requiem stared at the tray for a moment, seemingly perplexed at the amount of food he had in front of him. Damion smiled as he saw Requiem's mouth purse, then relax. He watched Requiem pick up a utensil and take a tentative bite of some of the meat. Damion chuckled when Requiem let out a small happy sigh. The tentative bites turned into a ravenous flurry of eating as Requiem began eating in earnest.

"Your stomach is probably a black hole." Damion laughed and ruffled Requiem's pale hair. "Good. You eat while I find you something to wear."

Nodding, Requiem continued to annihilate his food while Damion went to find the pile of clothes Athena had brought for the thin Core. He was only able to eat about half of the meal, but he polished off the ice cream. He stood on shaky but slightly steadier legs to put the tray on the table, keeping a sheet wrapped around his naked form.

"Feel a bit better?" Damion stood in front of Requiem, pulling the sheet away and tossing it back toward their bed before tugging the T-shirt down over his head. The shirt would be too big for him, but hopefully the jacket would be warm enough. "We can walk around. Their scientist can't wait to crack your brain open."

Requiem closed his eyes, letting Damion dress him like the doll Athena had called him. "I am slightly better. My head still aches a little bit. I believe it would be wise to expedite the doctor's process. I do not know how much longer I can suppress the signal. It would not be judicious for my vigilance to fail."

"Requiem, this is your choice." Damion sat down on one of the chairs, looking up at his lover. "If they try to take it out, you could die, or you might live, but you could never go back to the Corporation because they'd just kill you. I don't know if living here with them is any safer, but they won't expect you to be a slave like the Creators made you to be. If you don't want to take that chance, then we go back to the *Zeus*, somehow, some way, and hopefully giving them this ship will be enough to keep you from getting wiped and the Commander from killing me."

Requiem

REQUIEM STARED at Damion for a few moments, realizing that this was a monumental decision. Staying went against everything he believed in, and it was hard for him to understand that the choice was his to make. Letting out a long breath, he took the pants from Damion and slipped them on, not looking up at Damion as he buttoned them. "When I accessed the *Titan's* system, I learned many things. Things that I should just accept because of my loyalties to the Corporation. They created me, they own me, and they control me. Or at least they did. I have not been able to think clearly my entire life. My thoughts are still directed by facts and by the chemicals I have always been given."

He paused for a moment, running his fingers through his hair in an attempt to tame it. "But I have learned many things in the last day. I have learned that I will not sacrifice the lives of my fellow Cores for my created loyalties to the Corporation. Even if we turned in all this information from the *Titan*, they will find another reason to try to terminate you and have me completely under their control." Requiem raised his eyes to Damion's face.

Damion gave him a slow nod. "All right. Then you'll have to let them try to get that chip out within a few days."

"I request a condition." Requiem placed his hands on Damion's chest, soaking in the warmth that the larger man provided. "That if they are not successful, you do not terminate them. It is a very complex operation. Additionally, the chip in my brain was injected deeper than what is standard during my creation, for security. If the operation is not successful, then I request for you to continue living your own life."

Damion managed to conjure up a small smile. "Are you trying to comfort me?"

"I do not know. Am I?" Requiem was slightly confused as he thought about it.

"Can't I kill just one of them?" Damion half joked.

"In the end, that is your prerogative. I cannot order you to do anything. I can merely request it. I am yours to do with as you wish. If you say that I must go through with the procedure, then I will. If you say we are going back to the *Zeus,* then we will. I am your Core."

"No." Damion shook his head wildly. "No, Requiem, it's your life. You need to make this decision, and I think you already have. I don't blame you at all. You deserve freedom, or more freedom. I am not sure what else they want from you, but they definitely want your mind."

Now he was very confused. This went beyond his training or anything else he had ever known in his life. "I do not understand. I am your Core. I do what you wish of me. My life, my mind, and my body belong to you. My freedom is what you decide of it, not what I decide of it. I would not even know what to do with it."

"You've been doing what you truly wanted to do for a while now. Did I order you to blow the cameras in the room earlier? Did I order you to use the Barrier three times?" Damion chuckled darkly. "You are quite able to make decisions."

"Those decisions were in relation to you," Requiem replied, shaking his head. He pushed away from the man, going back to sitting on the bed, wrapping a blanket around his chilled body. "I am not equipped to be an independent entity."

"I know, and if you live or die, it still affects me. I just can't tell you what to do. Let's go see their crazy scientist. You can decide then."

"As you wish." Requiem stood, leaving the blanket behind and fighting the desire to wrap his arms around himself as they walked out of their room.

Damion frowned when Requiem almost tripped. "You okay?"

Requiem thought about not answering since he couldn't lie to the man, but he knew that would only make Damion angry. "The ache in my head will not desist, and I will admit to being chilled more than is usual. And... and I am slightly dizzy." He kept his eyes focused on the corridor floor as they walked, not looking at anyone they passed, even though they were being stared at. "Please do not concern yourself. I am certain that I will be acceptable."

"Keep hold of my arm," Damion insisted. "Please. I don't know where we're going exactly."

Requiem did as he was told, keeping a tight grip on Damion's arm. "Left at the next corner. There will be a lift at the end of the corridor. We will take it to the third level."

By the time the lift arrived on the floor they wanted, Damion was carrying Requiem tight against his chest. Requiem's movements had become more and more uncoordinated, and the pain had become more pronounced in the short time since they'd left their quarters.

"You are not okay," Damion growled.

Requiem didn't reply as he curled himself against Damion's body, soaking in Damion's warmth as he started to shake. His headache had increased to a blinding migraine, leaving his vision a blur and the lights around them piercing straight into his optical nerve center. His ability to hold back the signal was slipping, the agony in his head and chilled body preventing him from controlling it, blocking it. If he lost it completely, he was dead. Damion would lose him.

He knew what he needed to gain control once again. One word pounded through his mind as the killing migraine tried to wrest away from him. "Supplements" was all he finally croaked through dry lips, his narrowed eyes concentrated on Damion's neck.

"They don't have any. Or so they're telling us." Damion ran into Medical. "Where's that Lizzy girl?"

"That's Dr. Lizzy to you," said the familiar woman as she came out of her office, her brown eyes concentrating on a clear vid page in her hands. She finally looked up, eyes widening at the sight of the curled-up form in Damion's arms, quickly taking in the situation. And then she frowned, crossing her arms. "I'm not sure I want him back in here. Last time I saw him was through the window after he put us in quarantine lockdown. Took our tech nearly an hour to hack through the lock mechanism."

Requiem's skin was starting to go beyond clammy and straight into the sweats as his shaking became more apparent. He squeezed his eyes shut as he tried to control his body, but it just wasn't working. Yet again, he was being a burden on Damion, and he hated it.

"Look," Damion snarled, his lips pulling back from clenched teeth as he looked at Lizzy with the promise of murder in his dark eyes. "He's sick or something. Look at him! If you don't help him right now, you won't have to worry about him trapping you in your lab because I'll beat you to death in it and none of your fancy medical tools will be able to bring you back."

Lizzy arched an eyebrow. "Calm down, Captain Cranky Pants. Let me just say that if you're trying to sweet-talk me into helping you, you're going about it completely wrong." She put down the clear page on a nearby cart and waved a hand toward the medical table in front of them. "Put him down. I'm pretty sure I know what's going on, and there's not much I can do about it. But I'll check him out."

Requiem clung tighter to his lover, not wanting to leave the safety or warmth of Damion's arms, and especially not wanting to be touched by the strange woman again. He'd much rather just go back to bed and wait this all out. He let out a barely audible whimper as Damion gently laid him on the padded exam table, then placed a quick, soft kiss on the top of Requiem's head. Requiem grasped Damion's callused hand tightly in his own scarred one.

"What's wrong with him?" Damion asked, not moving from Requiem's side. "He wants stims."

Lizzy snapped on some gloves and grabbed a light scanner out of her pocket before forcing Requiem's eyes open. "I'm sure he does," she murmured as she pushed Requiem's hand out of the way while trying to get to his other eye.

Requiem shied away from her touch, but he was too weak to fend her off, so all he could do was turn his head away from her prying fingers. "Damion," he quietly protested.

"Dammit, Core, stay still and this will go a lot quicker." Lizzy placed her fingers on the side of his neck to read his rapid pulse the old-fashioned way. "He's like this because he's going through the DTs. I actually expected him to start going through them a lot quicker. If a Core misses even one dose of stimulants, they start going through withdrawal. When something that they've had every single day of their lives stops being administered, it causes their bodies to go into almost immediate shock. It's another way for the Corporation to keep them under their control. They start needing it, craving it. It's not as bad if they're weaned off the drug, but it is a severe shock to the system to abruptly be taken off it."

Damion let go of Requiem's hand, reaching out and grabbing Lizzy's shoulders in a tight grip. He spun the woman around to face him, moving so fast she didn't have time to react. "His name is Requiem!" Damion spat. "Now give him something to help! Now!"

"Hands off!" The doctor wrenched herself out of his bruising grip, not without a degree of difficulty. However, she managed to get free, slapping him in the process. "You screaming at me isn't going to help his damn situation!"

"Damion. Stop, please." Requiem reached out and loosely grabbed Damion's wrist, panting from the effort. "May we please just go back to our assigned quarters?" He pleaded with his eyes for Damion to take him out of the Med Bay, a place he loathed no matter where it was located.

"No way. You're not leaving here until you stabilize," the doctor said with a shake of her head, her long black braid swishing along her backside as she punched a code into the serum dispenser. "All I can give him is a flushing agent. Hopefully it'll flush his system of the remaining stimulants, but it'll also increase his reactions. Instead of going through DTs for days, he'll go through it in about an hour. It's not a pretty sight." She paused for a moment to let the facts sink in. "Are you sure you want to do this?"

"Ask him." Damion squeezed Requiem's hand, his thumb stroking the back of his lover's hand in comfort. "If he thinks he can tolerate it, fine; if not... then we'll think of something else."

"I'm sorry, I can't," Lizzy said as Requiem's tremors increased. "He's not in his right mind at this moment. He'll probably start hallucinating soon. You're the one who needs to make this decision." She lifted the dispensed needle, checking the dose in the reservoir as she waited for Damion to decide.

"Give it to him," Damion said briskly, without hesitation. "I wouldn't be able to watch Requiem go through this for days; it would be torture. But can't you give him anything for pain?"

The doctor didn't wait for Damion to change his mind, swabbing the inside of Requiem's arm and injecting the medicine into the vein. "I wish I could, but there are too many different chemicals in his system right now and it wouldn't react well. Especially with his heart still recovering from its own trauma." She disposed of the injection tube and yelled over her shoulder, "Simmons, grab me a bin!" before turning back to Damion. "You need to turn him on his side. He's going to start throwing up."

Requiem was already starting to convulse as the drug quickly worked through his system. His skin was slick with sweat dripping off him and onto the table. His lips mouthed Damion's name but nothing came out. His fingers had a death grip on Damion's hand.

Damion combed his fingers through his damp hair with his free hand as he whispered softly, encouragingly in his ear. "Hey, just take deep breaths. You'll get through this."

The nurse brought the bin right as Requiem began to expel everything he had in his stomach, his body heaving in near convulsions. His eyes were squeezed shut, tears trailing down his face, his nose runny.

For the next hour, his own body and mind betrayed Requiem. He vomited violently, sweated in rivulets, and fought against Damion's hands as he battled things only he could see. Visions of events that never happened, where he could've failed, but in actuality, he had succeeded. Or had he? He was caught in a loop of fear, of false and true memories. His former Fighters beating him, ripping him apart to bloody bits with bare hands. Except they now had Damion's face instead of their own. A twisted dark vision of what Damion might've become if Requiem hadn't chosen him. What he could still become without Requiem by his side.

The nightmare changed, the dark version of his lover fading away like a swirl of sand in an hourglass, only for the current Damion to take the evil one's place. A warm smile, dark eyes glinting with humor and an emotion that Requiem was slowly recognizing as deep affection— love perhaps? Damion was crouched over him, his long, darkly tanned muscular arms on either side of Requiem, his lean body hovering over Requiem's own. It was calming, and he relaxed a little as he stared up at the man who had become his world, his hand rising to touch the stubbled cheek above him.

Before he could do anything more than that, his attention was taken away from his lover as swirling ebony shadows appeared behind Damion, a giant hovering over both of them in the outlined form of the Commander. A cackling laugh surrounded them as lightning shot through the shadow, and a large hand, big enough to swallow them both, came for them. Requiem screamed something, he didn't know what, to the still serene form of Damion. But the larger man didn't seem to notice the danger.

Suddenly, he was the one on top of Damion, his arms wrapped around his lover, feebly guarding the larger man with his own inadequate form. He felt the cold hand grab them—no, just him—and Damion slipped from his grasp as Requiem lost his ability to move. Damion fell toward the darkness below, his features twisted in a rictus of terror, one hand reaching upward toward Requiem as he fell. The shadows below them changed to fire and carnage, as if a huge explosion had detonated. Requiem screamed, trying to order his unmoving limbs to reach for the falling man. They didn't obey him, and Damion disappeared into the roaring flames below just before everything went dark.

He screamed, shook, and had at least one seizure. Eventually, they had to strap him to the table to keep him from harming himself or others. For someone who normally showed no emotion at all, Requiem now ran the gamut from terror to panic to begging. In the end, about an hour and a half after it started, he quieted, tremors only shaking his body occasionally as he panted, his reddened, tear-glazed eyes staring at the ceiling. The wounds on his wrists had reopened from his struggles against the padded wrist cuffs. But he was finally quiet.

Damion

DAMION STAYED by Requiem's side the entire time. He had that cold empty feeling in his gut just like when he thought Requiem was dead in the Zodiac. He wanted to lash out, wanted to hurt someone. But he also wanted to hold his lover tight, even though it was impossible during the purge. He'd already hated the Creators, but now it was beyond that. He wanted them to truly pay for their cruelty to someone he cared about.

Everyone was exhausted by the end. Requiem had fallen into a restless sleep, and Lizzy deemed it safe to release the straps holding him. Her normally neat braid was almost completely unraveled, stray hairs sticking to her damp face as she released the cuffs. She took off the bloodstained bandages and looked over his wrists, examining the weeping cuts. She paused only to cast a quick, unfriendly glance at Damion before she silently cleaned, re-treated, and bandaged his wrists.

"He's out of danger now. He won't have any other problems from the stims, other than experiencing emotions in a way he isn't used to." Lizzy ran a scanner over Requiem's forehead, which Damion assumed meant she was taking a brain scan. "We're still going to have to remove the chip soon. I don't know how he's doing it, but the signal is repressed for now. However, it won't be for long. He's probably getting headaches from doing it, since the signal just continues to increase after a while.

I want him to be at full health when we take it out. He'll have a better chance of surviving. This is a deep one, but I know I can do it. Though I'm also not stupid enough to think there won't be difficulties."

Damion was sure he blocked out some of the woman's babbling as he rested his forehead on the cool table. So fast. Everything always seemed to go so fast.

Except for the last hour and a half. The last hour and a half had been painfully long. It was torture watching his lover suffer. Now they were planning the best way to crack his skull open. He was mentally and physically exhausted and couldn't even begin to think about the next surgery or he would snap. "When can I take him back to our room?"

The doctor looked from Damion to Requiem. Then she took a deep breath and let it out slowly before checking over Requiem's vitals. "He's out of the woods, and as long as you let him get a lot of rest, I think it would be okay for you to take him back down. I know he wouldn't get any sleep while in the Med Bay. I'm going to give him a dose of concentrated saline to replace what he lost, but make sure he drinks a lot of fluid today to flush the rest of the stims out of his system. I want him back here tomorrow morning for a checkup."

She took a prepped dispenser off a nearby tray and injected the solution into Requiem's arm. "If you have any concerns or worries, contact me immediately. If you can't get him to me, I'll be there as fast as my legs can carry me. If the headaches get so bad that he can't see anymore or they're just too painful, we'll have to do immediate surgery despite the dangers. I would like to wait at least two days, but no longer than that." She pulled off her gloves.

"Right, well, I hope he listens." Damion rubbed at his tired eyes with his knuckles. "He's tough and stubborn. So I can pick him up and go?"

"Make him listen or he'll be back here by evening call." Lizzy glared at Damion in a way only a doctor can. "You don't have to carry him. I can get a chair."

"No need. I have him." Damion replied.

"Damion?" Requiem's weak voice still managed to sound slightly panicked even in an unemotional state. Requiem was blinking and struggling to sit up as he looked for Damion. His obvious tension eased as he found Damion. His eyes were still red-rimmed, the dark circles underneath still showing against his paler-than-normal skin. He looked worse than he had when he died, but he was getting stronger by the minute.

"Hey, I think you purged all that yummy ice cream." Damion helped Requiem sit up, holding him close so that Requiem wouldn't tip sideways off the table. "Ready to go back to the room and sleep for a few hours?"

Requiem struggled to swallow, then licked his lips multiple times, seeming to try and add moisture to his mouth, as his weary eyes flicked to the doctor and then down to his own bare toes. "I am sorry to have been such an inconvenience," he finally said quietly in a raspy sore-throat tone. He didn't use the more formal word "apologize." He simply said "sorry."

"You did nothing wrong." Damion easily picked him up. "Let's just go get you to bed and where I can smoke."

"Remember what I told you about fluids," Lizzy called just before the door slid closed behind them.

Requiem

REQUIEM CURLED his smaller body against Damion's chest, resting his head on Damion's shoulder, relieved to feel the man against him. It was times like these that he felt especially fragile. He wasn't a weak man, quite the contrary. They were pushed to be their physical best, although they were only trained in basic self-defense, since they were supposed to rely on their Fighters to protect them. But right now he felt as weak as a two-week-old kitten. "I do not quite remember what happened, but I hypothesize that I went into withdrawal from the lack of supplements?"

"Yeah, but instead of taking days, they sped up the DTs, and that's why you feel like utter shit," Damion explained as he walked. "I didn't want you to go through days of it, and she suggested just doing it all today. I know it was tough on you. Sorry if I made the wrong decision."

"It was not the wrong decision. I would have been even more useless to you than I already am if the time frame was extended." Requiem wrapped an arm around Damion's neck, curling his fingers possessively in Damion's black hair.

"You are not useless, but you're also not out of the woods yet." He let out another long sigh as they stepped out of the lift. "That chip is going to keep giving you a headache."

"It is either a headache or having no head at all. I will be acceptable with just a headache," Requiem mumbled. He was exhausted, but his mind was too wired to go to sleep right now, and he was content in Damion's arms.

"The frazzled woman doctor says you're supposed to drink fluids pretty much at all times when you're awake. You think you could get down a cup of water to start?"

"Yes. My stomach has settled," Requiem replied quietly.

Athena was standing in front of their door waiting for them, her arms crossed and her mouth pinched in an expression of worry and unhappiness. "Is he okay? Lizzy let me know what was going on."

"Don't worry, your commodity is still alive," Damion growled at the woman. "But he needs some water and maybe a dry piece of toast."

"Lizzy was right. You are Captain Grumpy Pants today," Athena quipped, but her relief was obvious. "I'll have someone bring something up, along with a broth that should give him a little more energy. And I'll make sure that ice cream is saved for him when he can stomach it."

The captain rolled her eyes as her wrist communicator beeped insistently. She pushed a button and brought it to her lips. "Pull your pink panties out of your ass, Wolfe. I'm on my way. Let me know if you need anything." The last part was directed at Damion, and then she was gone.

"Next person to call me Grumpy Pants, I'm going to punch them," Damion muttered as he gently laid Requiem on the bed. "I need a smoke."

"You are a bit more... volatile than normal," Requiem said quietly as he wrapped himself in blankets.

"I haven't had a cigarette in a really long time, and you've been detoxing at an alarming rate. I'm allowed to be a bit peeved." Damion went to the bathroom and brought back a few wet towels to wash the sweat off Requiem's face and neck.

He knew apologizing again would only aggravate the man more, so he kept quiet, letting Damion clean him like a child. Despite Damion doing it for nearly a year and a half now, Requiem still wasn't used to being taken care of so tenderly. Even though he knew it would never happen, in the back of his mind, he kept expecting Damion to hurt him. And not like the night before, but truly hurt him. He blinked, his head still feeling a bit fuzzy and throbbing without pause. "I think it might be more expeditious if I just took a shower. I am capable of doing so while you smoke."

"You think you can stand without falling down?" Damion didn't sound so sure as he looked at him.

Instead of answering, Requiem crawled out of his cocoon of warmth and put his feet on the floor. After a moment's hesitation, he stood on shaky legs, keeping a grip on the nightstand. "Standing, I believe, is an acceptable movement. Walking, I am sorry to say, is another matter."

"I'll just hold you up." Damion pulled his shirt off and undid his pants, ready to jump in the shower with his him. "Then you need to try to drink something and rest."

"If you wish, but I only require assistance getting to the shower. I am capable of keeping myself standing in it," Requiem replied, blinking at how fast his lover undressed.

Damion walked over, put his arm around Requiem's waist, and helped him walk to the bathroom. "You don't know if your legs will give out."

He sighed but didn't respond, letting Damion encourage his weak legs to move. By the time they actually got to the shower, Requiem was panting and sweating again. His borrowed clothes stuck to his body, and he felt more than a little unpleasant from being in such a state. He leaned against the counter as Damion stepped into the large shower chamber to turn on the water. After finding a toothbrush, Requiem brushed his foul-smelling mouth with a determined focus.

"Feel a bit better?" Damion tugged Requiem's shirt off and then placed a kiss on his fresh mouth.

"Affirmative," Requiem replied. As soon as the shirt was removed, he started shivering again as the humidity from the hot shower hit his skin. His fingers shook as he unbuttoned his pants. He managed to get them off and almost fell only once, sliding along the counter to brace himself against the wall. He frowned, disliking the fact that he felt so weak. Damion helped him stumble into the shower, and he sighed in relief at the warmth of the water.

Damion smiled as he pampered Requiem by washing his body and hair—again. "I bet it feels good getting out of those clothes."

Requiem leaned back against Damion's chest for support, closing his weary, burning eyes with a small sigh. "They were… unacceptable," he finally murmured, letting the hot water wash away the none too pleasant smelling sweat from his body.

"Don't forget the drinking of water." Damion hugged Requiem to his chest tightly. "Damn, you scared me a few times in there."

Requiem hesitantly raised his hands to rest them on Damion's arms. "I do not remember much. I remember quick bits of memories." He let out an involuntary shiver, his head falling forward as the memories flashed through his mind again. "I remember trying to escape and accidentally injuring one of the nurses. And... I remember you telling me that it would be all right. Not much more than that. I am sorry if I harmed or concerned you."

"You didn't harm me. I'm just glad that part is over," Damion said. "Don't fall asleep. I might take advantage of you."

"You have never taken advantage of me, asleep or otherwise," Requiem replied. "Besides, while I am weary, I do not feel as if I could sleep." He rested his head on Damion's shoulder, taking relief in the water pounding on his cold and sensitive skin.

"Good, because I'd like to see you awake for more than an hour. You done?"

"I am acceptably cleaned, yes." Requiem dropped his arms and pulled away from him, feeling he should apologize again but knowing it would just annoy Damion to hear it.

Damion turned the water off. "Here, just stand still and I'll grab you the towel."

"As you wish." Requiem leaned against the damp shower wall, his eyes hooded as he watched Damion get out of the shower. He noticed the opened cuffs lying almost innocently on the counter where Damion had thrown them the night before. The bright metal was still stained with Requiem's blood, and he looked down at his new bandages, grateful to Lizzy for having the foresight to use waterproof ones.

"Now let's get you dry right away before you catch a cold." Damion smirked. "Because that would be the worst thing that could happen."

"I do not catch colds. As you say, they seem to catch me." Requiem grasped the towel Damion offered him, determined to do at least this much for himself. He carefully stepped out of the shower and leaned against the bathroom wall to dry himself.

A beep from the front room alerted them that someone was at the door trying to hail them. Damion looked up at Requiem and then out the open bathroom door, his face expressionless but his eyes nervous. He really did not like people he did not know. Which basically meant that he just didn't like people. He probably wished he had a gun. "Stay in here."

A girl of about fifteen stood smiling at the door and handed Damion a tray. There was water, broth, a biscuit, and a full meal for Damion as well. There was also a clear flask that held a liquid that looked suspiciously like what Requiem had seen Damion and Athena drinking the night before. Peeking around the bathroom doorway, still mostly hidden, Requiem looked closely at the deliverer. He could see there was a long, ragged scar on the young girl's neck, running from ear to ear, that was partially hidden by the collar of her dress. As soon as Damion took the tray, she waved to him and skipped away, disappearing from Requiem's view.

Damion put the tray down and saw Requiem watching from the door, towel still around his hips. "It was just food. Here, let me carry you."

"You carry me too much," Requiem mumbled, but he let Damion do as he wished.

"You keep getting hurt," Damion pointed out. "One day maybe you'll carry me."

"That would be… intriguing," Requiem replied as Damion gently set him down on the bed. Somehow he managed to keep the towel around his hips from falling as he scooted back to lean against the headboard. A small, fleeting smile tugged at his lips at the mental image. "I would think you would want to avoid that type of situation at all costs. It would not be helpful to your reputation."

Damion chuckled as he brought over the broth. "My man card might be taken away."

Requiem tilted his head inquiringly, but he decided not to ask, shaking his head. But his lips twitched again in response to Damion's laugh. The sound made him feel… well, yet again he didn't know what the feeling was, but he related it to what he felt when Damion touched, kissed, or really even just talked to him. Content maybe? Happy? He didn't know.

"Did you just smile?"

"I do not know. Did I?" Requiem looked up, his brow slightly furrowed. "I felt a minor involuntary raising of my lips. Is that what a smile is?"

Damion laughed. "Yeah. That's it."

Requiem carefully took the broth from Damion, his hands still shaky but not as bad as they had been. The nausea had gone away, though his appetite still hadn't returned. His mouth was horribly dry, so the fluid looked tempting. He took a sip of soup from the edge of the bowl, knowing that trying to use a spoon would have been futile.

"Good?" Damion asked as he began to eat his own meal.

Requiem took another sip of the slightly salty but very satisfying tasting liquid. "I am having no difficulties ingesting the broth. It is of agreeable taste." Plus it felt like a balm on his dry mouth and throat. "Do you wish me to stop this smiling thing?" He remembered how, when he was a child, one of the other Cores laughed unexpectedly and had been quickly taken away. They had never seen her again.

"No, I think you look good!" Damion cleaned his plate before leaning back on the bed and letting out a long sigh.

"As you wish." Requiem finished off the rest of his broth and put the empty bowl on the nightstand. He wrapped a nearby blanket around his shoulders, still a bit chilled with just the damp towel. His boxers had disappeared somewhere, and his new clothes were soaked.

"Feeling good?" Damion turned and pulled him into a hug.

"More acceptable, yes. The ache in my head is still there, but that is to be expected." Requiem curled his body around Damion's and laid his head on the man's bare shoulder. This was when he felt the most content, the most wanted, and it confused him, but not enough to question it.

"Yeah," Damion said with a hard swallow. "Want to sleep?"

"Negative. While tired, I do not feel as if I could rest. It is… odd," Requiem replied, his voice muffled from where his face was buried against Damion's warm skin. "You should rest if you feel you need to, however."

"I would like to sleep," Damion said.

Requiem shifted, finding himself uncomfortable, his legs twisted up in the sheets and his towel. Sighing wearily, he sat up again and took the damp towel from around his body. He folded it neatly and placed it on the very end of the bed before straightening the sheets and blankets, covering himself up, and lying back down.

"You okay? You usually never move around like that." Damion sounded surprised.

"I am acceptable. I was merely uncomfortable and did not want to cause the bed to be damp because of my towel. I apologize if I disturbed you." Requiem moved away so he wouldn't bother Damion with his movements anymore. He missed the feeling of Damion's smooth skin against his own, but it was better this way if his body decided to continue being restless.

Damion sat up. "Hey. Where do you think you are going?"

"I was disturbing you," Requiem explained, pulling a pillow to his chest and curling around it. "This way you can sleep in peace."

"I didn't say that." Damion reached over and pulled Requiem back to his chest. "You feel up to helping me?"

Requiem let Damion drag him across the bed, his expression confused. "I, of course, will help you with anything you need, but might I ask what that is?"

"Damn, you're smart but not bright." Damion leaned closer and kissed him, threading his fingers in his damp hair. He was no more true to his feelings, but Requiem was still learning feelings in a brand-new way.

Requiem inhaled through his nose in surprise, his hands splayed over Damion's bare chest as he melted into the kiss. "I see," he said when Damion released his lips so that they both could breathe. "I believe I am beginning to understand."

Damion grinned while pulling sheets away so that his body was exposed for him to see and touch. "Not so dumb, then."

"I beg forgiveness for my slow observations. I have been a bit below acceptable capacity." That fleeting smile appeared again as Requiem skimmed his hands lightly down the tan skin of Damion's chest and over his nipples.

"Then I am to believe you are fine with this?" Damion placed his elbows on either side of Requiem's head, leaning down and slowly rocking his hips against him.

"When have I ever denied you in the past?" Requiem replied right before he gasped from the contact of Damion's hot length against his own. "Have I ever denied you? There is still that space of time that is gone from me." Curious to see his reaction, Requiem slid his hand down Damion's chest and stomach to grasp Damion.

"Deny? Not really." Damion's voice was pinched as he held back a moan. "You never went right out and did that before, but don't stop."

"I do not know what you mean by 'not really.'" Encouraged by Damion's reaction, Requiem squeezed a little harder, stroking his lover like Damion had done to him in the past. Hesitantly, he raised his head to kiss Damion, a bare brush of lips.

"I want you to keep doing that," Damion said in a low voice, moving his hips forward slightly. "Just squeeze a little harder."

Requiem complied, increasing the pressure around Damion's need. He watched Damion's face, watched the pleasure roll across it, the mouth that was slightly open emitting the most arousing sounds. Requiem slowly cupped his lover's sac, gently rolling it as his other hand stroked him.

Damion bent his head down, panting against his lover's neck. "If you keep that up, I won't stay up for much longer."

"You were the one who ordered me not to stop," Requiem reminded him as his hand increased its speed, swirling the precome bubbling at the tip along the length to slick his path. Again hesitating, curious, he turned his head to nibble on Damion's ear. He couldn't remember a time when he had been so enthralled by another person's reactions, even Damion's. He was enjoying the pleasure he was giving his lover almost as much as if he were the one on the receiving end.

"All right, I want to come inside you, not on you." Damion licked his dry lips. "But damn, that feels so good."

"You are more than capable of stopping me at any point in time," Requiem pointed out before biting down on Damion's neck. He squeezed harder along the man's length, his other hand slipping underneath the sac to run a finger lightly between Damion's entrance and his tightening balls.

"Requiem!" Damion's hands curled into the bedding as he suddenly came. He bit hard into Requiem's skin.

He let out a choking gasp as Damion's teeth dug into the skin and muscle of his neck in an already marked place. The pain combined with the sound of Damion screaming his name shot a streak of pleasure through his body. His lips curled into a lazy smile as he lifted his now covered hand in front of his face. Curious, he brought one of the dripping digits to his mouth, tasting his lover's essence. It was a bit salty, but not an unpleasant taste, and he savored it. "You could have ordered me to desist."

"I'll just consider it as priming." Damion chuckled and gave him a quick but heated kiss. "That was pretty good. You ready for more?"

Requiem tilted his head, letting the throbbing from the bite to his neck pound pleasantly through his system and almost overrun the pulsing pain in his head. He felt the smile again. Small, fleeting, but still there and reaching his eyes before it all dimmed again. "As you wish."

Breathless, Requiem wrapped his arms around Damion's neck, kissing him back warmly while trying not to get the release on his hand in Damion's hair. Something seemed different now. More intense maybe. It had always felt good—no, amazing—in the past, but now it felt... more so. Requiem felt more sensitive, had more of a want to respond, and it baffled him.

Damion rolled them so Requiem was on top and grabbed his ass in his strong hands. "We need lube."

He squeezed his eyes shut as the world flipped, the pounding in his skull increasing momentarily. He landed straddling Damion's hips, their bodies pressed together. "All we have available to use is the lotion you implemented last night, and I currently do not know the location of it."

"Oh, the inconvenience of lust." Damion kissed Requiem again, not ready to leave the bed in search of lube.

"It did not work as well as other products" was all he could say before his lips were captured again. He sighed in contentment, his fingers digging into the sheets under his hands. Unconsciously, he shifted his hips, rubbing the cleft of his ass against Damion's half-hard cock.

Damion clearly wanted more, and he knew if he wanted to fuck his lover properly, he needed to get up. "Dammit!" he panted as their lips parted, the back of his head thumping against the pillow.

"What is wrong?" Requiem was panting as well, and he tentatively nibbled on Damion's bottom lip. He shifted again, stifling a moan as he rubbed his need against Damion's own.

He let out a groan. "We need some lube, which means I have to try and find some."

"I suppose that means you wish for me to move," Requiem inquired, but he wasn't about to do so until he ordered him to. He had never felt more... alive. He nibbled at Damion's lip again, his hips moving insistently.

"I don't want you to move, but we need to if we want a good ending."

"But you had yours, and I am content enough with that," Requiem replied softly, attempting to calm his body by stopping his wanton movements. "If you wish, think of it as my way of taking care of you."

"I don't think so." Damion finally moved so he could get off the bed, lifting Requiem easily off him and to the bed beside him before standing. However, it looked like it was rather difficult to walk with the insistent hard-on between his legs. "It has to be close."

Requiem flopped back onto the bed, watching Damion's efforts to walk. He felt… amusement… maybe? He didn't know what this feeling was. It was definitely one he'd never felt before, but it made something bubble in his chest, and his lips twitched again in that unfamiliar movement. He squashed it down to evaluate later. "Damion. I am fine. Content even. There is no need."

"I am not content," Damion growled, looking on the floor. Then he opened the bedside drawer and found a brand-new sealed tube of actual lube with a bow around it, mocking him. "Bitch."

Requiem wisely decided to keep his mouth shut. The last time Damion was close to one of his moods, he ended up bleeding. While it wasn't a bad experience, Requiem's wrists were still healing. He wrapped himself in the blanket.

"She was snooping again," Damion grumbled, tossing the note to the side. "I swear she's not human."

"I disabled all the cameras, but I did not check if she had more installed." Requiem slid out of the blanket and to the edge of the bed. His head swirled slightly and the pounding increased, but he ignored it to place his hand on the bedside console. Extending his senses to the electrical output, he winced as a stab of pain went through his skull and his hand began to shake. He had never before had a problem with jacking into any type of system, but apparently the effort of blocking the signal from the chip in his head and his decreased health were leaving him unable to do so.

"I… I am sorry. I cannot look to see if she has installed any more." He stared at the inaccessible screen, and his heart pounded at the thought of his sudden lack of abilities becoming permanent. What if taking out the chip made him unable to be a Core?

"It's okay." Damion sat down and ruffled Requiem's hair. "It's fine. If she wants to watch, I don't really care."

"I… always assumed that what we do is socially perceived as private. Something you did not do while others were watching." Requiem pulled himself under control, locking down his fear before he looked up at Damion. He dropped his hand from the console and tucked it under his bare leg so Damion wouldn't see its twitching. "I will search later. I do not like the thought of being secretly watched. Especially if she is listening in on our conversations as well."

Damion grunted. "I think she's just jealous. Can we get back on the better subject?"

"What is jealous? And what is it pertaining to Captain Athena?" Requiem's curiosities were cut off by the warmth and insistence of a sudden kiss. He leaned into it, noticing more vividly the feeling of Damion's lips against his own, the heat and wetness of his mouth, and the texture of his tongue. And it was heaven. "What subject are you mentioning?" Requiem mumbled against those full lips.

"The one where I put something very thick inside your very tight body." Damion urged Requiem flat onto his back.

Not having any strength to resist, nor the desire to do so, he flopped gracelessly back down on the bed with only the lightest pressure against his chest. His eyes opened widely and his legs flailed for a moment as he attempted, and failed, to catch his balance. "I see. I do believe that is a subject I can agree upon."

"That's a great thing to hear." Damion chuckled, moving until he was between Requiem's legs.

Requiem spread his legs a little wider so Damion's larger body could fit between them comfortably. He ran his hands featherlight down Damion's neck and chest as if afraid to put any pressure on the man's golden skin, so different in contrast to his own. Slowly, stopping once or twice as he hesitated, he lightly kissed Damion's lips. It was still a strange concept to act on his own without orders.

It was obvious that Damion was excited by Requiem's aggressiveness. He tried to open the lube while kissing and spilled some on the sheets, but he didn't seem to care. His fingers circled around Requiem's entrance before pushing in his middle finger.

Requiem pulled away from Damion's lips, gasping, his fingers losing that softness as they dug into the other man's hips. It was nothing like it had been before; it felt much more amazing. Even the very slight burning intrigued him, entranced him. "I… I do not understand. It feels… different," he breathed out, his eyes wide.

"Does it hurt?" Damion stopped instantly, sounding worried.

"Negative." Requiem shook his head enthusiastically, his soft white hair falling around his face. "Not at all. Please, if it pleases you, please… do not… do not stop." It took everything in him to say those words, to ask Damion that favor.

"Oh yes, it does please me." Damion moved his finger for a few moments before he added a second. "It's amazing. Your body seems to remember me the more we do this."

His toes curled into the mattress as he tried to keep his hips still when all they wanted to do was push down so Damion's fingers buried themselves deeper into his wanton body. "At least that was not lost as well, then," Requiem said in a strained tone before his eyes widened again and he let out a small scream of pleasure as the Fighter found that place inside him that felt oh so amazing. His hips moved involuntarily against Damion's fingers.

"You are so fucking sexy." Damion kissed him once again as he was able to push in a third finger. Requiem's body did seem to soften quicker today, or perhaps Damion was a bit impatient.

Requiem moaned against Damion's mouth as that third finger pierced him, heightening his pleasure. He cradled the larger man's head, his fingers digging into Damion's thick ebony hair. His hips were in constant motion now, uncontrollable.

Damion's fingers were slipping in and out easily, so he took his hand away and hurriedly coated his returned hard-on. "Can you spread your legs a bit farther?"

"As you wish," Requiem said, when all he was thinking was *anything you want, just don't stop.* He did as Damion requested, spreading his legs wide.

Damion guided his cock to his slick entrance, slowly pushing forward inside the gripping heat after the tight ring of muscle gave way. He let out a loud groan as he continued to thrust until their bodies were flush.

Requiem choked on a gasp, his fingers tightening in Damion's hair but not pulling it, as his eyes squeezed shut and his mouth opened wide in a silent scream, his breath stopping. "Damion…," he finally choked out, panting once Damion was seated. He opened his eyes to meet Damion's, a bit glazed and hooded in pleasure and… lust? Was it lust? He didn't know.

"Feels good." Damion moaned as he pulled out a few inches, then rocked forward and back into the velvet heat. "Goddess, I promised to take this slow."

"I do not believe this was an activity on the doctor's prescribed list. You have already gone against the rules. I do not know why you would not go further." Requiem let out a low groan, raising his legs to wrap around Damion's waist.

Damion snapped his hips forward. "You just tempt me beyond reason."

Requiem let out a yell, his head falling back. The only thing holding him up was his grip around Damion's shoulders. He had never been vocal before—a trained fear keeping him silent—but now he just couldn't help it. Damion's cock slamming into him pushed the sounds past his lips. "I admit, I will not apologize for that fact," he finally managed to pant, licking his dry lips as his eyes met Damion's again.

"You look different. You even talk different." Damion shook his head and began to feast on Requiem's neck, leaving marks on the opposite side while bracing his hands on the bed and continuing to thrust deep and hard into Requiem's clenching body.

As he tilted his head to the side, pants and moans fell unbidden from his mouth even when he bit down on his lower lip to stop them. He could still feel the cut from Damion's teeth on his lip and tried to avoid reopening it. It was only then that Damion's words sliced through his growing haze of pleasure. "I do… do not mean to be different. I do not notice what you mean," he panted out before Damion hit that glorious place inside of him and he let out another soft scream. The heat was building quickly in his body, his need so hard between them it was almost painful.

Damion left a large bruise on Requiem's shoulder and looked up to see his face. Requiem's hands slid down and clutched Damion's biceps tightly, blunt nails digging into the muscle as he finally fell back on the bed. His hips moved to meet the other man's, his lip between his teeth as he tried to stifle his outbursts. His eyes were closed, head tilted back as the fire built up from the pool in his groin and spread through his body. "Damion…." He was unable to hold it in anymore.

Damion slammed into that spot once more, sending him over the edge with a scream and starbursts. His body arched in ecstasy, his fingers squeezing Damion's arms hard enough to bruise as he came so violently he could almost taste the orgasm. And it felt better than anything ever had in his entire life.

"Gods." Damion didn't wait for permission and thrust faster and harder against that spot, clearly enjoying Requiem's screaming and the mild pain from his nails.

Requiem didn't have time to wallow in the haze of pleasure as Damion started pounding into him again, straight into that spot that fired all of his pleasure synapses. It was almost too much, beyond what his body and mind could handle. The throbbing in his head was currently a distant memory, overpowered by the pounding of his heart and Damion's harsh breath in his ears. Pulling his body up using Damion's hands, he crushed his lips against Damion's, his tongue demanding entrance to the man's panting mouth as he squeezed his lower muscles around his hot need.

Sweat slid down Damion's back, but it didn't deter him from his wild thrusts.

Requiem nibbled on Damion's bottom lip for a moment before his need to breathe overcame him and he released a moan into the delectable mouth touching his own. He thought he would have been done after that one explosion, but his body seemed to be heating up again, and quickly. The feeling of Damion overtaking him, owning him, claiming him. The harsh, almost violent sounds of wet skin slapping together, the feel of Damion's sac bouncing off his ass, the smell of sex, and the overwhelming feeling of contentment, need, and... something else that Requiem couldn't name was a heady combination. Using his legs, he slammed his body back down on Damion, meeting him thrust for thrust.

"Requiem!" Damion wrapped his hand around Requiem's dripping cock.

The large hand wrapping around the center of his heat was just too much for Requiem's sensitive and overwhelmed body to handle. He let out a gasping cry and cut it off as he bit into Damion's shoulder, his arms and legs wrapping around his lover tightly as his world exploded for the second time that day. It was no less amazing than the first.

Damion collapsed on top of him. "Whoa. The room is fucking spinning."

Requiem grunted softly at the sudden weight but didn't move to push him off. His legs were still loosely wrapped around Damion's hips, his fingers tangled in his lover's hair as he tried to catch his own breath. His eyes were hooded, swollen lips slightly parted, trying to find out where his brain went and not really caring at the same time.

It took Damion a few tries to roll to the side, and Requiem shivered when Damion pulled out of him. He took a deep breath once he was off him, his lungs filling gratefully. He started and failed to speak a few times before getting the hang of it again. "That was... a lot different."

"Different?" Damion raised his head to look at him. "How?"

Requiem licked his lips. "More... vibrant, I suppose is the correct word." He thought about it for a few minutes, feeling very much like he had been well fucked—which he had. "I believe it was similar to a man that has only ever seen in monochrome finally being able to visualize colors." He furrowed his brow for a moment, wondering if that had made sense.

"Right, okay." Damion let his head flop back down and closed his eyes. "You definitely responded differently."

"I apologize if I acted in a way that you do not approve of," Requiem replied with a subtle wince. He hadn't been able to control himself, and a Core was supposed to excel in control.

Damion let out a lazy chuckle. "No, I approve."

"Very well." Requiem wasn't so sure about it himself. He didn't like these new unfamiliar feelings, especially since he didn't understand what they were. For example, how his stomach fluttered and his heart beat harder, a warmth spreading through his body, any time Damion touched him. He raised a trembling hand, rubbing at his eyes, the pounding in his head making itself known again now that the endorphins had worn off.

Damion sat up. "What's wrong? Pain? Want some water?"

"If you do not mind, water is a good idea," Requiem said, ignoring the other questions. He sat up slowly and leaned back against the headboard, looking at the mess slowly drying on his stomach. He reached for a towel at the end of the bed and cleaned himself off.

Damion grabbed them some water and put the tray of finished food by the door. "You don't look good."

"I would not expect to after nearly expiring yesterday and going through withdrawal today. Even I will admit that I am not at operable best." Requiem took the water from Damion and nearly drained it dry in one pull, before closing his eyes and leaning his head back against the headboard. Without the minimal light in the room shooting into his suddenly light-sensitive eyes, the headache eased a little bit. "I apologize. It seems I am not much use to you again. I was feeling more acceptable for a short time."

Damion sat next to him, brushing his hand over Requiem's hair. "You are the only person I truly trust and depend on, so don't talk about yourself like that."

Requiem slid along the headboard, leaning against him. Damion's words warmed something in his chest, but it was a good feeling. He took another sip of water. "You do not truly trust Fighter Juni?"

"I trust him, but it's a different trust," Damion said. "I trust him to back me up, to watch my back, to not slip me a mickey and tie me up naked and take pictures. But I trust you solely with my life."

One of his eyes cracked open a sliver to look at Damion. "Slip you... a mickey?" He went to shake his head, winced, and then stopped. "I do not understand." He paused for another moment before continuing. "I believe I have already made it quite clear in the past that my life is in your hands, to do with as you wish."

A knock at the door interrupted anything else he might have said, and Requiem felt a small flash of panic. He'd always been able to know who was coming, who was at the door, through the vid system. However, he was currently blocked from accessing that because of the pain in his head. He leaned harder against Damion.

"Just stay here and relax." Damion got up to check it out. "You really don't look so good. I guess I pushed it too soon."

"I was not unwilling," he pointed out, fumbling momentarily for the edge of the blanket to cover himself. He finished off the last of the water before carefully placing the empty glass on the edge of the bedside table.

"Hawk, hurry up. I don't have all day," Athena called through the locked door.

Damion punched in the code, allowing the door to open. "What the hell? You can't give us a few hours of peace?"

Athena's eyes automatically flicked to the bed. "I don't know. Can you let your butt buddy have a few hours peace so he can heal?" She pushed past him easily with a shake of her head and moved toward the bed. She pulled a full syringe out of her pants pocket and popped the cap. "Gods, Hawk, have you no bloody sense? I'm here by doctor's order, and it looks like I should have been here sooner."

"What the fuck are you doing?" Damion snapped, grabbing her wrist and squeezing it so tight that the bones ground together. "What are you trying to give him?"

Athena attempted to twist her arm out of Damion's grip, but he was too strong and had years of martial training to rely upon. He effectively held her arm and prevented the unadorned needle from going closer to him. "It's something Lizzy concocted. It's to help with his head and has nanos in it that will help suppress the bug in his gray matter without any side effects." She nodded toward Requiem, who was watching them through half-opened eyes as he slid farther away from her and toward the corner where the bed met the wall. "You want him to continue to be in pain?" She paused, looking Damion up and down. "Or perhaps you do with the way you won't let the poor thing rest, along with bruising him and handcuffing him to the bed."

"Captain, please stop. Damion did nothing against my will," Requiem said softly from his corner. "I am acceptable. I do not need any treatment." Just because he couldn't lie to Damion did not mean he couldn't stretch the truth to Athena.

"You'll take it," Damion insisted, giving Requiem a look that told him his words were nothing short of an order. "She might be a bitch, but she doesn't want you to die."

Requiem's half-opened eyes flicked to him, and he considered protesting. Then he deflated and closed his eyes again. "As you wish."

"Now that that's settled." Athena twisted her wrist out of Damion's loosened grip, finally reaching the bed and crawling on it to get to Requiem. She sat down beside him. "I just want to warn you, this is going to knock you on your ass for a little while. You need to be sleeping for it to take effect. It helps the nanos get through your bloodstream faster or some shit, I don't know." Instead of grabbing his arm, she held out her hand to him. He didn't move, and she frowned. "Requiem?"

Requiem opened his eyes again, looking to Damion and effectively ignoring the woman.

"That's my name for him," Damion said. Damion moved to the bed and pulled Requiem to him protectively, watching Athena closely. "Go ahead," he encouraged Requiem. "Let her put it in, and then you can get some decent sleep."

Requiem immediately relaxed when Damion's arms wrapped around him. "As you wish," he stated again, holding out his hand to Athena.

The captain frowned as she took the offered hand, curling it into a tight fist as she placed the needle down on the bed and reached into another of her vest pockets to extract a tourniquet. "Then what the hell should I call him? I can't keep calling him 'doll,'" she huffed as she tied the rubber around his upper arm. She waited until the vein she needed appeared, which was pretty quickly in such pale skin. She lifted the needle again and slipped it under the skin and into the vein with the efficiency of someone who has had a lot of practice. She pushed down on the plunger and the blue fluid emptied into Requiem's body.

"Call him 47, at least for the time being. He's used to it." Damion gave her a poignant look. "It's not like we'll be separated anytime soon."

Athena pulled the needle out of Requiem's vein and popped the tie on the tourniquet. She pushed her thumb over the small wound in his arm as she released his hand. "You really are pushing for time here, Hawk."

Requiem's eyes flicked to Athena and Damion, knowing there was an underlying conversation going on but not understanding it. "Damion, what are you speaking of?" His words started off clear, but by the end of the sentence, they began to slur. His body felt warm as the drug quickly spread through his veins, his eyes glazing over. "Damion?" He didn't like the feeling of slowly slipping into hazy oblivion. He gripped Damion's wrist tightly.

Damion gave Requiem a tight hug. "It's okay, just fall asleep. I won't leave you."

Damion

DAMION WAITED until Requiem slipped into a drug-induced unconscious state before speaking with the captain. "Pushing? I don't think I'm the one who is pushing," he growled. "You kidnap us, thrust us into this situation. I think you're the one who's pushy."

"Perhaps, but that's only because I need an answer." Athena popped the cap back on the syringe and put everything back inside the pockets of her vest. "Time is running short, and if you're not going to help out with this mission, we're going to have to replan. And if you're not going to be any use to us at all, then we'll just have to return you to the Corporation. With a few modifications, of course." She slid off the bed and stood next to it, her hands on her hips and her expression determined. "You know too much now, so we'd have to wipe both your memories, and I'm sure they'll love getting a Core back without his chip. I'm sure it'll go over well."

"See, I knew you weren't that different from them," Damion sneered. "Still use him as leverage and use threats to get what you want."

"Ah, but we are different. Because that's what we *could* do, but we're not going to." She shrugged, letting her arms fall to her sides. "If you decide to join us, I'd like to know sooner rather than later. If you decide not to, we'll drop you off wherever you want when we pass it. Jasper and I both know you've been trying to figure out how to get Requiem out. We have our sources." The redhead turned and walked toward the door. "You have five days. That's when Jasper is going to be back and we'll have to put the mission into working status. Let me know by then." And with that, she was gone.

"Women." Damion sighed. "They're definitely a pain in the ass." He was almost jealous of his lover's oblivious nature. "Five days... I guess it will depend on if you survive."

He placed a kiss on Requiem's head, then tucked them both into bed. What a hell of a day—again. He wondered what tomorrow would bring.

Tuesday, October 25, 455 MC
1316 GMT
Damion

DAMION WAS done with medical bays, because here they were again in the medical bay two days later. Requiem was sitting on one of the examination beds, his eyes shut tight against the pounding agony in his head. Lizzy's serum had worked wonders to help him detox, but the headaches lingered. Damion didn't even want to think of what his head would feel like if he didn't have that in his system.

"It hurts to think," Requiem whispered.

Doctor Lizzy was running a scanner over the back of his head, mumbling readings to herself. "Well, it definitely has to come out soon. Like now. It's on its final signal. They only try so much before they release a signal so strong that it just destroys the chip. A mini-explosion in the brain. The signal that's emitting now would have just fried his brain. The next step is that they blow up his head."

"Requiem." Damion put a hand on top of Requiem's head, and as much as he tried to look and sound calm, he was obviously anything but. "You have to let them do the surgery. Are you ready?"

He set his glazed eyes on him. Since Athena had first given Requiem the drug, he had to be injected with it once a day. He would sleep for about five hours, and then when he woke up, he was like a zombie. Damion had the feeling Requiem knew what was going on but was slow to react and understand.

Requiem licked his dry, chapped lips and nodded slowly. "Do not want to, but I understand the need." He paused for a moment as Lizzy stepped away. "It may not be successful," he stated. "What if I don't make it through?"

"It's a choice of going back to the *Zeus* and you getting wiped and me kicked, secretly killed, or letting them try to get it out and maybe you die," Damion said. He did not hide the lack of joy he felt for either option.

"As you wish," he whispered, his fingers falling lightly on Damion's forearm. "I would prefer dying to being wiped."

Damion gave him a smile. "It's okay if you're scared."

"Is that what the emotion is?" Requiem let his hand drop along with his eyes. "Then I am not scared for myself, but for you." He slid off the table and started to walk carefully toward the surgery room where the doctor was waiting.

"Don't worry about me. I'll be fine," Damion reassured him. "You just do your best to get through it."

Requiem looked over his shoulder, a sad smile flashing across his lips. "As soon as I am on the table, it is out of my hands and in Doctor Lizzy's." With only a brief hesitation, he took the doctor's offered hand and let her lead him into the room.

"Take good care of him," Damion said as nausea rolled through his stomach in waves. "Please."

Lizzy's lips thinned as she looked at Damion, understanding the seriousness of the situation. She nodded before leading Requiem to the table. "Hawk, there are scrubs and a mask in the cabinet if you want to watch. I know it's important to you," she finally said.

Damion saw the eyes of the technician widen as the man looked from Lizzy to him. From the look, he assumed the doctor was normally pretty strict about letting people in the OR.

At the doctor's gentle direction, Requiem sat on the table and let the nurse put monitoring sensors on his chest and back before lying down on his stomach. His face was directed to an open space in the table that was fitted with a mask.

Damion found the scrubs and got dressed, but he was hesitant to go into the surgery area. He'd never had to wait on someone like this before, and the anxiety was new. He wasn't usually an anxious person.

Somehow sensing the dilemma Damion was having, Requiem said, "I do not believe Damion should watch. I would not want him to see if something went wrong." Her only reply was to gently push his head back down, motioning for the technician to start the drug that would knock Requiem out.

Damion hesitated for a few more seconds before taking a deep breath and walking into the room. "Now what?"

Lizzy absently waved to the other side of the table as she gathered up a scalpel and a small drill. "Now you sit there and hold his hand and wait for him to fall asleep. Which shouldn't be much longer now." She raised her eyes to look at him. "If at any time you have to leave, do so quietly and without jostling him. And don't lose your temper, please."

"Why would I lose my temper?" Damion sat and held his Core's—his lover's—hand tightly. "Try not to just dream of me while you're napping."

"I have never dreamed of anything else," Requiem slurred right before his body relaxed completely.

Lizzy watched the holographic monitor for a minute or two before nodding to one of her nurses. The man walked up with a needle, gently brushing Requiem's hair aside to reveal the small divot below the tattoo on the back of the Core's head. He carefully inserted the needle directly into the center of the divot and injected a clear liquid.

"See, I am dreamy." Damion tried to make a light joke since he wasn't sure what the hell they were doing other than poking his lover.

Lizzy looked down at the back of Requiem's head, pushing his hair about with the opposite side of her gloved hand. Then she sighed, putting the scalpel down on the tray before picking up a shaver. She neatly and efficiently shaved the back of his head, brushing aside the falling white hair once it was severed. He soon had a straight line of white hair that stopped right above the tattoo horizontal across his head to end at his ears. She put the shaver down, changed her gloves with the help of the nurse, and picked up the scalpel once again to cut a thin line right across the divot.

"He's gonna have a cold neck," Damion muttered, trying to make a joke again. "And be a bit upset."

"Knit him a scarf," Lizzy commented dryly, lifting the small drill, placing the tip of the bit to the right of the divot. "You mentioned that he dreams?" She looked up at another screen, tilting the back of the drill farther to the left before starting up the drill at an angle, the tip going underneath the divot. She held the device completely still at that perfect angle until she seemed to get to where she wanted and immediately shut it off. She handed it to a waiting nurse before picking up a scalpel and pushing up the hair above the mark, waiting. "He dreams?"

"I guess," Damion said. "He never really told me about them. I know the first time he had one, it really upset him and he slept in his capsule afterward. Then the morning came and they wiped him." He wondered if that had been worse than this moment.

Lizzy's brow furrowed, her frown unseen beneath the mask. "They wiped him and he's still coherent?" she murmured. She cut another line across the other and then picked up a small bottle of liquid. She put a small dot of it on the back of Requiem's now bare head, one above and below the cut flesh, and one on either side. Then she grabbed a pair of forceps and carefully peeled each triangle of flesh back from the skull, sticking the tips to the liquid, where they adhered. Without the skin there, a small tube of indeterminable material was exposed, approximately a quarter inch in diameter.

Damion squeezed Requiem's hand tightly again. "When will we know?"

"Know what?" the doctor mumbled, inspecting the tube with a light.

"If you're going to make his head explode, what the fuck else?"

"You know how I mentioned not losing your temper?" she replied with a glare, shutting off the light and turning to grab a fishing-line-weight wire from the nurse. "We'll know if it happens."

"That isn't my temper," Damion said. "It was just a question." He watched as she slowly inserted the wire into the hole she had drilled beside the tube, feeding it through until it nearly hit the end of the tube where the second hole was made with deft precision for a camera. She looked up at a holo-screen that was emitting the feed from the camera. The chip could be seen on the screen, about the length of a grain of rice before being magnetized. A red light was blinking.

Lizzy let out a small growl. "The fucking thing has shifted. It's moved beyond the straight line of the insertion tube."

"You aren't going to paralyze him, are you?" he asked.

"Paralyzing would be a middle ground. We don't have a middle ground to choose from." Lizzy shifted the filament camera around so that she could see more of the chip. Sighing, she reached for a long, very thin rod on the tray. A tiny pair of pliers was on the tip of it with a loop at the top of the rod used to control the mouth of it. "Here we go." She carefully slid the rod into the tube, keeping her eyes on the holo-screen.

Damion was holding his breath and hadn't even realized it until he gave a loud sigh. "It's okay?"

Damion was answered by a sudden shrill of alarms, and the numbers on the monitor next to Requiem began plummeting.

"Nope." Lizzy cursed as she pulled the rod out and dumped it on the tray. "Shitshitshit," she chanted like a mantra. She quickly grabbed a needle with the same liquid as the one the technician had injected Requiem with earlier. "Hold him!" she ordered.

One technician was already holding his head still as he started to convulse. Others rushed over and pushed Damion out of the way to grab his arms, legs, hips, and shoulders, trying to keep him still.

"What's going on? What happened?" Damion screamed above the alarms with a cold ache in his chest.

Lizzy didn't answer, too intent on trying to keep the thrashing Requiem still as she lined up the tip of the needle with the exposed hole in the back of the Core's skull. Finding an opportunity, she quickly slipped the tip in and depressed the plunger. Almost immediately, his vitals slowed back to an appropriate rate. She watched the screens anxiously.

Then after a minute she let out a long breath, her body visibly sagging. When she nodded, everyone let go of the now quiet body.

"The injection we gave him earlier should have neutralized the chip until we could get it removed," Lizzy explained as she dropped the emptied syringe on the table. "There's a pulse that emits around the chip that serves as a warning device. Only a code held by the Creators can turn it off so that the chip can be accessed. Anyone else who attempts it will hit the barrier and the chip will immediately shut down Requiem. The only reason it didn't happen that way this time was because we had confused it with the earlier injection and it was slow to respond."

"He's okay?" Damion asked, looking at the unconscious man and back at the doctor. "Right?"

"I think I neutralized it before it did any permanent damage, but unfortunately I can't be sure. Once we're done, he either wakes up or he doesn't. There is no paralyzed. The chip goes for higher brain functions first. The fact that he's still breathing and his heart's still beating under his own power is a good sign, though." After picking up the rod again, she started over, sliding it down the tube and watching the screen.

"Great, so he might wake up blind or mute," Damion grumbled as he sat back down, looking at the unconscious man. "If he doesn't wake up, there's no hope."

"No, what I'm saying is he'll wake up fine, or he won't wake up. Like I told you before, there aren't any middle grounds here." Lizzy's voice was faint, obviously not following her own words. She slowly released one hand from the rod to gently grip the ring. She carefully pulled up on it, her eyes glued to the screen, her body tense. Finally she let out a long breath, slowly pulling the rod out of the tube with a slight tug.

A nurse was immediately at her elbow. As soon as the rod was clear of Requiem's skull, Lizzy turned. The nurse held a jar of liquid, and with a quiet plop, the chip dropped in and immediately began to dissolve.

"Well, that won't be doing any more damage."

Damion's left leg bounced up and down quickly. He felt helpless—utterly helpless.

"Turn the gas off," the doctor mumbled to the tech as she grabbed a small spray bottle off the table. She gently misted the adhered flaps of flesh opened like a four-petaled flower on the back of Requiem's skull. The telltale hiss of gas in the room slowly quieted as the skin came free.

With gentle fingers, Lizzy folded the flaps back in place before taking another bottle with a thin spout and running it over the lines her scalpel had made. With a needle and clear thread, she slowly sutured the cut flesh. Once done, she picked up the same bottle and squeezed a liberal amount in the drill hole before putting it down along with the bandages.

Letting out a long sigh, she pulled off her gloves and turned to the orderlies in the room. "Go ahead and take him to the tank for recovery."

"Are you sure that's the best?" Damion didn't know why, but the idea of submerging a man who just had something pulled out of his brain put him on edge. "He hates that thing."

"I understand that," Lizzy growled, but it lacked the bite it usually held as she yanked off her mask and walked out of the room, following the wheeled bed holding the Core. "But it's the fastest way for him to recover. The liquid in the submersion tank will heal him faster than lying around in a bed." She stopped before the tank, crossing her arms and sighing as she watched Requiem lifted gently to the top of the tank, still lying on the bed. "Besides, right now all we can do is wait until he wakes up."

"Waiting is something I really suck at." Damion turned and left Medical, feeling he was going to need a drink if he was going to make it the next few hours.

Chapter Seven

Tuesday, October 25, 455MC
1453 GMT
Damion

DAMION WALKED all the way to his room, found the bottle Athena had dropped off two days ago, and broke it open. He wanted to be in the room with his lover and wanted to be there when he woke up. But he didn't want to be in the room if Requiem didn't wake up. He took two large drinks of the potent alcohol and sat on the edge of the bed. What would he do if Requiem didn't wake up?

A soft knock on the frame of the open door tore through Damion's musings. Athena leaned against the frame with her arms crossed over her chest, her expression sympathetic. "Lizzy gave me a brief report of what happened. You doin' okay?"

"Super." Damion gave her a large, fake smile. "How are you doing?"

"Hiding currently. Wolfe is a fucking harpy about shit." She gave him her own small smile back. After pushing away from the doorframe, she slowly walked into the room. "You know it was the only option, right?"

Damion sipped from the bottle for a few moments before answering. "Yeah, and he wanted it—wanted to not be wiped by the Creators again."

"The doc said you mentioned that once. She wanted to ask you a little more about it, but she was kinda in the middle of brain surgery at the time." Athena pulled a chair from the table and plopped onto it. "She was surprised that he was wiped once and still has a personality or a brain. How'd that happen?"

Damion shrugged and tilted toward the right as the liquor hit. "He was getting on my nerves really badly after they wiped him, so I pushed sex. And maybe it was bordering on violent, but it was that or lose him. It seemed to snap him out of the robot state a little bit at a time."

Athena quirked an eyebrow at him. "Do you always violently fuck him when he pisses you off or annoys you?"

Damion gave her a blurry-eyed look, and he knew it was time to stop drinking if he hoped to be sober at all the rest of the day. "I guess I do."

"Why? Why do you feel you have to punish him?" Athena tilted her head. "Hasn't he been through enough of that in his life?"

"I wouldn't say it's punishment." Damion chuckled. "It feels good for both of us, and for some reason he does respond to actions and pain better than words. You can talk at him for hours or just shag him, and it seems the shagging does the trick." He winked at her with false bravado before leaning back onto the bed. "He's not like other Cores, or even other humans."

Athena stood and plucked the half-empty bottle from unresisting fingers and took a swig herself. "You ever think that it may be because you trained him that way? Cores are very susceptible to their Fighter's wants and needs and respond and act how they feel their Fighter wishes them to do so. They don't have the nickname of pets for nothing."

"He'd follow my orders, that is true. But if they were orders he doesn't like, he'd make this face." Damion sighed as he closed his eyes, enjoying the relaxed feeling, since before it felt like his jaw would break from clenching it. "He is stubborn."

"But he'd still follow them." Athena tapped the bottle against Damion's hand, forcing him to take it. "I must admit, I've never met another Core with more personality. And the fact that he even had it on the stims is amazing. He'd *have* to be stubborn to fight against them."

"I tell him not to do something and he'd do it anyway if he thought it would help me in some way. Stubborn. There has to be another word for that asshole." Damion sat up so he could drink and not choke.

"Protective. Caring. Obstinate." Athena listed off words, ticking her fingers for each one. Then she shrugged. "He only does it to keep you safe, from what I've heard. And yet you punish him for it. It's just a guess, but I'm fairly sure if it wasn't for you, he would have let that chip just blow up and kill him."

"It's not his job to protect me; it's my job to protect him!" Damion screamed, not meaning to snap at the captain. But he couldn't hold back his frustration. "He thinks that even his death is warranted if he believes my life would be easier or safer. Fuck him for thinking that! If I have to do something to drill in the fact that my life is not any more precious than his, and it involves smacking him or fucking him, I'm going to do it."

Athena's eyebrows rose at the venom in Damion's protests, and she leaned back in her chair. "You ever think there might be another way to go about it, other than making the poor boy bleed?"

"Like how?" Damion asked, still a bit angry. "I told you, talking to him doesn't do any good. He just talks right back in circles."

She shrugged. "You know him best. I can only make observations and suggestions. Just think about how his life was before you came into it. I only know pieces and parts, and I'm sure a lot of the previous Fighters' indiscretions were never reported, but I do know that it was brutal."

"I've never beaten him or raped him." Damion felt as if he had to justify himself to her, and it was getting on his nerves. "I always knew he was human."

"Never said you didn't. Anybody can tell you think of him as such." Athena stretched. "But there are many different ways to beat a person. It doesn't have to involve fists. And while I'm all into kinky sex and all, generally my partners don't bleed from cuffs or have bruises all over them afterward."

"Generally?" He gave her another smirk. "Look, if he told me to stop, I'd stop. And if he was scared, I'd stop. He likes it rough and I like it rough. It was almost a full year before I even fucked him the first time, and then after he was wiped clean, it was months before I did it again."

"You held out for a year?" Athena blinked at him and then shook her head. "Why? One of the duties a Core is supposed to perform is sexually satisfying their Fighter. So why'd you wait that long to do it again?"

"Why? Because he'd already been used as a fuck toy by three other Fighters, and really even those scientists on the *Zeus* were fucking him in another way." Damion scratched the back of his head. "I didn't want to force him. I wanted to wait until he was ready, but I couldn't use anyone else or he'd give me those guilty eyes."

Athena snorted in disbelief. "I think you were imagining things. When he walked in on us, all he had was a blank unemotional stare."

"You saw blank." Damion gave her a frown. "But I knew he was upset."

"He always seems blank except for the occasional flash of comprehension." The captain shrugged again. "But like I said, you know him best. You can take a blank canvas and get something from it."

"So what is your plan?" Damion wanted to know what torture he'd agreed to.

"Plan? Which one? I have many, so you'll have to be a bit more specific." Athena's brow furrowed.

"The one involving me." He gave her a snarl. "You want me to go back."

"Ah, that one." Athena stretched her long body, her vest coming up to show her well-toned stomach as she let out a breath and shifted in her seat. She propped her boots up on the table. "Drink more. You're still ornery as fuck."

She was quiet for a moment and then switched gears. "We have to wait until Jasper gets back, which will be in about three days. In the meantime, the *Ares* is being partially repaired. If we do a full repair, then it'll look suspicious. We're just fixing the engines so that you can take Jasper and limp back to the *Zeus*. From the reports we've received, his security force is making the *Zeus* their base while still looking for him."

She gave Damion a long up-and-down look. "Sorry to say, but we may have to rough you up a bit to make it look authentic. There's no way they're going to believe that you were captured and escaped without a scratch. Though it pains me to mar that pretty skin."

Damion laughed. "Admit it, you still want to hurt me for leaving you hot and bothered."

"Well, there is a tiny part of me that will take some pleasure in it, I'll admit." Athena's lips twitched in a grin. "Anytime you want to finish what we started, let me know. But I'm not going to risk being fried in my sleep." Her fingers picked invisible pieces of lint from her pants. "Anyway, once you're back on the *Zeus,* Jasper will insist on you getting a promotion. Obviously you'll no longer be a Fighter since they think your Core is dead, but you'll still need access to confidential information. You'll have a contact there who you'll report to as well."

"Depending on the outcome," the captain went on, "Req… 47 will stay here and be your direct contact to us. We'll give you a device, and he'll be able to receive communications from you via a jack-in tech that we're developing. That way, you'll still have minimal contact with each other."

Damion shook his head. "He won't like it. And how long will I have to stay? I know you're keeping him as leverage."

Athena did not try to deny it. "Perhaps, but it is also for your protection. If you two went back, one or both of you would die. You'll have to explain it to him if he wakes up before you leave." She sighed, running her fingers through her ruby-toned hair. "As for how long, I don't know. It all depends on what happens. What intel is retrieved, or if it becomes too much of a sticky situation for you to remain there."

"He's going to give me that look." Damion felt heavy as he lay back down. "And if shit goes wrong, I'm dead."

"It's a risk we all take. I asked you if you wanted to help, and this is how we need it. You'll potentially be saving thousands, perhaps millions of lives with the intel you will provide."

He rolled to his side and laughed. "Me, a savior of lives? You better reread that dossier!"

"Before you joined the Chrysalis Corporation, you worked in the mine back on Mars. One day, there was a line of explosives and they went off. The mine collapsed, trapping twenty-seven workers underground. When rescuers pulled you out from the collapsed entrance, you turned right back around and started pulling out rock. About two hours into the rescue, a dust storm hit, leaving no visibility and making it hard to breathe, on top of being poisonous. Everyone knew they had to evacuate, but you also knew that if you did, the dust would cover whatever air was left in the chamber that held the trapped miners. You continued to pull rock even when others gave up. That night you saved twenty-one of those workers while suffering injuries and dust inhalation. You were in the hospital for nearly a month and then went right back to work."

Athena sounded as if she was quoting his file. "That's only one example. I have plenty more, the least of all being saving Requiem's life from a fate worse than death."

"That isn't hero bullshit; that's just doing what my gut told me was the right thing to do." Damion stood up and walked unsteadily over to the captain. He leaned forward and put his hands on the armrests of the chair, looking her straight in the eyes.

"I didn't join the Army for fame and glory, babe. I joined because I didn't want to die in that stinking sand trap of a planet like most of my family before me did or some shit. I wasn't expecting to make a difference, but I figured I'd rather die fighting as a soldier than die as a worker ant under someone's shoe. Even if I died as a Fighter, they would send my parents a year's worth of severance pay. That might not be a lot to you, but it could do some good for my mom. I just know you're about to send me back into the lion's den, and the only reasons why I am not fighting are because you saved my Core, you promised me the Commander on *Zeus* is sure as dead, and I suppose a small part of me doesn't think you're completely wrong."

He couldn't help but look down her vest, a grin on his face. "That doesn't make me a hero, and I'm not planning on dying for anyone's cause."

The captain quirked an eyebrow at him, her lips twitching into a grin. "Ah, but that's the definition of a hero. Doing something because it's right and not just running to save your own ass. Saving lives. It doesn't matter what the road was that got you there; it's what you do when it comes down to the wire."

She crossed her arms under her breasts, effectively bringing them up and giving Damion more to look at. "And does drinking always make you want to jump the thing closest to you? I told you, I'm not going to start it for fear of being fried by your little friend, but I'll sure as fuck finish it."

"He's a silent killer." Damion chuckled before going back to the bed, not wanting the temptation. "He might even wake up."

"All the more reason. It might goad him into waking," Athena said with a soft laugh. "Such a shame. All the handsome ones are gay or taken. In your case, both."

"I am not gay." Damion gave her a weak glare.

Athena rolled her eyes. "Sure, you just choose butt sex over straight sex."

"He's the first man I've ever had sex with. Before that it was only girls."

"Oh sure, blame him for turning you gay," Athena teased. "And I'm guessing you'll never have sex with another woman in your life."

Damion's head listed to the side. "I can't say that, since I can't see the future, and I would greatly enjoy fucking you once in my life if I didn't have to worry about him getting upset. Also, we have different views on sex, I think. Me, I don't even have to know a girl's real name to fuck her. For him it's different."

Athena made the sound of a whip. "It's amazing how that little man has you so wrapped around his finger by just existing."

Damion crossed his arms. "He is my partner."

"Partners don't give a shit if the other fucks other people. And generally the one doing the fucking doesn't care what his partner thinks," Athena pointed out, using her pinky for emphasis.

"It's different. He's different. If he was just another hole it would be simple, but he actually feels pain and remorse and hurt." Damion rubbed his eyes with the palms of his hands. "When will we know?"

"Every Core feels those things in some way, shape, or form. They are just forced to repress it and not acknowledge what they're feeling." Athena sighed. "We'll know when he wakes up, Hawk."

"How?" Damion didn't want to go into the room and just sit and wait because that would drive him just as nuts. At least here he didn't have to listen to the monitors and watch Requiem float.

"How what, Captain Vague? How do Cores feel, or how will we know when he wakes up?"

Damion rolled his eyes. "How will we know when he wakes up?"

"When Lizzy tells us." Athena leaned over Damion. "You know, maybe you should get some sleep. You look like hell."

"You want to help me fall asleep?" He gave her his most charming grin.

Athena shook her head. "We've already had this discussion, pretty boy. You don't have the balls to do anything about it. Your Core has them. Besides, I've already helped by supplying you alcohol."

"He doesn't have them. And you could always try and change my mind again." He didn't know why he liked to bait the woman, but he did.

"I think I'll save myself the frustration, thank you very fucking much." She frowned. "Are you looking for an excuse? You goad me into molesting you and then when 47 finds out, you blame it all on me?"

Damion laughed. "I take credit for my own mistakes, don't worry about that. But no, goading you is pretty damn fun."

Athena pointed her finger at him. "Bullshit! You blamed me and the alcohol last time."

"No I didn't. I blamed him for being dead." Damion reached out to grab her wrist and drag her down to the bed. "I do blame you for flaunting your naked body and getting me all hot and bothered."

Athena's eyes widened as he dragged her out of the chair. She landed on her stomach across him. "That's exactly what I'm saying! You took no blame for yourself!"

"All right, if Requiem wakes up, I'll walk up to him and blame myself for your tight ass and you handcuffing me to a bed. Will that make you happy?"

Athena's eyes eventually trailed to Damion's face. "My tight ass, as you say, is off-limits. I know it's been a while, but women have another hole for you to use."

"Very funny." He looked at her with a deep curiosity. "Perhaps I just have an addiction to using sex to make myself feel better. What do you think?"

"I think you're drunk, insane, and a sex addict," Athena said. "I think it's also a good thing that your Core is unconscious right now."

"If he were awake, I would be trying to nurse him into a healthy state." He hummed. "Probably not drunk with you over my lap."

"Mmm, I would be tossed aside like yesterday's trash yet again." Athena crossed her arms. "Does nursing back into a healthy state involve screwing him senseless?"

"Probably." Damion was surprised at the truth of his answer. "You know, if he wasn't around, this would be a great moment to prove that I am still one hell of a man in bed with any woman. Especially when the woman is as hot as you."

"Wow, how do you get into the *Ares* with an ego like that?" Athena laughed, shaking her head as she flipped over so she was actually sitting in Damion's lap instead of draped over it. "So was there any point in dragging me into my current position, or were you merely being all macho man on me?" She slowly ran a fingernail over Damion's lower lip.

"At some point I thought that, if he wasn't going to wake up, I could just drown my rather repressed emotions with hours upon hours with an incredibly sexy pirate woman." Damion grinned ear to ear, but it quickly faded. "But I'm not sure if he's going to get up or not."

"Well, *you've* certainly gotten up," Athena drawled, moving her hips slightly so that her ass rubbed against the anatomy poking her. "So what you're saying is, that if it was brought to our attention that your Core was never going to wake up again, you'd immediately have sex with me?"

"You wouldn't comfort me?" He couldn't help but flirt with the woman.

"That's just cold," she said, shaking her head.

"I guess I don't do well when he's almost dead." Damion brushed her hair back. "I really wish he'd stop that."

"Do you ever do well?" Athena moaned. "And this time it's not his fault."

"Good point; he didn't put that thing in his head." Damion grinned. "You getting frustrated again?"

She curled her fingers around his shoulders. "I'm still wondering if you're going to cross the line again, because I know you'll just whine about it later, even if it is a good time. And I assure you, it will be."

Damion looked at the prime, warm, willing woman on his lap. But then an odd feeling began to creep into his chest. It was the same damn ache he felt the last time they were together. Why did he care what Requiem would think? Damion wasn't sure if Requiem was even going to survive!

"You think I'm going to regret this?" he asked.

Athena nodded. "Yes. Yes, I do. Especially when he wakes up and opens his eyes and looks at you. I think guilt will hit you like a ton of bricks."

Damion's face turned sour with rising anger. "Why? If it wasn't for him, but I can't stop…. I mean, me and you could be good."

"Can't stop what?" Athena placed callused fingers over Damion's hand. "And yes, we could. Gods, we could. But you need to decide if you want to risk it."

"I can't stop worrying about him." Damion choked out his confession to the one person who could order both of their deaths. "Ever since he fucking appeared, all I do is worry about him."

"Out of duty or out of personal feeling for him?" Athena asked gently. "You carry a little love for the Core, even if you don't want to admit it."

Damion pulled at the captain's hair. "I don't know. All I can think about is how good it would be to just do it with you, but then something hurts when I think how pissed he'll be. And before you say anything, yes, he'll be pissed. Not to mention hurt."

"I don't deny he has feelings, Damion. Just that he doesn't know what they are. You'll have to teach him them. I have a few liberated Cores on board who will attempt to help him acclimate while you're on a mission. But you need to figure out your feelings for the man before you leave." Athena pulled her hair out of Damion's grasp with a wince.

"I know that doesn't leave you much time, but it might be important. He'll be here alone, without you, and he'll need something to hold on to to keep him grounded."

"That being said, him finding out we had hours of sweaty sex will just make it harder on him." Damion fell back onto the bed, pressing the heels of his hands into his eye sockets. "Fuck, fuck, fuck!"

Athena flailed as she fell back across Damion's body as her support disappeared. Her hips were elevated as her ass rested on Damion's hips. "That is the action in question, isn't it?"

She paused for a moment, staying where she was but putting her arms under her head. "Now the question is, would the amazing sex outweigh the guilt you would feel afterward? Are you just horny and don't have your usual fuck buddy so you're looking for the next best thing? Or are you trying to prove something to yourself?"

"You're not making this easy on me," Damion muttered.

"Only because I'm making a point and making you think about your feelings. Very emasculating, I know. But I'm a woman, it's my job. Now answer the questions."

"I don't know!" Damion growled, pulling his hands away from his face and glaring at the ceiling. "I don't want him to die and I don't want him to hate me or be disappointed in me. I've never been in love."

"Sounds like you hold him and his opinions in high regard," Athena said calmly. "Love is a risk."

"I am not gay. I could fuck you. Means I'm bi. It's not that big of a surprise anymore." He had to get over himself. He was starting to get on his own nerves.

"You trying to prove it to me or to yourself?" Athena rolled her eyes. "It doesn't matter who you want to fuck or who you love, Damion. Leave off the labels. I know you find me attractive; that was never the issue. The issue is what you're avoiding. You're avoiding the fact that you have strong feelings for 47, and you have them buried so far up your ass that they're blinding you from the truth."

"You just like looking at my ass." He couldn't help the sarcasm; it flowed out naturally. "Do you think he'll live?"

Athena was quiet for a moment. "He didn't die on the table. But there's living and then there's living. I don't really know. He may never wake up. Or on the other side of the coin, he may wake up today, tomorrow, next week. I just don't know."

"I can't leave without knowing." Damion clenched his jaw.

"Damion…." She paused. "If a Core doesn't wake up after two days, they usually don't. Ever."

"Two days?" He rubbed his eyes. "Two days. Just fucking wonderful. Then you better stay the fuck out of my room for two days."

"If he wakes, he may wake before then." With a grunt, Athena sat up, sliding to sit on the bed. "So you've decided on trying to control yourself? Have you realized why yet?"

"I guess I'm waiting on him." Damion chuckled as he sat up. "And I think you're a foul temptress and a kidnapper."

"Mmm, and you keep avoiding the questions and the truth. Besides…." Athena looked over at him and grinned. "You're so easy to tempt." She stood then, stretching.

Damion rolled his eyes. "There's the ball-busting bitch I've been expecting."

"I aim to please." She walked to the door. "And I hate to disappoint."

"Something tells me that you never disappoint," Damion yelled at her departing back while glaring at the wall across from him.

A laugh and then a pause of footsteps met his yells, beeping filling the hall. Athena started talking to someone on her communicator, but it was muffled until she let out a surprised "Holy shit!" She ran back to the open door, eyes wide, mouth twisted up like a grinning idiot. "Your Core doesn't like to disappoint either. His vitals are showing he's going to wake up soon."

Damion's shock lifted the heaviness in his chest. "Soon? How soon?"

"Lizzy says if his vitals continue on the path they are, perhaps in about an hour or so." Athena was grinning ear to ear, her eyes shining.

"How in the hell does he do that?" Damion rubbed the back of his head.

"You're the one who said he's stubborn. And he's not awake yet," Athena pointed out, still grinning. "This just gives you an opportunity to tell him how you really feel before you leave."

"*I* don't even know how to explain it to myself," he said. "But I'm happy that he's going to make it."

"Well, he's not completely out of the woods yet. But his chances just got a whole lot better," Athena explained. "Do you want to be there when he wakes up?"

He nodded. "Yeah. But just sitting there would drive me nuts. I don't even have my books."

Athena leaned against the doorframe. "It's completely up to you, of course. I'm sure I can find you something to read, but in the end, I think you're just scared."

"I am not afraid," Damion claimed defensively. "I don't allow myself to be afraid."

"Mm-hmm. Keep telling yourself that." Athena pushed away from the frame. "Well, I'm going to visit sleeping beauty. You wallow here."

"No, I'm going too." Damion stood up and combed his fingers through his hair.

"I thought you would be bored." She gave him a knowing grin. "Are you sober enough?"

"I'm not that much of a lightweight," he grumbled. "You just wish you could drink like me."

"I could drink you under the table anytime. We'll just make sure your chaperone is there to carry you to bed." Athena grinned and motioned for him to leave the room.

Damion grabbed her hand. "One day I will have to prove my manly self to you."

Athena looked down at their joined hands and then back up to his face, eyebrow raised. "Oh really now? I'd say you already have. I've already seen the manliest thing about you."

"Can he have a shuttle to himself, at least?" Damion frowned, the thought suddenly coming to him. "Requiem would want his own space."

"I don't think that would be a problem. He'll have to be stationed outside of the ship to get in touch with you. A shuttle attached on the outer hull should work," Athena told him. "And of course, he'll be able to keep your current space."

"I don't think I'll be coming back to the ship often, I'm guessing, so no need to keep a room open just for me." Damion reasoned that if he were supposed to live and be treasonous, it would not benefit him to visit the head of the pirate fleet often.

"We won't, he will. That will be his room until you come back if he chooses to use it," Athena corrected.

"I think you've thought this through well enough." Damion shook his head.

She shrugged as the lift came to a stop. "It's my job to take care of my crew, and now you and Requiem are a part of it. I try to think of every problem and every possible solution."

Damion grinned. "You just don't want me to die before you get one more chance to have me naked for hours."

Athena threw her hands up. "Good Gods, you have an ego on you. How the hell do you get through doorways?"

"You already asked me how I get into my ship, and the answer is always the same. With skill." Damion felt in a much better mood so suddenly it was almost unnerving.

The captain snorted. "Perhaps. Or perhaps you just believe in it so much you get by with amazing luck."

Chapter Eight

Damion

THEY WALKED out of the lift and into the hallway, toward the medical facilities. Damion frowned when he saw the flashing lights. "What the hell is going on?

"Fuck!" Athena bolted down the hallway. "It means something went wrong!" She slammed her palm against the key to open the Med door.

They stepped out of the hallway and into chaos. Medical techs were running all over the room, and Lizzy was standing beside the monitoring system in front of Requiem. She was pointing and shouting orders like a hardened battle commander. The tank itself was covered in a giant dark cloth from top to bottom, effectively keeping out all light and sound to give the person inside a calm environment to recover. Even with the mayhem in the room, Damion could hear pounding coming from within the fluid-filled cylinder. Fluid lapped over the unseen top of the tank to soak the cloth surrounding it as Requiem thrashed. Damion's chest constricted as he stood, uncertain what he should be doing. He was so far out of his depth. All he knew was that he needed to help Requiem. Requiem was his priority.

Requiem

REQUIEM DREAMED. As soon as darkness invaded his mind, the gas dragging him into unconsciousness, the images started. Or really, the memories. Pieces, fragments of his childhood—or what he had to consider his childhood. He had never really noticed how dark it had been.

The first memory brought him to a classroom. He and nine others were there, all staring straight ahead, perfect posture in their seats. He couldn't hear the words that were spoken, only saw the movement of the Creator's mouth. Holo-screens were on either side of him, showing the different parts of a capsule and what each input affected. Fade out.

Fade in. He saw himself as a child, perhaps eight years old, strapped face-up on a chair. There was a gag in his mouth and his eyes had been forced open, the eyelids pulled back. His body was tense, pulling against the bonds that kept him in the chair, corded muscles straining against his pale skin. A Creator was standing over him in medical scrubs with a port in between forceps as another pried cut skin apart in the left side of his chest to install it just below the skin, in the muscle. Blood trailed down his ribs. Red against white. Fade out.

Fade in. Fifteen years old, standing in a line with others of his age. They watched without flinching as another of their age group was strapped to a chair, screaming, blond hair thrashing about. The Creators plugged a jack into the back of the child's skull and turned to look at the line. Watching them, the Creator flipped a switch. The child's screams increased in volume, ragged, in agony as the body bowed. And then suddenly—silence—his body collapsing. Glassy eyes were open, chest rising and falling, but there was no more intelligence. No one was home anymore. They had wiped him completely. Fade out.

Fade in. Darkness. Complete and utter darkness. No sight, no smell, no touch, no sounds. Nothing. They had put him in the desensitization tank again. He had been injected with a numbing agent so he couldn't even feel the thick liquid around him, or the plugs in his ears and nose, or the air from the circulator strapped to his mouth, or the blindfold over his eyes. Nothing. He felt like he was being crushed, the air growing thinner and the walls closing in. He couldn't move, couldn't breathe, couldn't scream. He was trapped, and he couldn't move a finger to try to get out. So his screams were in his own head. He had always had a mild distaste for the desensitization tank. But now he felt something else. He felt fear. The unimaginable terror that squeezed his heart, constricted his lungs, and made him go mad.

Requiem crossed from unconsciousness to full wakefulness without ever knowing. He woke still trapped in his dream, not even acknowledging that he could move, that he could feel the liquid around him. All he knew was complete darkness and silence. Except now he could fight. He screamed against the rebreather, his hands coming up to feel glass walls around him, and he pounded against them, kicking them to try and get free. He had to get out. He would do anything to get out. Tears flowed from his eyes, mixing with the solution around him. He ignored the pain that rocked his body, head, and hands as he pounded against the glass.

Finally, there was sound—the distant sound of splashing. The water curled around his body as something fell into the water with him. A tickle of bubbles caressed his skin as he backed away from whatever it was but quickly came up against the side of the tank. Turning, he beat against it, feeling even more claustrophobic now. But it hadn't been something—it was someone. Arms wrapped around him, pinning his arms to his sides as he was pulled back against a hard, clothed chest. He struggled for a few more moments until he felt a familiar pain of teeth digging into his shoulder, familiar arms surrounding him, letting him know who it was. Requiem immediately calmed, his body sagging in Damion's embrace. Safe. He was safe. Damion had him and wouldn't allow him to come to harm. Unless, of course, the Fighter was the one doing the harming.

He felt Damion's strong legs start to kick, and suddenly they surfaced, both of them taking deep breaths. Requiem opened his eyes, staring at the blinding lights above them, not caring that they hurt his eyes. He continued to stare at them as Damion pulled him out of the tank and they collapsed to the platform beside it. He clung to the man, his arms wrapped around one of Damion's arms, pressing back against the man's warm body as they both shivered. He curled into a ball as he tried to stop the panic that pulsed through his body, tried to stop the pounding of his heart. He couldn't seem to get enough air.

"Damn it all to fucking hell, you stupid jackasses!" Damion continued to curse at the lab techs as they ran around. "Get me some towels, you worthless shits! And get these lines off him!"

The techs all jumped at his words. One knelt down to disconnect Requiem, pulling the lines out of his jacks. She gently tried to pull the air circulator out of Requiem's mouth and nose, but Requiem's teeth were clenched around it and unwilling to unlock. "I can't get the rebreather," the woman said to Damion, while another tech ran over with blankets and wrapped them both in multiple.

"What the hell happened, Hawk?" Lizzy demanded, appearing behind them on the platform. "One minute he was fine, and the next he was trying to break my damn tank!"

"He's having a panic attack, you stupid bitch." Damion put his free hand against Requiem's forehead. "You open your mouth right now. You hear me? Requiem? Open your fucking mouth now!"

Requiem whimpered, shying away from both the tech and Lizzy. But hearing Damion's orders, he immediately opened his mouth, releasing the circulator abruptly. The tech fell back on her ass and then scrambled away.

Damion appeared scared and panicked. "The deprivation tanks... they're like this."

"We always use this method with Cores after removing the chips, and none of them have ever had a reaction like this." Lizzy knelt next to the tech struggling with the air systems and taking Requiem's pulse.

"Hawk, calm the fuck down," Athena called up from the lower level. "He'll be fine. How the hell were they supposed to know he's claustrophobic? Did you even know?"

"You want me to give him something to calm him down or you want to try first?" Lizzy asked Damion, completely ignoring his foul mood.

Requiem twisted to wrap his arms around Damion and curl his body around him as he trembled, taking deep, panicked gulps of air.

"He's not claustrophobic! He was just scared!" Damion took a deep breath. "Knock him out. He won't snap out of this without help. Just dose him up."

"I'm telling you she's right. This looks like a panic attack brought on by claustrophobia," Lizzy stated. She grabbed a syringe and knelt down again, reaching for Requiem's arm.

Somehow Requiem found enough breath to scream, bat her away, and cling closer to Damion. Any time he found more breath, he continued a barely audible mantra of "Nononononononono."

The doctor huffed as she got up. "Control him so I can get the needle in. He keeps thrashing around like that, I can't inject him. I fucking swear, biggest pain in the ass patient I've ever had."

"Just shut up and give me the needle. I'll do it," Damion snapped.

"Don't make me sedate you too, asshole," Lizzy threatened but handed over the needle. "It won't knock him out, but it'll calm him down."

"Please, no. Do not send me back there. Please, Damion, do not send me back to the darkness," Requiem whispered, shaking his head. His arms clenched down even tighter on Damion's midsection. He kept his eyes wide open, almost afraid to blink, lest he go back into the nightmares.

"Even in the darkness I'll be there, so you have nothing to fear. We don't fear," Damion said sternly as he found a patch of pale skin to inject the medication into Requiem's muscle.

Almost immediately, Requiem's grip loosened, his body going slack and rolling off Damion's lap and onto the cold steel of the platform. Tears were still in his eyes as they found Damion's face. "Then where were you in my nightmares?" he whispered, a slightly accusatory look on his face.

"You must have forgotten about me, because I was right there trying to get to you, obviously." Damion put a hand on Requiem's back. "You look like a pale drowned rat, and I don't think I look much better."

"I could never forget you. Even if the Creators got ahold of me again," Requiem promised, his words slurred, his eyes half closed as he fumbled with numb fingers to pull the blanket around his shoulders.

Lizzy gently turned Requiem's unresisting body on its side so she could check the wound in the back of his head. "It's healing nicely." She looked up at Damion. "Let's get you guys into a warming chamber and into some new clothes. You want to carry him, or should I ask them to bring a stretcher?"

"It'll be better if I just handle it, in case he wakes up again. He hates med clinics." Damion sighed. "He might be a pain in the ass, but he's my pain in the ass." He picked up Requiem's limp body and slowly stood. "Lead the way."

"Not asleep," Requiem slurred, his eyes still open even as he buried his face against Damion's neck.

Lizzy supported Damion's arm so that they all didn't go ass over teakettle down the stairs. "The heating room is next to the surgery room. One of my techs is already setting it up. There's clothes waiting for you there as well," she instructed, her tone clipped.

"All right, but then we're going back to our room and you can stop poking at him for a few weeks," Damion joyfully said. "Thanks for not scrambling his brain."

"My pleasure, but I think next time I might try to scramble yours. You turn into such an asshole when it concerns him," Lizzy mumbled, shaking her head as she led them to the room. "And I don't think it's wise for him to leave Med Bay yet. He just had brain surgery, for God's sake."

"Besides," Athena chimed in as she joined them, a pack of smokes in her hand, "any time you take him back to your room with orders to rest, you never let him rest."

"This is one part of women I don't miss." Damion ground his teeth. "He's just going to flip out again if he stays here, because something will set him off, and that'll delay his healing even longer. We don't have that time."

"And this is why men are stupid. Time shouldn't matter when we're talking about his health," Athena said with a roll of her eyes while Lizzy keyed open the door. Steam and humidity immediately poured out of the room.

Lizzy ushered them inside. "I suggest getting undressed before you laze about. There's a bathroom off to the right where you can dry off and get changed. And there's a door that leads out here so you don't have to go back through the heat. Take your time, and we'll discuss things when you're warm and hopefully less cranky."

The door slid shut behind them, leaving Requiem alone with Damion. "Women." He pulled Requiem to the side and began stripping the scrub pants and boxers from his thin body. "Hey, you. You understand me?"

"I attempt to," Requiem replied lazily, his body near dead weight as Damion tugged his boxers off and pulled his blanket closer.

The room was hazy with steam and dimmed with red lights. There were benches lining the walls and a bed with bars on it off to one side. Off to the other was the door for the bathroom Lizzy had mentioned.

Damion sat them down and pushed back Requiem's long bangs. "You're free from the Corporation. One hundred percent."

"Never be free," Requiem mumbled, leaning heavily against Damion, shivering every once in a while. "Can never go back."

Frowning, he slowly lifted a heavy arm, his hand falling to the back of his head. His fingers ran over the creases of the healing cuts and the smoothness of the back of his shaved skull. Bleary eyes looked to Damion in confusion.

"They had to cut in the back there and probe pretty deep, so they gave you an odd haircut." The Fighter laughed. "I guess you do look a bit weird that way, but it will grow back. Are you able to move all your fingers and toes, and are you still the smartest person in this part of the galaxy?"

Requiem moved his fingers and toes to prove to Damion he could, but he shook his head in answer to the second question. His brain still felt fuzzy, even as his body warmed up. "I very much doubt that I am the most intelligent being in any galaxy," he stated as he slid down on the bench, laying his head in Damion's bare lap. His body was too heavy to keep upright any longer.

Damion petted Requiem's head lightly. "I was almost convinced you wouldn't wake up, ever. Now here you are. You are something."

Requiem shivered again, but it wasn't from being cold. It was the images from his nightmare coming back to haunt him. "Were there complications?" he asked.

"Your head almost blew off into small pieces." Damion leaned his own head back. "You started to seize and jump around, and then you seemed okay."

Requiem was silent for a few minutes, going over that piece of information, pushing it through his hazy brain. "I am sorry to have caused you any distress," he finally said. "May I ask what you would have done if I had not woken?"

"I'm not really sure," Damion answered. "I was trying to think of that right before I had word you were about to wake up."

"I would hope that you would live your life. To go back home, or anywhere else besides the Chrysalis Corporation." Requiem shifted slightly to get more comfortable. The back of his head was throbbing, but anything was preferable to the blinding headaches he'd had before. He was on his side facing Damion, his eyes on Damion's toned stomach. "But I also understand that the Corporation is everywhere and that would be difficult."

"The pirates want me to spy on the Corporation, actually, but yeah, I had thought a few times of just going home. At least I know what's killing me there." Damion shrugged as he rested his hand on Requiem's shoulder. "I'm glad you woke up."

"They want us to go back?" Requiem frowned, his fingers idly caressing Damion's bare thigh. "But I cannot go back. They will kill me." His brain slowly went through the facts, his thoughts moving like molasses until he realized what Damion was really saying. Somehow he managed to push himself up on leaden arms, his eyes wide as he looked at Damion's face. "You are leaving me." The words were whispered and slightly accusing.

"Not leaving, really, just paying my share for your freedom. I suppose we're already traitors in the Commander's mind, and I'll be lucky if he doesn't try to kill me on sight." Damion shook his head. "We'll be able to contact each other, or they're going to try, at least."

If he hadn't already been dosed, Requiem was quite confident that he would have been panicking again. "I do not trust these people, Damion. While I do believe in what they are doing and what they are fighting for, I do not trust their intentions toward us. They have lulled us into a false sense of security by helping me, and also with the Captain's seduction of you. Their cause is legitimate, but I have found evidence of Captain Athena doing anything and everything for her cause."

"All good rulers do that, and I'm not saying I trust them, but we can't escape from here. And even if we could, like you pointed out, where would we go? We can't go back to the *Zeus*, and if we ran back to Mars someone could report us, and then we'd still end up dead or worse. Hate feeling trapped. Until we can find a way to get out of this on our own without one of us ending up dead, then we have no choice but to follow along. I told the captain she needed to give you space and to leave you alone. Once you're back up to 100 percent, I'll have to hope you can booby trap your room so you'll be safe no matter what happens. I also want you to have a shuttle."

"How long?" Requiem's voice was hoarse, his eyes still boring into Damion's. "How long will you be in danger? How long will I be left here?" He didn't want Damion to leave, he didn't want him to be in danger, and he certainly didn't want to be left alone with a ship full of people he didn't know or trust. Damion was the only one he had ever fully given his trust to. People he didn't know—besides Juni and 108— were just out to hurt him. And he was tired of being in pain.

"I don't know. I know you don't like being lied to," Damion said. "I just don't know."

"Too many contrasting variables," Requiem mumbled, slowly lying back down, his body too heavy to hold up anymore. His fingers went back to tracing idle patterns on Damion's skin as he attempted to think through the fuzziness of his brain. The heat was making him drowsy.

"Isn't that life?" Damion smirked. "Hey, be a bit happier, okay? I had to fight off that woman again."

"I am sure it was a difficult battle," Requiem responded dryly. "Death-defying, even."

He looked at Requiem as if the man had grown a third head. "What the fuck? Did they inject you with a smartass function?"

Requiem actually had the grace to look embarrassed. "I apologize, that was uncalled for. I have no right to say anything on the matter of yours and Captain Athena's relationship. Please forgive my words."

"I just wasn't expecting that from you. Hey… are you always afraid of closed-off places?" Damion said.

"I promise I will not speak so out of turn again." Requiem was grateful for the subject change, if not the subject matter. "I do not know. I have always felt uncomfortable in small spaces, especially dark ones, even though I shouldn't have been able to feel that way. But I have never had such an extreme reaction before." Just thinking of the darkness, of the walls closing in on him, caused his heart to beat faster.

"You never told me."

"There was not anything to say." He shrugged, his bleary eyes trailing to his own fingers, which were still lightly tracing designs on Damion's skin. "I believe I had mentioned my dislike of the tanks, but that was all. Just a distaste. I never had the emotional capability to properly feel fear."

Damion pulled Requiem up and into his arms. "There will be a lot of things you're not used to feeling. For now, let's go to bed."

"Teach me, then. Help me understand." Requiem laid his head against Damion's shoulder, his body still mostly limp as Damion carried them into the large bathroom.

Damion nodded. "I'll do my best to help, but I sure as hell don't know everything."

"More than me." Requiem was silent for a moment, nuzzling Damion's neck. "I do not want you to go. I understand why you must, but that does not mean that I like it."

Damion grinned from ear to ear as he dried his lover's damp body. "I like to hear you say that."

Requiem gave him a small smile back and then licked his lips, looking down. "Whose orders will I follow while you are absent?"

"Your own and mine." Damion ruffled his cut hair. "Even if she's captain, you look after yourself."

Requiem didn't have any answer to that, so he let Damion finish drying him off and then attempted to help get himself dressed. The shot was starting to wear off, but he was still very shaky.

"Hey? You understand what I said?" Damion said.

"I understood. I just did not know how to respond. I have taken care of myself, although not too successfully, before you arrived on the *Zeus*. But I was still following the orders of someone else. I have never been left to my own means for so long before."

"They want to implant something inside me, and they promise it will let us keep in contact." Damion rubbed his face. "Am I able to have surgery and then travel? I'm a good pilot, but if any part of my brain gets scrambled flying might be out of the question. Not that it matters, I'm not getting much of a choice."

Requiem thought about it for a moment, wrapping his arms around Damion's neck as the man helped him walk toward the exit of the bathroom. "More than likely, a cochlear implant. It is surgically implanted into the ear so that there will be no scars and no indication of a communications device. It cannot be detected."

"I hope you're right, because I hate surgery." Damion walked out into the hall, looking to see if anyone was waiting on them. "Let's get you to bed and rest. Real rest, this time."

Lizzy caught up with them before they could get out the Med Bay doors. "Athena said you forgot these and said you would probably need them." She put the stim cigs in Damion's shirt pocket. Then she lifted up Requiem's black top and slapped an adhesive monitor to his chest. "If that comes off, he will be back in here within five minutes. Also, if anything happens, it will also go off. It's there to monitor his vitals." Lizzy's eyes dared Damion to protest as Requiem shied away from her hands.

"You know, creepy women like you need to get laid more often and stop being jealous," Damion shot at the woman as he continued to walk.

"My sex life is quite active, thank you very much. And who the hell would I be jealous of? Just keep your dick in your pants," she shot back, closing the door after them.

"She's jealous." Damion helped Requiem all the way to their room. "Gods. I almost wish we were back on the *Zeus*. Since we came here it's been one disaster after another."

"Of whom?" Requiem inquired, leaning heavily against Damion.

Damion smiled. "Of you."

"Why would she be jealous of me?" Requiem asked, honestly confused. His eyes widened as his bare feet slipped along the corridor floor and he had to grab on to Damion tighter. "It must not be because of my gracefulness." He scowled at his feet as if they had betrayed him.

"Because I'm your lover."

Requiem looked up at Damion for a moment, blinking before he silently shook his head and looked back toward his feet. He had no comment to offer that wouldn't get him in trouble, so it was better to keep silent.

Damion seemed happy to get back to their room and didn't appear upset at Requiem's silence. He led his lover to the bed and sat him down. "Want water?"

Requiem immediately flopped backward onto the bed, drained. He winced slightly when the back of his skull hit the bedding. "Yes, thank you."

Damion went to the nightstand and picked up the small bottle of water. "They must have stocked up while we were in the steam room."

"It would be another way for Doctor Lizzy to silently insist on my treatment," Requiem said.

"She silently insists on a lot." Damion sat next to him and handed him the bottle. "Can you sit up?"

Instead of answering, Requiem grabbed the bottle with one hand and Damion's forearm with the other, using it to pull himself up. "Affirmative," he mumbled as he popped the top on the water and began to down it.

Damion smiled. "You can just say yes or no."

"It will take getting used to." Requiem wiped his mouth with the back of his hand, the bottle almost empty from his chugging.

"You'll have time." Damion went to reach for his soft locks and frowned.

"But you will not be here to teach me." Requiem finished off the rest of the water and then lay back down, curling on his side with his head in Damion's lap.

"I will be able to talk to you. At least that's the plan," Damion said.

Requiem made a noncommittal noise and wrapped his arms around Damion's waist. His head was still in his lap like he was trying to pull Damion's warmth out of him. He wasn't freezing anymore, but he was still slightly chilled. "When are you leaving?"

"I think two, maybe three days." Damion covered Requiem with the blankets. "You just want to sleep right like that?"

"Affirm… yes. But I know it will not be comfortable for you," Requiem answered honestly, pushing himself up with shaky arms and lying back down on the bed so that Damion could move. "I did not know it would be so soon."

"Hey, I didn't say I minded." Damion actually pouted. "And I know it's soon. That's one reason I'm happy you're up now."

"If I fall asleep, you will more than likely be stuck like that for many hours. In the end it would be painful for you," Requiem pointed out, and then he was silent for a few moments. "If I had woken up after you left, I would not have believed them if they said that you went back to the *Zeus* for any reason. More than likely, I would not have even looked for evidence either way." Requiem's tone was slightly ominous.

Damion frowned. "Then what would you have done? I mean, if I just disappeared you wouldn't find out why?"

"I was not in the right frame of mind when I awoke, Damion. I believe I was only seconds from jacking in. If you had not jumped in the tank, there would have been consequences."

"I don't know if I could have left you in that tank."

"I will not go back in there, Damion, unless you order it. I do not care if it helps me to heal faster, I will not willingly go back into the tank." Requiem's words were whispered, tinged with fear as his body trembled in remembrance.

"I won't make you unless it's to save your life." Damion moved behind Requiem, pulling the man close to his chest. "You can sleep and be safe."

"I would rather you just let me die," Requiem grumbled, but he moved so that his body was perfectly in line with Damion's. He curled his fingers around the Fighter's arm as his eyes closed.

"That's never going to happen," Damion growled. "If you hadn't noticed, I want you alive."

Requiem's lips twitched in sad amusement. "I am observant enough to have noticed that. Perhaps I should clarify. I meant that I would rather die than be put back in the tank." Although he didn't quite know why Damion wanted to keep him around so much when he had options like Athena and Doctor Lizzy available.

Damion gave the back of Requiem's shoulder another bite. "I make no promises for that."

Despite his tiredness and the numbness wearing off, Requiem gasped at the feel of Damion's teeth through his shirt. "Well then, perhaps there is one positive aspect to you not being here. Not that I plan on having to go back into the tank, but now I will have options."

"Options?" Damion rose to look down at his Core. "What do you mean, options?"

"If I do not want to go into the tank, I do not have to. Nor will I." Requiem could feel Damion looming over him but didn't open his eyes to acknowledge it.

Damion lay back down, seeming to feel a bit better. "You better not let anyone else bite you."

"If anyone attempts to bite me, I assure you it will be under extreme protest. I have a problem with people even touching me. Biting is certainly beyond that casual intimacy." Requiem shook his head against the pillow. "Besides, with all the marks of ownership you leave upon my skin, I doubt anyone would be able to find a place that you have not already claimed."

Damion grinned. "No other man or woman can have sex with you."

That made Requiem open his eyes, and he looked over his shoulder at the man with a raised eyebrow. Then he blinked and laid his head back down. "I did not know that needed to be said," he murmured.

"Because people will try to take advantage of you again once I'm not here to protect you."

"I do not expect to put myself in a position to be seen often. I was able to avoid confrontation on the *Zeus* by becoming completely undetectable. Only the Creators could find me because of the chip," Requiem explained.

Damion gave him a hug. "Remember, we can't trust them."

"I am aware. I do not trust anyone except for you, so it will not be hard to keep that in mind." Requiem breathed in Damion's warmth, tucking himself even farther against Damion's body.

Chapter Nine

Requiem

IT WAS odd, these thoughts he was having. It never would have concerned him before if Damion had decided to sleep with other people. It simply wasn't his business. But the recent events with Damion, and Athena and Lizzy's obvious interest, caused Requiem to feel… not unwanted, but *less,* when in the past the Fighter had always made him feel *more.*

It was obvious that he had only been a convenience. Damion preferred the female body; he always had. Requiem had read the reports of Damion's personality before he reached the *Zeus.* But men and women were kept separated on the *Zeus.* Except for the occasional passing by, they never saw each other. So without his usual supply, Damion had turned to the nearest thing on hand, Requiem himself. He had not been unkind, not at all. And Requiem knew Damion cared for him in some way. He had to, or he wouldn't have risked as much as he had. But now he had what he truly wanted available to him, and Requiem wouldn't be surprised if Damion ended up on top of one or both of the women before he left here. If he hadn't already, that was. He understood this logically, but that didn't mean he had to like it.

"You okay? You're all stiff," Damion said. "Are you upset?"

He took a minute to answer, licking his dry lips. He couldn't lie to Damion, but he didn't think it wise to reveal his thoughts. He knew they would make Damion unhappy and perhaps even angry, but he had to tell the man something. "Am I… acceptable to you?" he finally asked, not knowing how else to phrase the question.

"Acceptable? What do you mean by that?" Damion asked.

"Pleasing. Am I pleasing to you?" Requiem attempted to reword the question, sighing softly in frustration. He kept his eyes closed, his back to the man, not wanting to look him in the eye while he asked this.

"You want to know if I think you're attractive? Yeah. I wouldn't have sex with you if I wasn't attracted to you, and I wouldn't go through all of this if I just wanted sex," Damion grumbled. "I am shit at this conversation stuff, that's why me and my girls didn't last long. I don't know how to take myself apart for someone with words."

He bit the inside of his lip as he heard the impatience in Damion's voice. That wasn't actually what he'd meant, but he couldn't figure out how to ask what he wanted to ask. He wanted to know if he gave Damion what he needed, because it seemed clear that he didn't if the man was going to get it from Athena. He wanted to know what he could do to keep Damion with him and prevent him from going to back to the captain.

But how did one ask that type of question? "Do I... do I satisfy you?" Maybe that would work.

"You're being cryptic as fuck today. Satisfy?" Damion sounded frustrated. "You mean do I like having sex with you?"

"No, it is obvious you enjoy it. But do you get everything that you need out of having sexual relations with me? It is also obvious that you wish to have sexual relations with Captain Athena, so I am wondering what I am not doing correctly to still leave you with those needs. Or is it because I am not female? I know that is what you prefer." Requiem finally had to lay it out for Damion because subtlety was not working. For a highly intelligent man, Damion could be dense sometimes.

"Requiem." Damion sat up and moved to the edge of the bed, tugging harshly on his own hair. "It's not about what you're lacking. You are really good at having sex, but I'm not used to having sex with just one person. It's been different. I'm attracted to the captain, I admit it. But she's hot, and she's just the type I'm used to. Quick sex a few times, then the next morning we get up and go on with our lives. I could have had sex with her plenty of times, but each fucking time I have to stop."

Requiem cringed at the loss of Damion's warmth. He knew he should have kept his mouth shut. He always had to see what would happen if he pushed a little bit further. It was his experimental nature, he supposed.

"Why do you have to stop?" he asked quietly. At least he was learning something—he was learning that it wasn't because of him; it was just Damion's habits.

"Because of you!" Damion turned and yelled. "Because I can't stand to see that face you make when I hurt your feelings."

Requiem's eyes flew open and he cringed, the mild throb in the back of his skull increasing at Damion's volume. Somehow he managed to focus his eyes on Damion's face, which was flushed and annoyed.

"Until recently, I did not have any feelings to hurt," Requiem replied, his eyes meeting the Fighter's. "I did not even know that I 'make a face,' as you say. I apologize for letting my new emotions get out of hand. And I am sorry that I got in the way of your sexual activities. It was not my intention. I should have never brought the subject up."

"Stop that! Stop acting like you don't care when I know you do!" Damion grabbed Requiem's upper arm and tugged the man toward him. "I don't want you to be sorry. I just want you to admit that it's worth going through all this."

Wincing at Damion's bruising grip, Requiem sat up so his whole weight wasn't on his arm. He kept his head down, and his hair fell forward to cover his face. "I am afraid that is a question I cannot answer. Was it worth escaping being wiped or you being terminated? Yes. Was it worth being captured by rebels and used for their plans? Yes. I cannot answer the other scenarios." Requiem's reply was unemotional but to the point.

"Hawk! What's going on?" Doctor Lizzy's voice came through the intercom system. "47's heart rate just jumped through the monitor. Is he doing okay? Or are you being stupid and not letting him rest like I told you to?"

"Will you leave us alone, you harpy. We're talking!" Damion snarled. "I swear there isn't any privacy on this ship."

"Well, perhaps if you had some consideration for your Core's health, I would leave you alone, Captain Asshole," Lizzy snapped back.

"I am acceptable, Doctor Lizzy. As Damion said, we were talking. I apologize for alarming you," Requiem spoke up softly and respectfully.

"All right, then. If you need anything, let me know. I'll send security in there to plug the asshole full of holes. Medical out."

"I really hate it that people keep accusing me of abusing you." Damion shook his head and looked at Requiem. A question in his words, Requiem realized.

"I do not accuse you of that," Requiem said as Damion squeezed his thin arm tighter. "And I believe my opinion is the only one that matters when it comes to that subject."

"True." Damion's face appeared sad. "I want to do right by you, Requiem, but I'm not sure what that means."

"I do not know either. Perhaps it is one of those questions that only you can answer. Similar to the one where you need to decide whether putting up with 'all this crap' was worth it?" Requiem shifted so his legs were tucked under him, his eyes searching Damion's face. "I did not mean my questions to disturb you so."

"They were questions I had been asking myself already. I just want to make sure we're both doing this for the right reasons." Damion rubbed the back of his neck. "I need a smoke."

Requiem plucked the pack from Damion's shirt pocket and held it out to him before grabbing a lighter off the side table and handing that to him as well. "I cannot help you figure out your feelings. I do not even know what I am feeling, so I am afraid I am useless to you in this aspect."

"You have never been useless." Damion quickly lit a stick and slowly blew out the plume of smoke. "It's not that I don't believe in monogamy. I've just never been one to practice it until now."

Requiem knew his initial thought would only anger Damion, so he decided to go with his second one. "We do not know how long we will be separated, Damion. I would not expect you to remain monogamous."

"Yeah, you would," he grumbled. "You're the loyal sort. You would do anything I ask of you. I saw how you were when you were off your stims before and you still followed my orders. It's not that I don't care about you. I do, it's just difficult for me. Fuck, this is why I can't stand talking about relationships. This shit is complicated."

"Is that what you call it? A relationship?" Requiem asked. "And as I told you before, even though I was programmed to be loyal, I am not loyal to you because I'm required to be. You were the first person who was ever truly kind to me, who asked for my opinion and my permission. And the first person I ever truly trusted. It's natural for me to have strong… feelings for you. That does not mean you should reciprocate, and I understand that."

"You're the first person I wanted to work so hard to protect that wasn't blood," Damion said with conviction.

Requiem really didn't have a response to that, so instead he gently pulled his arm out of Damion's grip and lay back down, his feet on the pillows and his head in Damion's lap again. "You do so quite successfully, and I appreciate it."

"I do, huh?" Damion brushed his hands along Requiem's hair. "Thanks. I do my best."

"You are the best," Requiem countered as he realized Damion probably was avoiding the real conversation topic. He hadn't expected to get as far as he did with his inquiries, so it didn't really matter, even if he still wanted answers.

"I feel like I'm less than perfect in your eyes and I hate it," Damion admitted.

"Why does my opinion matter to you? Maybe your answer lies in that question beyond the usual answer of I do not know." He skimmed his fingers under Damion's shirt, wanting to feel the warm, smooth skin of Damion's side.

"I guess this just might be my way of falling in love." Damion touched Requiem's cheek.

Requiem looked up at Damion. He had heard that word before, but he didn't know what it was, what it felt like, or how to recognize it. "What is love?" he finally asked, his gaze dropping, his fingers continuing to take pleasure in the feel of Damion's skin.

"I think it's when you care about someone more than yourself to a very unhealthy extreme." Damion shrugged. "I think."

Requiem was silent for a few moments, letting the words sink in. "But... evidence points to us both being guilty of such actions. I thought that was something that partners did, not those who are in love."

"Partners look out for each other and put our lives on the line, but being in love is worse than that." Damion touched Requiem's cheek. "Makes you much worse."

"As in... enjoying each other's company and wanting to spend time together? Wanting to see that person a lot? Like being nervous when you do not know where that other person is and they are possibly in danger? Not liking when they show affection or attraction to another person?" Requiem was honestly curious if love and these ideas had anything in common.

Damion smiled. "Where did you hear all of that stuff? Reading some love novel?"

"Cores are not allowed to read recreationally," Requiem pointed out as he let his hand drop out from underneath Damion's shirt. "They are examples of how I feel." He sat up slowly and stood up even slower, his body still leaden as he worked his way to the table to grab another bottle of water.

"Hey, I could have gotten that if you just asked," Damion grumbled. "You're so damn stubborn."

"I needed to see if I could do it myself. You cannot carry me everywhere." Requiem was out of breath as he flopped down in a chair and popped the top on the water bottle.

"For the next few days, I damn well could, since you're so damn skinny." Damion let out a snort as he got up to walk to the bathroom.

"I need to regain my strength," Requiem replied, noting that the subject had changed again. And that Damion had completely ignored what he had said. He didn't mind and had expected this.

Chapter Ten

Damion

"WHAT ARE you thinking?" Damion asked as he walked back into the room. More than ever before, there was light in Requiem's eyes. It was as if before there had been someone just peeking beyond thick curtains and you were never sure if someone was home. Now the curtains were gone, the windows were wide open, and the lights were definitely on in those wintry eyes.

"That this phobia is annoying and inconvenient," Requiem promptly replied.

Damion knew he would have to be calm for Requiem to help him through the next few bumps. Being inside the *Ares* would be hell for them both. He knew Requiem's attachment to the ship and knew Requiem's claustrophobia had become worse. Requiem was there leaning into the chair as he sipped his water with seemingly no cares in the universe.

Requiem finished the water and used the table to push himself to his feet. "And that, to hide from the crew here, I will have to do so in small spaces, so I need to get over it."

"Don't push it." Damion sat next to him. "I was never afraid of much, but it was hard going in the mines when I was young."

"How did you deal with it?" Requiem stood there, supporting his shaky position by leaning on the table.

"Just kept having to go down day after day, and my dad helped." Damion watched his lover quiver, not sure if he should make him sit down or let him go. "He said that I needed to face my fears."

"I have never really felt fear before. An appropriate definition and therefore synonym for what I was aware of would be wariness, yes, but not… terror of that magnitude." Requiem's eyes shut as he visibly shivered. "I could not breathe or think. I felt like I was bound, and it was so dark. I could not hear anything. It reminded me of the chambers. No sight, smell, touch, taste, nothing. Just utter nothingness." Requiem bowed his head, his face hidden behind his hair as he carefully moved to the bed. "I was dreaming beforehand, and when I woke, I thought I was still dreaming until it became a reality."

"You need to find yourself an anchor, or focus when it happens." Damion reached forward and helped Requiem the last few inches to the bed. "Something you can say or do or think about to get yourself out of the cycle."

"An intriguing thought." Requiem accepted Damion's help, clinging to him. "And possible, eventually, with work. The problem is that I lose all ability to think when it happens. All I can do is scream in my head and try to get out. Even if I knew the exit was up, I might still go down."

"You'll have to notice when it is beginning to happen, so that you can start focusing before it gets too bad." Damion was worried. In their short time together, he knew Requiem and his dependency on one another had grown. "Will you be able to get into a ship?"

Requiem looked at Damion out of the corner of his eye as they sat down on the edge of the bed, the doubt obvious before he looked away and leaned against the headboard. "Nothing is impossible."

Damion laughed. "That's the first thing you said tonight that sounds like the old you."

"I apologize if my change in personality bothers you," Requiem said softly, looking down at his hands.

"I didn't say it bothered me. It will just take a bit to get used to." Damion sighed. "Hopefully you won't realize how big of an ass I can be and turn toward girls."

"I have had nearly two years to get used to your personality, while mine keeps changing on you. It is I who will have to worry about you turning from me once you realize that you do not like the new me." Requiem's lips twitched in a small, brief smile.

"We both have things to worry about," Damion agreed. "What should we do now?"

"In what way? I do not believe I can leave the room. The doctor probably has a tracking device imputed in this monitoring equipment." He rubbed his chest, the scratching sounds of his shirt rubbing over the plastic device stuck to his chest reached his ears. "However, that does not mean that you are required to stay here with me."

"I'm not leaving you." Damion said as he shook his head, "We could try and sleep." He looked around the room, searching the bare shelves. "I really miss my books."

"I doubt you are tired. There are virtual books on the console." Requiem pointed out, slipping farther down the bead until his head reached the pillow. He pulled the blankets up to his neck in an attempt to get warm.

"Yeah, but I have a soft spot for the increasingly rare books made of paper. The pages feel so good in my hands." Damion sighed, turning to help tuck Requiem into a cocoon of blankets.

"I have never read anything that was not an educational report or manual in nature." Requiem said, pulling an arm free to grip Damion's own, tugging down gently. Damion took the hint and as soon as he was lying next to him, Requiem curled his body around Damion, soaking in his warmth and comfort.

"You should try and read something other than that. I think you'd enjoy it." Damion rubbed his eyes as he yawned. "It's nice to just … let go sometimes and escape into a book."

Requiem made a noncommittal sound, wrapping his arm around Damion's waist and burying his face into Damion's chest. He thought he had heard Damion say something, however the words were muffled and sounded far away, becoming fainter as he drifted off.

Thursday October 27, 455 MC
1114 GMT
Requiem

TWO DAYS later found them back in the Medical facility, except this time they were there for Damion instead of Requiem. Doctor Lizzy was waiting for Damion in the surgery room, even though what they had planned wasn't a major procedure. She motioned for him to sit on the table, her back turned to him as she prepared her tools on a nearby tray.

"This should only take about ten minutes. Unless you whine, and then I may purposefully puncture your eardrum," she warned him.

Requiem followed Damion into the room, looking glad to be on his own feet this time instead of being carried or pushed in that awful chair. He sat down to watch the procedure.

"You girls make a man feel real at ease," Damion grumbled.

Lizzy turned around, a large needle in her gloved hand. It was about two feet long and a quarter inch in diameter. "All right, tilt your head to the left," she said with a completely straight face.

"You have to be joking." Damion frowned and looked at Requiem. Requiem looked at the needle and quirked an eyebrow, slowly shaking his head. "What?" he asked, but Requiem grinned.

"No, Hawk, I'm completely serious." Lizzy pushed his head to the side, bringing the needle up. "This may hurt a bit."

"Hey! Wait!" Damion didn't move, but his voice pitched high. "What the fuck?"

"Hold still or it's not going to be comfortable," Lizzy said. But then she started laughing hysterically. "Oh Gods, you should see your face." She doubled over in laughter, her eyes tearing up.

Requiem stood and walked around the table to where Lizzy was having hysterics. He plucked the needle from her fingers, showed it to Damion, looking him straight in the eye as he stabbed himself in the palm of the hand with it. The needle retracted in on itself until it was only an inch long.

Damion growled as he spun to glare at the doctor. "What the hell are you trying to pull?"

This doctor was crazy. He was beginning to think she was some sort of mental patient before becoming a doctor.

"Lighten the hell up, Hawk," Lizzy managed to get out, her hands on her knees as she tried to catch her breath. "Oh wow, that was priceless."

Requiem handed the needle back to the doctor and walked back to his chair, squeezing Damion's shoulder on the way.

"Your humor sucks," Damion grumbled.

"Only because you have no sense of humor," Lizzy replied, wiping her eyes before picking up a thin fiber cable.

"Is this thing really going to work? Have you done it before?" he asked, failing to keep the nervous tremor out of his voice.

She tilted his head to the side, a little more gently this time. "Yes, many times. Ask your friend Collins."

"Shitty bastards," Damion said. "You've been watching me that long? What about his Core?"

Lizzy paused, her eyes staying on his ear as her hands stilled. "We still haven't found him, yet. He may have been sold into a black market sex ring, maybe dead, but we promised Collins proof. The official story from the Corporation is that he's still onboard, plugged into the system."

She shook her head, placing her left hand on Damion's jaw and feeding the cable carefully into his ear with the other. "This is going to feel strange. It shouldn't hurt, but let me know if it does."

"It just feels like pressure," Damion said, pushing the palm of his hand into his left eye. "And how do you know for sure that his Core was sold?"

"Collins found the paperwork for the transaction. He was transported to a vessel outside of Venus and then taken to a pleasure colony on Neptune. We lost the trail after he was taken off the ship. We haven't heard any word since." Lizzy was concentrating on what she was doing. She looked up at a screen, watching the progress of the device.

Damion felt his eye twitch involuntarily. "You know, I have no idea how you think we're going to be able to stop all the crap you say is going on."

"Do the best you can. That's all you can do. All any of us can do," Lizzy said, the mad scientist facade gone. She sounded sadder and less manic and hyperfocused.

"You know that's a hell of a non-plan." Damion let out a small groan. "Okay, that is uncomfortable."

Lizzy's eyes remained on the screen. "I, in fact, warned you that it wouldn't be comfortable. Now hold very still. I'm almost done."

Requiem reached over and gripped Damion's hand, squeezing it gently.

"You liked getting a lot of ports put in?" Damion asked Requiem. He couldn't understand how people could get addicted to surgeries.

"The moving of your mouth constitutes moving," Lizzy grumbled.

"No," Requiem replied softly. "But it was necessary, and I learned to endure. Especially since we were allowed no anesthetics or other drugs that would make it easier."

Lizzy let out a breath and began carefully pulling the cable out of Damion's ear. "Okay, it's in. It may feel weird for a day or two, and your equilibrium may be off for that length of time, but you'll get used to it. It won't be activated until you leave for the mission. Jasper should be back tomorrow, so plans will be made then. More than likely you'll head out the day after."

"Aren't you going to tell me how it fucking works?" Damion felt a headache beginning, but it would be fine.

"You won't be in control of it; your Core will or the captain will. It works as a receiver and a recorder. Everything that you hear, we will hear. Requiem will be able to speak to you through it and you back to him. He'll be the main one in control of it. It also monitors your vitals, so that if the auditory function on it goes, we can still see that you're okay. It's disabled right now, as I said." Lizzy shook four pills into her hand. She handed two to Damion along with a small glass of water and then took two herself.

"What are these?" Damion asked. Requiem released Damion's hand after another small squeeze.

"Something to help with the pain," she said.

Damion tossed back the pills, trying to stay calm and not freak out. "The captain going to fry my brain?"

Lizzy began cleaning up her tools. "She would do it up close and personal. Not like your friends in the Corp, who are cowards and do it from afar. The chip isn't even connected to your brain, just the bones in your ear."

"At least my head won't explode." He got up and took Requiem's hand again. "Let's go get some food."

Requiem nodded and got up, keeping his eyes on either Damion or the floor.

"Question, does he talk to anyone but you?" she asked without turning around. "When he's not giving demands or pushing us away, that is."

Damion hummed as he considered his lover. "When he wants to talk to someone else, he will. I'd rather him not get too friendly with anyone here, since I don't really trust pirates."

The doctor's hands slammed down on the tray, metal clattering as tools jumped, but she still didn't turn around. "After all we've done for you and him? After all we've shown and trusted you with? You still don't trust us? How stupid can you be?"

Now she whirled around, her face furious and her eyes full of angry tears. "It's the Corporation who is the evil one here. They kill, steal, and sell to their hearts' content and no one is wiser. Everyone thinks that we're the evil ones when we're just fighting to save lives, to take back what's ours! But no, you don't trust us. Fine." She turned away again before the tears fell. "Fine, do whatever the fuck you want. Just realize we could have killed you both ten times over already. I didn't have to save your Core or put up with your shit."

Requiem looked at Lizzy and then up at Damion, quirking an eyebrow as if to say, "Well, now you've done it."

Damion gave Requiem a baffled look in return. See, this was why women were no easier to figure out than his own feelings for Requiem, a man. "I never called you evil," he muttered. "I just can't trust someone after five days. I'm glad you saved his life, but it's not like I know any of you either."

Lizzy was silent for a few moments, only moving once to wipe her eyes. Finally she took a deep breath, her shoulders rising and falling. "You're right. And I'm sorry. I wouldn't trust someone that quickly either. I didn't mean to lose it like that. It's just been a rough day. Go, get something to eat. You need to fatten up your Core before he blows away with the circulation system."

The pale man tugged on Damion's hand, pulling him gently toward the door before looking back.

"Thank you," he said softly to the woman.

Damion stayed quiet as they left, since he always found it safer with women to shut up when you were in trouble. "Why did she bite my head off like that anyway?"

"It is the anniversary of her son's death," Requiem explained softly, his fingers lacing with Damion's. "He was seven years old when he was killed by an invading force on one of Saturn's moons, Rhea, three years ago. Chrysalis Corporation wanted the mineral deposits on that particular moon at the time. It was a mining city. His school collapsed under the assault."

Damion nodded. "Ah. But why the pain pills?"

"Unknown. Perhaps she had a headache?" Requiem shrugged as they walked toward the lift.

"Or she has a problem. It's common too." Damion didn't want to start rumors, though. "Just keep that between us, all right? Crap, which way was the mess?"

"One level down," Requiem replied promptly, even though he had never been there. He had memorized the schematics for the entire ship. "There is no record of her having a drug problem."

"Why would they keep a record of it?" Damion found the lift and pushed the summon button.

Requiem stepped inside. "There are records on everything."

Damion rolled his eyes. "You can't tell everything from someone's personal files."

He looked up at him, a small smile on his lips. "You are right. But there is a lot you can."

"That's true," Damion had to admit. "I just don't know how to react to people here. I don't know what to do when I go back to the *Zeus*."

"Just be yourself," Requiem suggested, his eyes drifting down again as the lift door opened. "I do not know if you should inform Fighter Juni. However, it may concern him if they decide to take 108 away. I was teaching him what I know, and he might be the next best possible option for the Creators."

"That utterly sucks, because Juni's going to be a basket case." Damion could barely tolerate the shit Requiem went through, and he knew Juni was a bit more detached from his Core, but it wasn't by much.

"I do not predict that he will believe you once you tell him that I am dead. 108 cannot know that I am alive. If the Creators interrogate him, he will not be able to hold back information," Requiem reminded him as they walked down the hall.

"Damn." Damion sighed and his shoulders dropped a few inches. "I mean, I've kept secrets, sure. And bullshitted my way through a lot of problems, but this is different."

"You will be fine, I am sure," Requiem said softly as he squeezed tighter to Damion's back when someone came too close. They finally reached the refectory, which was bustling with people between shift changes.

"You going to lock yourself in the room when I leave?" Damion wondered if Requiem would become reclusive.

He was quiet for a moment, probably swallowing a lump of fear in his throat from all the unknown people around him who were looking at him curiously. "It is a distinct possibility."

"They told me the other saved Cores are going to want to be all buddy-buddy," Damion warned as he shuffled into line.

Requiem's only response was to shrug. Besides 108, he had never spoken on a regular basis with any other Cores, except for professionally. Socializing wasn't banned, but it was frowned upon. Perhaps the Creators worried they might be able to get past their brainwashing and revolt. But it was the furthest thing from any Core's mind. Until now, that was.

"What you hungry for?" Damion asked Requiem. "You okay? You look even more fidgety."

"I… I think I am nervous," Requiem replied, watching the tips of his boots as if afraid to look up. "You seem to know what I favor more than I do myself. I am still not used to eating anything with flavor."

"You can now eat until your stomach explodes." Damion put a warm hand around Requiem's shoulders. "There's nothing to be nervous about. No one usually starts anything in the mess. You're smart enough to walk away if you see trouble starting."

"You had a fight in the cafeteria," Requiem pointed out blandly, leaning into Damion's body. "Why would they start a battle? I know that we are recently from the Corporation, but we have not participated in any raids or takeovers."

Damion shrugged as he started to load up their tray. "When someone starts a fight, it's not always for the right reasons."

"When you fight, is it always for the right reasons?" Requiem asked quietly, grabbing a water and a fruit-like drink that seemed to intrigue him.

"I try to make it for the right reasons, but even I make mistakes." Damion couldn't stand there and pretend to be some chivalrous knight.

Requiem was silent for a few moments as they moved through the line, staying close to Damion. "Could you… could you teach me how to defend myself?"

"In a day?" Damion blinked. "I don't know how well, but sure, I can teach you a few things."

"Maybe two. I know the basics, we are all taught those, but I do not want to always rely on you," Requiem confessed as they walked toward an empty table. "It does not have to be now. It can be after you return."

"Not like we have a lot to do between now and when the president shows up, so I don't mind not staying in our room." Damion sat down and took a drink to wet his throat before starting to eat.

Requiem opened the juice and took a tentative sip. His next sip was a little more enthusiastic. "I am not saying I will be a good student, but I will try my best since you will not be here to protect me later. It seems even more imperative that I learn." He picked up his fork and took a cautious bite of his meal.

"You are a damn quick learner, but I don't want to overdo it and send you to medical for a concussion." Damion shuddered. "That woman would kill me."

"Despite recent examples otherwise, I am stronger than I look. I have taken a hit to my head before and I was able to push through it," Requiem stated before digging into his food with exuberance.

"You've been through a hell of a lot and lived," Damion said with a mouth full of food. "Trust me, I know you're no waif, but I'm also not used to teaching."

"Nothing short of attempting to terminate me will hurt me too much. That was proven when I was stabbed by—" Requiem stopped abruptly, realizing his mistake, and tried to play it off by shoving more food in his mouth. "Do you think the room assigned to us will be enough room to practice in?"

"Stabbed?" Damion frowned. "What the hell are you talking about?"

"It is of no consequence. My last Fighter before you reacted badly when I said something he did not like, that is all."

"You never mentioned that." Damion sighed. "How bad?"

"There was never any point in mentioning it. It was inconsequential." Requiem shrugged before finishing his food and taking a sip of his juice, his eyes not leaving the table. "I should not have mentioned it in the first place. As much as I do not like to admit it, I did not think."

"Don't blow me off like that. If I ask you something, I want you to answer it." Damion poked at his food.

"He stabbed me. Clipping my left kidney because I didn't want to bend over and let him do whatever he desired to me. So he stabbed me and did it anyway." Requiem's eyes were everywhere but meeting Damion's as he finished off the drink. "Hence, why I do not trust others. One of the many reasons."

"I don't blame you." Damion really wished a few of those pilots were still alive so he could kill them. "Not everyone wants to kill you either, remember that. Or fuck you."

"That is true. But everyone wants something." Requiem stood, gathering the tray and his trash, then walked toward the compactor, then threw it down the chute.

"Yeah. Look at me and Juni. All he wanted was just someone to watch his back and drink with, and then we got him mixed up in our drama." Damion looked around. "Where are we going to train?"

"I do not know. I do not know if there's enough room in our quarters, or if we should go to the recreational room. I would prefer not to be watched."

Damion tipped back and emptied his water. He ate more than Requiem, but at times, it seemed Damion ate slower. Or maybe it was because Requiem didn't always finish his plates. "Our room is too small, and it would distract me."

Requiem frowned, tilting his head. "Why would it distract you?"

Damion shook his head. "I'm sorry. I don't think I could explain it."

"As you wish. I suppose that the only choice is the training rooms."

"All right." Damion looked around once again. "Which way?"

Chapter Eleven

Requiem

REQUIEM LED Damion down the long corridors. They walked in silence while navigating past the people passing them. He immediately moved again as someone passed by too close to him, a pale slip of a girl with input ports who gave him a small smile as she moved by. A former Core, he guessed. He moved closer to Damion to avoid running into anyone else.

"Lead the way." Damion sounded concerned. "This whole feeling stuff is really freaking you out."

"I am not used to it. I do not know how to handle it or what I am feeling," Requiem admitted.

"First part is just understanding that there is nothing to fear."

"There is a lot to fear. The Creators, for example," Requiem pointed out.

"I'm sure they'll want to beat my brains right out of my head for getting you 'killed,' but at least I can tell them the truth." Damion gave him a firm look. "You killed yourself trying to use the pulse three consecutive times."

"That is true. Even if I did not remain terminated," Requiem said. He could feel the man's eyes burning holes in him. "And I did not simply try. I succeeded in using the pulse three times."

Damion went through the door marked Training. "You will never do that again, correct?"

Requiem let out a small sigh and didn't answer. Instead he scanned the room. It was large, with mirrors on three of the walls, and half of the floor was covered with mats. The other half had exercise machines and also training VRs. A few people were in the room, some working on the machines and a pair practicing a fighting technique on the mats. Requiem took a step backward out the door, reconsidering his desire to learn.

"Well, it's big enough." Damion blindly reached back and grabbed Requiem's thin wrist. "Come on, we'll start with the basics."

Requiem dug his heels in for a moment, shaking his head. But Damion was too strong, and he eventually gave in, bowing his head as Damion dragged him to the edge of the mats.

"What's your problem?" Damion asked with a frown. "No one here is going to hurt us, right?"

"I do not like… people. And I do not like being stared at," Requiem replied quietly and honestly, his eyes still down as the tips of his boots reached the mats. He twisted his wrist out of Damion's grip, then knelt down to take off the boots.

"Hey, I'm here, right? I won't let anything happen, and people stare because you're new. Give it a few days and the newness will wear off."

"You are here, for now," Requiem stated, stepping onto the mat in his bare feet, as far away from the other occupants as possible. The other two on the mat had stopped their sparring and were watching him and Damion in unabashed curiosity.

Damion took off his own boots and stepped onto the mat. "Hey, even if I'm across the damn system, that doesn't mean I won't come back to help if you're in trouble."

Requiem appreciated the words, even if there was no way this could happen. If he was in so much trouble that he needed to call Damion back, by the time the man got there, it would be too late. He started stretching, remembering that much from his basic fighting class.

"All right, I guess we'll start with what you know. I'll attack you in some basic ways and you defend. Good?"

Requiem nodded, shaking his hands down at his sides and getting into a basic defending position. He balanced on his legs so he couldn't be pushed over and fisted his hands in front of him, his arms and elbows blocking his sides and torso.

Damion took two steps forward and lifted his left fist, following through with a rather weak punch toward Requiem's face.

He easily blocked it with his right forearm and a slight turn of his body, returning it with a punch of equal strength. His eyes were glued to Damion's shoulder, knowing that he would be able to tell Damion's movements from his torso.

Damion used his knees to tilt away from the punch and grabbed Requiem's forearm. Then he pulled him forward while raising his knee. Requiem clenched his teeth as he stumbled, but he twisted his body in time to take the knee harmlessly against his thigh, his other hand punching toward Damion's stomach.

"Good." Damion smiled and let Requiem go. "But try not to overextend, and make your punches quick so you won't be grabbed. Now let's try it if I grab you from behind."

"We were not taught how to get out of a situation like that. Fighters generally do that when they want to use us, so they did not want to teach us how to get out of this position. What are the basics?" Requiem concentrated on the man in front of him instead of the people watching them curiously.

"You know defensive maneuvers, a few solid kicks, and even how to disarm." Damion rubbed the back of his neck. "You know those, right?"

Requiem nodded in confirmation, stretching a little as Damion talked.

"Let's keep going until I teach you something new." He chuckled.

"How do you get out of someone grabbing you from behind?" Requiem inquired with a slight tilt of his head. "As I stated, they refused to teach us something like that."

Damion turned around. "Try and grab me."

Requiem quirked an eyebrow at Damion's back, mostly because of their drastic differences in height and body type. Shaking his head, he looped his arms under Damion's, his shoulders basically resting in the man's armpits as he laced his fingers behind the Fighter's neck and waited. He cringed as he heard amused laughter from the other occupants on the mat, but he held his position.

"Good. Now most people will try to wrestle you back or forward depending on if they are trying to pull you into a dark corner or push you into a room. Either way, while they're trying to move, you can still use your legs." Damion moved his right leg back, easily tapping it against the inside of Requiem's knee and then lightly on top of his foot. "Or you can become dead weight and it's harder for them to move you."

"I do not believe the last option will work so well. Especially if the differences in height and weight are as great as they are with you and me. If I attempted to use dead weight on you, it would not affect much," Requiem pointed out as he released his lover, stepping back slightly and already missing the warmth of being pressed up against Damion's back.

"You will have to try everything if you are fighting to survive." Damion smiled as he turned around. "All right, now you turn around and try."

Requiem turned obediently and let Damion grab him from behind. He licked his lips, appreciating the familiar warmth of the man against his back before dropping his complete weight to prove a point.

"See, I can still drag you." Damion began to walk backward. "But your hands are close to the ground, and it's easier if you need to pick up something or grab a gun from your waist or a knife."

"I see. So it is useful in some cases if an additional weapon is close by or if an electrical panel is nearby for me to conduct." Requiem attempted to get his feet under him, but Damion was still dragging him. He sighed in frustration and finally got it.

Damion stopped, but he had a proud expression on his face despite Requiem's annoyance. It seemed Damion couldn't help but be happy that Requiem was thinking about fighting back. At times in the past, Damion had expressed his worry about Requiem just letting others walk over him. "Yeah. Want to continue?"

"Yes, if you do not mind," Requiem said as he worked his way out of Damion's loosened arms. "We do not have much time."

Damion spent the next hour working up a sweat going through multiple moves and scenarios. Requiem wasn't strong, but he was damn fast and also a faster learner.

Eventually Requiem reluctantly had to call it. He was panting, sweat trailing down his spine as he stood across from Damion. He was tired; his head was throbbing from the activity, his surgery wounds having not fully healed yet and his body still recovering from everything he had put it through. "I do not want to, but I believe we should stop and continue tomorrow, if you do not mind."

"I think we need more water, and I need a smoke, then a shower." Damion held out a hand to him. "How does that sound?"

Requiem nodded as he placed his sweaty hand in Damion's, only letting go when they reached the edge of the mat so he could put his shoes back on. He grasped it again as soon as they were on, and they left the training room and started down the corridor toward the lift.

"See, they only watched. No one hurt us," Damion said in a low voice.

"You were one of the highest scorers in hand-to-hand combat in the Corporation. It would be illogical for them to attempt to harm me while you are present," Requiem pointed out, his eyes on the corridor floor again as they walked.

"They don't know my scores. They barely know who we are." Damion sighed. "Anyway, let's get that water."

"No, but they can read your body language and see how you carry yourself, and that would give them enough reason to pause," Requiem stated as they walked into the lift. Two other people were in there, so Requiem clammed up, looking down at his boots.

"You can do the same, sort of." Damion clenched his jaw, grinding his teeth for a long moment before he continued. "Don't fear."

"Read body language? Yes, it is true. But carrying myself in the lethal way you do is not something that I can accomplish," Requiem whispered.

Damion stepped out of the lift and quickly headed to pick up five bottles of water from the mess hall. "I guess I can rest well, knowing you will be in our room most of the time."

"There or in the shuttle, yes, I would assume so," Requiem replied as soon as they stepped out of the mess hall and back into the corridor to head to the lift again. "Unless you order me otherwise."

"I won't order you otherwise unless that is what you want," Damion said.

"There are no other orders that I should follow. I am your Core." Requiem looked up at Damion in confusion as he pushed the directional button for the lift.

"Requiem… you're not a Core anymore. I mean, don't get me wrong. I like that you'll do what I say more times than not. But you don't *have* to. Do you see the difference?"

Now Requiem was really confused, leaning up against the lift walls as he stared at Damion. "Not a Core? How can I not be a Core? It is what I am. And if I do not follow your orders, whose do I follow?" Requiem shook his head, his eyes sliding from Damion's, confusion mixed in with a plethora of other emotions, causing him to feel mildly upset. "No, I do not see what difference you think there is. There is nothing else I could ever be." When the doors opened, he nearly ran out into the hall.

"Requiem." Damion hurried after him. "I said that wrong. I suck at this." He waited until they were back in their room to continue.

"Look, what I mean is that a Core is what you are, yes, but it's also a label the Creators made. You can still do everything you did before—and probably better, now that you're not constrained—but you're not a machine."

Requiem kept his back to Damion, standing in the center of the room and looking around as if he was lost, his hands clenching and unclenching. What was he if he wasn't a Core? He was nothing now, even with his abilities. There was this mission and monitoring Damion and then what? What was his purpose? He couldn't voice those... fears—yes, fears, to the Fighter because he wasn't sure if he would understand.

"You need something?" Damion put the bottles down. "I wasn't trying to upset you."

"I know you were not. You have just... brought things to my attention that I have not thought about until now." Requiem ran his fingers through his hair and then over the back of his shaved head. It still felt strange. Damion may not have understood, but Requiem had never kept anything from him before. "I do not know my purpose now. I do not know what I am if not a Core. It was what I was raised and augmented for, nothing else. I know nothing else," he finally confessed, shaking his head and stripping off his sweat-dampened shirt. He tossed it down the laundry chute.

"I suppose that means you have a chance like many of us don't have." Damion sat on the bed. "You can be anything you want. Damn, I mean you're smart. If you wanted to start being a doctor you could, or maybe you would want to actually fly the plane instead of just manage it."

"I do not exist in the system except as a number, Damion. My ports and branding mark me as a Core. If I go anywhere on my own, I will be brought back in as a runaway or captured and sold to a ring or the highest bidder. Even being freed, I still will not have freedom. You will not always be with me to protect me." Requiem finally gave Damion a small smile, shaking his head. "Nothing is impossible, but some things are improbable." He bowed his head and walked toward the bathroom.

"You confuse the hell out of me." Damion followed Requiem. "I'm not going anywhere. I mean permanently. I'll be back or I'll be dead."

"I am not only talking about now. You cannot stay tethered to me forever." Requiem sat on the counter and took his boots off, letting them fall to the floor, followed by his socks. Then he hopped off the counter and turned on the shower. "You will want to do more with your life than babysit a Core… or whatever I am now. More than likely I will end up staying on this ship until I die. The rest of the galaxy is not free to Cores, except through data and vids. I am comfortable with that since it is all I ever expected. I just do not know my place in it anymore." He should not have said anything. He had known Damion wouldn't understand his predicament.

Damion rubbed his eyes with the heels of his hands. "By the Goddess, I don't know what to do with you. Requiem, I'm doing all I can to figure out what it is that I'm feeling for you, and you're saying that it's not worth it."

Requiem paused in unbuttoning his pants, confused again at Damion's words. His eyes flicked over the man, and he inhaled deeply through his nose and let out a long breath. He tentatively reached for Damion's face. "I do not want you to be trapped by my limitations. You are as smart as I am, perhaps more so, since you have the ability to use your emotions in your judgment calls and decision making. Any path could be open to you. I am not saying that… figuring out your feelings for me is not worth it. I only want to make you as aware of your situation as you have made me of mine. I do not want you to regret in the future watching over me or even to start… disliking me strongly for it." He let his fingers slide off Damion's chin before he continued to get undressed, steam filling the small bathroom.

"I'm not going to hate you, as long as you don't try to kill yourself again," Damion threatened. "My life isn't much better than yours. Let's be honest, we're right now under these pirates' clutches until they let us out, and even then I don't have anywhere to go."

"It was not my intention to attempt to terminate myself. And you did not kill me last time I was brought back, so that is an idle threat." Requiem folded his pants and boxers, then placed them on the counter. "And then perhaps you should be thinking as strongly as I am about what to do besides fight in a war we do not completely understand anymore." He stepped into the shower, the hot water almost immediately soothing his sore muscles. "And then, perhaps, we may both be on this ship for the rest of our lives. Too many variables to consider."

"I don't think I could stay on this ship forever." Damion watched Requiem before undressing and joining him.

Requiem was silent for a few minutes, stepping out of the way of the warm water so that Damion could use it as he ran soap through his hair. "The thought does not bother me. I was expecting to never leave the *Zeus* again, except for when out in the *Ares*. And then you took me on leave with you and we ended up here. But I also do know that you like your independence and freedom, and staying here would be uncomfortable for you."

"Staying on the *Zeus* wasn't much better. It's just choosing who you want calling the shots." Damion ducked his head to wet his short hair.

He waited for Damion to move before rinsing his own hair. "But eventually you could have left the *Zeus*. Once your assignment is over, then what? It will all depend on the circumstances of how you return here. If your death is faked or you have to escape, either way you will not exist anymore. Just like me. But you will be able to achieve a new identity and go wherever you want." He closed his eyes under the spray. "I am sorry. We can end the discussion if you wish. I am aware I will analyze anything until there is nothing left, and I must admit to still being confused about the new situation."

"I guess I never saw myself really leaving the *Zeus*." Damion shrugged. "I mean, I really thought we were going to die during that fight."

"I would not have let you die," Requiem said quietly as he leaned against the wall under the showerhead so Damion could have the water. "A Core's number one order is to take care of a Fighter at all costs. But I will not follow that command simply because it is an order, but rather because it is what I want."

Damion quickly rinsed off before pulling Requiem into his arms. "You are stubborn."

Requiem nearly lost his balance sliding along the shower floor, but he caught himself by grabbing Damion's arms. Sighing, he laid his head on his shoulder, closing his eyes. "I suppose, if that is what you want to call it," Requiem mumbled against the man's damp skin.

"How about this for a deal? I don't think of a future without you as a part of it and you don't think of a future without me as some part of it?" Damion gave him a tight squeeze. "We'll play our parts and try to find our own way in the meantime."

A smile worked its way over Requiem's lips. "I think that sounds most agreeable," he said, wrapping his arms around Damion's waist.

"We should get out of here soon before we get yelled at for overusing the water rations." Damion turned off the water and then reached for towels.

Requiem took a towel and stepped out of the shower and onto the cool tile floor. He moved out of the way so Damion could also get out of the shower as he dried himself off. Then he wrapped the towel around his waist and walked back into the main room, desperate for that bottle of water now. He promptly drained most of the water before he felt he could put it down.

"How is your head and equilibrium?" he asked Damion.

"I won't lie; I have a bit of a headache." Damion sat on the bed and rubbed his arms and legs dry with his towel.

"You should lie down and rest. Perhaps if you do so, it will go away. Doing energetic activities probably did not assist in getting rid of it. I am sorry for my thoughtlessness," Requiem said as he sat down next to Damion and finished off his water.

Damion squeezed Requiem's hand. "I hate being bored, and just sitting here would have bored me. I enjoyed our sparring."

"Now you realize how I feel when I am forced to merely lie in bed staring at the ceiling," Requiem replied with a small smile.

Damion gave a snort. "You don't listen that often. Or do you mean when I'm having sex with you, you're bored?"

Requiem shook his head, a brief grin on his lips. "When we have sex, I generally cannot see anything."

"I'm glad I don't bore you." Damion tossed his towel across the room and pulled Requiem in for a kiss.

"I do not think that is po—mmph!" Requiem's words were cut off as he was suddenly sprawled across Damion's naked lap and his lips were otherwise occupied. His hands had gripped Damion's arms in surprise, but they slowly loosened as warmth flowed through his body.

"Hmm, well since I'll be away for a while, I might as well get my fill of you now," Damion said, eyes glittering with happiness and lust.

"I did not think there was a limit for you. Is it possible for you to get your fill?" Requiem asked quietly, the look in Damion's dark eyes causing his heart to skip in an odd way and a tickle to brush the inside of his stomach. He released Damion's arm to run his fingers over the man's lips.

"No, not really. I just can't seem to get you out of my damn mind." Damion went back to kissing him.

Chapter Twelve

Requiem

REQUIEM MANAGED to get himself untangled from Damion before the man fell sideways. It was difficult since his body felt like jelly. He licked his lips, his eyes hooded and unfocused. "I do not believe I would be able to withstand two hours or more of that. I think, perhaps, I would perish, but it would not be an unpleasant death."

Damion's laugh was a bit dry from his own exhaustion, but the levity was still there. "I think it's still a good goal to have in life."

Grabbing his discarded towel, Requiem proceeded to clean himself up before anything more messed the bedding. "Perhaps," he replied with a smile that was slow to disappear.

"You okay?" Damion asked with a grin.

"At the moment, more than." Requiem rolled onto his side, wrapping his arm around Damion's waist, slightly unsure if he would like the intimacy. "But it brings to mind that… after tomorrow I will not be able to touch, see, or smell you anymore. I also won't have you here to hide behind any longer."

Damion let out a long sigh. "You know that doesn't make me happy. I mean, I don't want to think about leaving at the moment."

"I apologize. I did not mean to upset you. I cannot help but think the way I do, and part of that is constantly thinking of all variables." Taking an initiative, even though he did not feel fully confident, Requiem sat up and leaned forward, placing a warm kiss on Damion's frowning lips.

"You always think of all the scenarios." Damion shrugged. "I guess we will have to figure this out. We don't have a choice."

Requiem pulled back, leaning against the headboard. "I cannot be anything other than who I am, and that includes thinking of the scenarios. What do we need to figure out? I did not think there were other options."

"I mean figure out how to be apart," Damion said. "What if you keep changing? What if you need me and I can't be here to help you?"

"I see." Requiem stretched his thin body as he thought. "We will still have communications on a daily basis, but… it will be odd to be separated from you for the first time in nearly two years." No capsule, no Damion, no longer able to call himself a Core. He was quickly losing what made him who he was.

Damion's hands began to make slow circles on his pale skin. "You might enjoy your freedom without me looming over you."

"You never, as you say, loomed." Requiem was unable to repress a shiver of pleasure. "And you have given me more freedom than I ever thought I would be granted. More freedom than I even wanted or know what to do with."

"Guess we are still not really free, but it's better." Damion combed his fingers through Requiem's hair.

Requiem sighed, his eyes slipping closed as he shifted closer to Damion. "I never knew what it meant to be free. Did not even acknowledge the word because it meant nothing to me. Except for the freedom to pick you, and they tried to take even that away from me."

"Free men breathe air much sweeter than those who wear chains. Well, that's what one of my books said." Damion chuckled at his own words. "I will take freedom with you."

"What do you mean by that? I do not quite understand." Requiem opened his eyes, his head tilting as he tried not to be too distracted by Damion's hands on his skin and hair.

"I don't think we'll understand it until we are free." Damion smirked. "One of life's mysteries."

"Mysteries. I am used to mysteries and attempting to solve them." He slid down in the bed and laid his body over Damion's, his fingers playing along the man's bare stomach.

Damion chuckled. "You do like proving people wrong. You get a thrill out of it."

"I do not know if that is the case. I only like proving that the impossible is truly possible," Requiem replied with a shrug, nails idly sliding over Damion's skin.

Damion shivered. "Hey, that could get you into trouble."

"What? Proving the impossible?" Requiem raised his head, looking at Damion with confusion as he thoughtlessly ran his fingers lower over Damion's skin, skimming the trail of hair above his groin.

"No. Touching me like that." Damion grinned. "It makes me feel a bit too good."

Requiem quirked an eyebrow. "Do you wish me to stop?" he asked, but his fingers kept moving.

"Only if you don't want to have sex," Damion said bluntly.

"I have never denied you before," Requiem replied with a casual shrug. "And I think by this point in time it would be obvious if I minded."

"Yes, but you get yourself in a ton of trouble quickly." Damion tucked Requiem underneath him. "Still don't mind?"

Requiem swallowed a surprised squeak as he was suddenly on his back with Damion's warmth covering him. His hands were flat against Damion's chest as he blinked up at him. "I do not know how you came to that conclusion. I attempt to keep myself out of trouble." He shook his head. "Why would I mind?"

"Because you're getting sick of me? But how could you, since I'm so handsome?" Damion teased. Then before Requiem could reply, he kissed him with a great passion.

Requiem had opened his mouth to answer, but forgot what he was going to say. His hands slid down to Damion's hips, his fingers kneading the skin there as he moaned softly into his lover's mouth. Requiem would miss this. This warmth, this closeness, and the feelings that he didn't recognize. He liked how it made his stomach flip and his heart pound.

Damion continued kissing him until they were in need of air. "Damn, you are learning how to kiss."

"I have a good teacher with a big ego, so I could not help but to learn." Requiem smiled with a hint of amusement.

"Big ego?" Damion made a sound of mock surprise. "Do I?"

"Sometimes," Requiem admitted, soothing the comment by leaning up and nibbling on Damion's ear. "But I do not mind, and you deserve to have one."

"Now see, if you say things like that, I will get a big head." Damion rubbed his hips into Requiem's.

Requiem sucked in a breath, his eyes fluttering for a moment before he focused them again. "Too late, I believe."

Suddenly, two beeps sounded throughout the room, signaling that someone was calling over the vid comm.

"Hawk, you there?" Athena's voice was clipped as it came through the speakers.

"You have the worst timing." Damion growled and nipped Requiem's chin. "What is it, Athena?"

"Any time I don't have you both in sight is a bad time. I have to get my words in while I can."

Requiem tipped his head back, his fingers tightening on Damion's hips as his own hips rose involuntarily to rub against Damion's.

Athena continued. "We're meeting in the morning so that you can be briefed and prepped for going back to the *Zeus*. You and the president leave tomorrow evening Earth time."

Requiem froze in his actions, his head tilted fully back by this time, his eyes staring unseeing at the ceiling.

"Tomorrow?" Damion frowned. "But you said we had another day!"

"Jasper said he has to be back earlier than anticipated," Athena replied in a no-nonsense tone. "So plans proceed ahead of schedule. He has to get back in time for a major senate meeting or they'll declare him lost or dead and the Chrysalis Corporation will put another puppet in his spot."

Requiem wrapped his arms tightly around Damion's waist and kissed him on the neck before burying his face against his Damion's warm skin.

"Fine," Damion barked. "Then let us be until we need to meet."

The comm was silent almost long enough for them to believe the captain had gone before a quiet voice spoke again. "I am sorry, Damion."

And then two beeps signaled that she was really gone. Requiem didn't move from his spot, clinging tightly to his lover.

Damion growled. "She has the worst timing. She's either watching me or she's taping us again."

Letting go of Damion, he stretched his arm out to the bedside console. His eyes lost focus for a minute as he did a quick check in the *Titan's* system. It was... colder than the *Zeus's* system. When diving into the *Zeus's* system, it was as if he were talking to a friend, one that played in the entire ship with him. It had taught him to do so many things within the system that he never would've discovered while exploring it himself or with the Creators' narrow instructions. The *Titan* was like jumping into an ice bath where he was completely alone and had to fumble his way through to the correct information. He was relieved when he exited the mind of the *Titan,* blinking repeatedly while shaking his head. "No, there are no more video inputs in the room."

"I will miss having you around," Damion admitted. "But right now we're together."

"We should use our remaining time wisely," Requiem replied with a small smile. "And I do not think you will be too sad. You will not have to watch over me or keep me out of trouble. You will no longer have to deal with your, as you say, pain in the ass."

"Aren't I a pain in your ass?" Damion had on a cocky grin as he reached to take Requiem's member back into his hands.

"Only when you do not prepare me enough. But that is the kind of pain I enjoy." His voice was breathy as he arched into Damion's hand.

"I try to please." Damion stroked him slowly. "We were interrupted right when it was going to get good."

"I am sure that this will not detain us long," Requiem replied, running his fingers over Damion's ribs.

"Hm." Damion smiled. "No more trying to break my record?"

"That is your personal achievement. Not mine. Do or do not challenge yourself, it matters not in the end to me." He leaned up and nipped at Damion's lips before lying back down, gazing up at him, warmth and slight amusement filling Requiem's chest.

"You are a troublemaker." Damion kissed him deeply while focusing once again on getting Requiem's body ready.

Requiem practically purred as their tongues slid against each other, a slow battle for supremacy. His long fingers trailed down Damion's back to eventually grip his tantalizing ass, kneading it as a cat would. "I attempt not to be one, but it seems more often than not, I fail at my attempts," Requiem said when they pulled apart for air. Bending his knees and planting his feet flat on the bed, Requiem lifted his hips wantonly as Damion's slick digits made sure he was still open enough. He dug his fingers deeper into Damion's muscular ass, ranging over the top of the cleft and to his hips in eager circles. He raised his head, nibbling on the Fighter's neck and shoulder, his breath coming fast, his heart pounding.

Damion took his fingers away and gave Requiem a grin as he slowly pushed into his quivering hole.

Requiem's breath hitched, his lungs straining as his lover entered him. Anticipation filled him, his teeth digging a little deeper into Damion's shoulder as his body trembled.

Damion didn't hold back. He moved quickly in and out of Requiem's willing body.

Fingers tightening in Damion's straining flesh, Requiem let out his breath in a whoosh of air, unable to hold it anymore. His pants were interspersed with barely audible cries, even more muffled by the skin between his teeth. He finally relaxed his jaw, whispering Damion's name in a pleading high moan as his hips moved against him. It was good, but not enough.

"Requiem." Damion's voice was a strained whisper before it turned into an inflamed roar of lust and his hips began to move harder.

Requiem's head fell back as he let out a sharp cry, his feet coming off the bed from the force of the thrusts. Eventually he rested his heels on Damion's ass, using them to encourage the man as his nails drew red lines up Damion's back. The feel of Damion pounding into him, filling him completely, nearly caused Requiem to lose his hard-earned breath. He never wanted to lose this, to let it go, to let Damion go.

Damion kissed every expanse of skin his lips could reach and then bit the softer areas.

Requiem's cries became louder as teeth sank into his flesh, only heightening his pleasure. His own shifting caused Damion to hit the amazing gland inside of him that created white bursts of pleasure behind his eyes. He dug his fingers into Damion's hair, dragging the man's mouth to his own as his hips met Damion's, increasing the brutal sounds.

Damion pressed a bruising kiss to his lips, and Requiem swept his tongue along Damion's lips, demanding entrance by pulling back and nibbling almost harshly on the soft flesh. As his hips met Damion's, his body arched against the man, almost coming fully off the bed, his arms and legs holding him there for a brief time before resting back against the mattress and starting all over again. His weeping cock rocked against the Fighter's undulating stomach as they moved.

"Requiem," Damion moaned again.

Requiem was amazed how much more attentive Damion was when they had sex. The man pushing into him had a limited vocabulary while they had sweat rolling down their arms and backs.

He tried to push down his impending orgasm, his body trembling with the effort of doing so. Tears burned his eyes, so he closed them to hide, not wanting this to end so soon. The sounds in the room were distant, from flesh slapping against flesh, to the bed squeaking in protest and the headboard banging against the wall. All he could hear was Damion saying his name, his moans, grunts, pants, and cries. Only Damion.

Damion kissed Requiem's wet cheek, then his lips, finally letting both of them tip over that edge that would push away all emotions except pleasure.

It was the tenderness and the determination that caused Requiem to finally hit the crescendo. He let out a choking sob against Damion's lips, their hot breaths intermingled as he screamed softly. His body went rigid except for a few involuntary jerks of his hips as he exploded between them. The feeling of Damion filling him only caused him to tremble more, his body clenching around Damion's spurting cock filling him with hot seed. Perhaps the last time for a long while.

Damion slowly rolled to his side as if he didn't want to break their contact. Still, Requiem did not want to suffocate under his lover so appreciated the space. "Damn, that was good."

Requiem softly hissed as Damion left him, letting his arms and legs fall. He managed to keep contact with the man's skin by laying his hand on Damion's wrist as he panted. He let his head fall to the side, away from his lover, as he got his tears under control. Tears that were a combination of several different emotions that overloaded him. His body still occasionally trembled, feeling euphoric and well used in a fantastic way, despite the sweat covering him and the fluids on his chest and stomach and leaking out of him. It just seemed to add to the experience.

Damion pulled him into his arms and hugged him close. "You speechless?"

Grateful for the warmth, Requiem twined his form with Damion's, wrapping his arms around the man. "There is not much more to say than you have already that I do not agree with," he replied, glad to have finally gotten the water in his eyes under control.

Damion pulled the sheets up to their waists. "I don't want to fall asleep, but even I have to admit I need a breather."

"Are you admitting that your never-failing stamina is finally giving out?" Requiem asked as he buried his head under Damion's chin.

"Never." Damion grinned from ear to ear. "But I don't want to overdo it."

He nuzzled Damion's neck. "I see. Forgive me for my assumption, then. It will not happen again."

Damion smiled and hugged Requiem tightly. "I'll miss this."

"I will as well. I keep trying to think of different scenarios and other possibilities so you do not have to go. But... I cannot. The option presented to us is the most logical." Requiem tightened his hold around Damion, inhaling the man's scent deeply.

"Something impossible?" Damion teased as he kissed the side of his head.

"No. Merely improbable. Illogical. But not impossible if we choose the options we must from the evidence we've been provided." He ran his fingers featherlight over Damion's side.

Damion looked at the wall across from them. "I want to hope for a better future."

"Then, unfortunately, this is the path we must take. As much as we both may dislike it, it is the most logical movement," Requiem whispered, closing his eyes and burying his face against Damion's skin. He wanted to remember him. The feel of him, the scent of his skin, his voice, everything in case they failed and he never saw him again. That thought sent a burst of pain through his chest that confused him but felt appropriate.

Chapter Thirteen

Damion

DAMION HAD never dressed so slowly in his life. He didn't want to leave the room. He didn't want to face the president. After he combed through his short hair and sighed for what had to be the hundredth time, he glanced over at his lover.

Requiem had already procrastinated getting dressed as well, in borrowed jeans and a plain black zip-up vest. He was now sitting at the table, staring at the floor. Since they had gotten out of bed—another slow venture—he hadn't spoken a word, his face vacant of expression and his eyes wide with lack of sleep and a hidden sorrow.

Damion went over and put a hand on Requiem's head. "Nothing on your mind? Or are you pouting?"

Requiem's eyes closed, and he leaned into the affectionate touch. "I do not know what pouting is. I… my mind is uneventful. Blank. I suppose you could call it numb."

"Really? That isn't normal for you." Damion smiled sadly.

"My concept of normalcy is in the process of being reevaluated," Requiem reminded him, his eyes still closed as he leaned a little to the side, resting against Damion.

Damion chuckled. "Yeah, I guess mine will be too in a few hours. Hopefully this thing in my ear will work as they promised and I'll be back in a few months."

"It will work. I have already inspected it. Using a simple terminal with a strong signal, I will be able to access it. The shuttle they plan to provide me is in actuality docked securely on the outside of the ship, therefore increasing the signal. I will be able to contact you from anywhere as long as there is power to boost the signal."

Damion tugged on the back of the man's short hair and pressed a kiss to Requiem's lips. "Hey, enough of that pouting, you hear me? This has to work. I mean, we're still alive. The Gods must have something planned for us."

"I reiterate. I do not know what pouting is." Even as he said this, Requiem attempted to hide the small shiver that Damion's kiss afforded him. "And how do things that I do not believe in have something planned for me? We should depart. They are waiting for us."

Damion shrugged. "Let them wait for a minute longer. They're pirates; it's not like they have a schedule. Let's walk slowly."

Requiem favored him with a small smile that could have been construed as loving. He nodded in agreement as they moved out of the room and into the hallway. Their footsteps were ambling as they traveled toward the lift, Requiem's fingers brushing against Damion's in an unconscious attempt for continued contact.

Damion let his fingers intertwine with Requiem's. It wasn't something he usually did, but it felt right and comfortable.

Despite their slowness, eventually their walk had to end and they came to the meeting room that the captain had directed them to. Requiem squeezed the fingers he held tightly, swallowing audibly as the guards at the door granted them entrance.

There was a large wooden table in the center, holo-terminals in front of each seat, and a display of the sector they were in spinning in the center. He could see the captain and the president at the end of the table going over some paperwork, their heads together as they planned. As Requiem and Damion entered, they stopped, looking up at them expectantly. Athena's gaze seemed angry at first due to their tardiness, but then dropped to the couple's held hands and looked almost sad, before falling back to the papers in front of her.

"Why do you two look so damn glum?" Damion asked in his normal smart-assed tone.

Requiem squeezed Damion's fingers tighter, reminding him not to take his unhappiness out on the other two. Then he let go.

"We're just finishing up some logistics of the mission. It's not going to be easy, and it's going to require all of your skills," the president replied, standing and stretching. The man looked tired and worn, dark circles under his eyes showing the toll his position took on him. "Thank you for agreeing to it. Your involvement will help greatly. I'm sorry to have to put this burden on you."

"You sort of saved his life and mine, and I guess helping you find your son isn't all that bad of a deal either. I'm not sure I'll be a good infiltrator." Damion wanted to put that out there right away. "I'm a soldier, so you better tell me real well what not to say."

"Why don't you and your Core have a seat?" Jasper said, waving a hand toward the chairs near Athena and him, his face pinching only momentarily in old pain at the mention of his son.

Athena leaned back in her chair. "What not to say is fairly easy. Don't mention that you're working for us or your true objective. Try to find out information that would benefit us, but don't be too obvious about it. Learn subtlety; that'll be the hardest part. Just go about your business like you used to. Except this time you'll be an officer and you'll have to act as if Req… 47 is truly gone. You have to figure out how you would act if that were true. You'll more than likely be questioned about it, and you don't have to lie. He was technically dead for a little while when you first arrived. Just go with that."

Damion sat down with a heavy sigh. "How did I survive again?"

"After they captured the *Ares* and your Core died in the attempt to keep that from happening, they kept you for questioning." Jasper began to recite the planned story. "You were placed in a cell next to mine, and we planned an escape. It was an altogether simple plan. Wait until someone came to gather you for questioning and then knock them out, grabbing the pass key access to the cells and the ship. From there we made our way to the docks, meeting some resistance on the way, which you dealt with fairly easily because of your martial skills and by purloining a weapon from one of the guards. We managed to blast our way out of the dock, damaging the ship's release controls so that they couldn't come after us. From there we limped our way back to the *Zeus.*"

Requiem remained standing against the wall behind Damion's chair, keeping his silence as he listened, his eyes downcast.

"Of course, part of your questioning would involve torture of some sort," the captain added, wincing sympathetically. "So unfortunately we're going to have to emulate that type of evidence on both you and Jasper before you leave."

"Yes, well, the roughing me up has been mentioned before, so I'm sadly ready for the appropriate ass-kicking." Damion was not looking forward to it at all. A question about a certain security guard that he had spent hours with when the Creators wiped Requiem entered his mind. "How long has Alexander Collins been working with you?"

"Since he found out his Core was terminated," Athena replied without hesitating. "He went on a bender when he was on leave afterward, and I ran into him in a bar. He couldn't give up hope that his Core, 162, aka Red, was still alive and his hatred for the Chrysalis Corporation had already been born. I didn't even have to ask for his help."

"I can't wait to give him a friendly thank-you." Damion grinned. "Since I'll be even higher rank than him, it wouldn't be out of character for me to push him around a bit."

"It'll be easier since he'll be under your command," the president replied with a smile. "He was quite taken with you and thought you would be a good addition. Said you reminded him of himself." Jasper's eyes flicked up to Requiem in obvious curiosity.

"We've fixed up the *Ares* enough so that it'll go, but not much more than that," Athena said. "It'll be difficult to control without a Core, but we know you have the skills to do so. The repairs aren't obvious, so if it's deeply searched it'll look like damage done in a fight."

"I can get it back to the *Zeus*." Damion wasn't worried about the flight. "What information am I looking for exactly? I mean, being the president's lackey will get me further, but I'm not even sure what I'm looking for to begin with."

"Anything damaging to the Corporation, really. Along with any information on human trafficking, obvious evidence of genocide, drug trade, weapons trade, etcetera." Athena stretched in her chair. "Anything we can use to convince the general populous of their crimes."

Requiem finally pushed away from the wall and slid into the chair next to Damion's, listening silently with his leg pushed against Damion's leg.

Damion gave Athena an even look. "And the assassinations you want me to do?"

"That task will not fall on you squarely." The president steepled his fingers. "The only one we're planning for is the Commander's, and that will have to be done at a certain time so that you, and possibly Collins, get out right away with no prior suspicion. Or that it can be done with no suspicion at all."

"I am the one more skilled in doing subtle terminations," Requiem said, his voice barely audible.

Damion gave Requiem a small smirk. "I don't think you can remotely access *Zeus* anymore. But you can definitely help plan."

"Nothing is impossible," Requiem said with a small shrug.

"Wait. Can he be subtle at assassinations?" Athena looked at Requiem and then Damion, her expression confused.

"He's had to deal with past Fighters." Damion frowned, hoping they would leave it at that.

"We know about the three before he chose you, but those killings were fairly blatant with no subtlety needed." Athena crossed her arms and leaned back in her chair, her eyes traveling to Requiem, assessing. "They were deserving of it. That was obvious even from the nepotism of the reports."

Requiem merely sat there, his eyes on the table.

"He's smart, quiet, and able to do a lot with electronics." Damion looked at the president and then Athena, trying to stare her down. "It's not that relevant."

"The situations are not relevant, but the execution of it is… intriguing," Athena admitted with a sharp smile.

"Back on track, Athena," Jasper said, his tone both calming and slightly chiding. He nodded toward Requiem, speaking to him instead of around him. "Obviously we will need your abilities as well, to keep in contact with Fighter Hawk."

Requiem nodded silently, still not looking up.

"How long will it be until I can come back and check on him?" Damion looked over at his lover. "Don't you have questions?"

Athena and Jasper looked at each other, seeming to go through some sort of silent communication before looking back to the partners. "At this time, we don't know," Jasper admitted. "It depends on the situation and need. When you leave it will be for good, because anything less would be suspicious. Could be months, could be over a year. It all depends."

Requiem shook his head to Damion's other question, and Damion could tell that Requiem wasn't going to allow any of his emotions on the proposed plan to show. "I will figure out everything else once I am in the shuttle," he told Damion. "Besides that, what questions should I ask? I am used to being told."

"No one tells you what to do while I'm gone." Damion reached out and pulled Requiem's chin up. "If the captain gives you an order which makes sense, then go ahead and follow it. I want you to remember that no one controls you any longer."

Requiem opened his mouth to reply, his sad eyes meeting Damion's, but Athena interrupted before he had a chance to. Requiem pulled his chin free from Damion's grasp, which took some work since, in Damion's anger, his fingers had tightened, biting into the bone.

"While he's on my ship, he follows my orders. Even if they do not make sense, there's always a reason for them." She stood with her hands flat on the table and leaned forward, glaring.

"Not if you tell him to kill himself," Damion growled back, almost coming out of his own chair. He didn't like Athena's tone and didn't care if she didn't like his at the moment.

"Then it's a good thing I'd never give him that sort of stupid order," Athena hissed. "He seems quite capable of doing that all on his own. With or without your order. You seem to forget, he almost died under your command. I think I'll do better at it."

"Look, you overconfident wench." Damion's jaw hurt from clenching it so hard. "I have always done my best trying to keep this man alive, but you'd kill him if it suited your purpose."

"And it would never suit my purpose to have him dead. If you're so worried about it, why are you allowing him to stay on my ship while you go on the mission? Why did you even agree to the mission? We've done nothing but help you, heal you, and keep you safe!" Athena shouted, her fury matching her blazing hair.

"Athena, Hawk, that's enough," Jasper said in a low tone. "We're supposed to be on the same side, and fighting over whether or not the Core will kill himself is not helping our cause."

Requiem just sat rigid in his chair, his eyes on Damion. Damion knew he hated to be the center of attention and he disliked the anger involved in the conversation.

"The only reason I'm doing all of this is to protect him!" Damion sat back down with a hard grunt. "Doesn't mean I want to leave him behind either. Let's continue. When do we have to leave?"

Requiem placed a hand on Damion's thigh, squeezing tightly in understanding.

"In about three Earth hours. It will give both of us time to prepare. You're not the only one who's going to be getting roughed up today," Jasper replied.

"We thought you'd be more comfortable with letting 47 do the maiming required," Athena added, sitting down in her own chair and glaring.

Requiem's eyes widened, his icy gaze going to Athena and then Jasper, his head shaking wildly.

"Let him kick my ass?" Damion's voice actually raised an octave.

"Would you rather I or a stranger do it?" Athena asked with a quirked eyebrow, looking at Requiem's still insistent shaking of his head. "We figured letting someone you trust do it would be better. You would know the person wouldn't truly harm you. It doesn't have to be something done with malicious intent. It just has to look like they tortured you. Restraint marks, possibly a few broken ribs, and of course, bruises to the chest and face."

"I really think…," Damion started, then stopped as he looked over at Requiem.

Requiem's eyes were still wide as they met Damion's, and he licked his dry lips. "I cannot hurt you," he whispered.

"Oh bullshit, he hurts you all the time. Think of it as getting revenge," Athena said with a snort.

"He does not do anything that he would not stop doing if I asked him to," Requiem clarified for her, still not looking away from Damion.

"I don't hurt him like that." Damion really hated that he had to keep defending himself. "It's not like I'm some backwater wife beater. Look, if you're the one that wants to kick my ass and get it out of your system, fine."

"I have no desire to kick your ass, Damion. And I may tease you, but I've never met a Fighter who treated his Core better," Athena admitted with a sigh.

"Former Core," Requiem muttered under his breath.

"I honestly thought you'd prefer having Req… 47 do it."

"I would really like no one to try and kick my ass, since I won't be able to really fight back, but I understand that it has to be done." Damion looked at the president. "You ever let your ass get kicked before?"

"A few times. For the cause," the man answered with a nod. "It's not easy to let yourself take pain, to not guard yourself against it. But it's easier when someone you trust does it because you know they won't go too far."

"All my beatings were due to drinking, fighting, and work." Damion chuckled. "I never even let my brother kick my ass without trying to kick his right back."

"Then how do you propose to go about this?" Jasper inquired, his voice calm, with none of Athena's impatience.

"Great. Such a complicated plan and he gets hooked up on the beating part of it." Athena threw her hands up in frustration, eyes rolling.

He gave her a wide grin. "It's not the complicated parts that worry me, since if I fuck up, I'm dead. Just get a few of your boys together, and Requiem will stand back and make sure it doesn't go too far."

"If that's what you wish to do, I'll arrange it," the captain said with a shake of her fiery head.

Requiem didn't look as confident about the idea, and his head shook, but a bit more slowly. "That would not be wise. I do not know if I could watch you take one hit and take no action. In the past, perhaps I might have been able to. Now I cannot know what my own reactions might be. Even if it is your duty to protect me...." He paused. "*Was* your duty to protect me, it was also programmed in me to do the same by whatever means possible." His hand left his lap and caressed the console in front of him, as gentle as a lover would sensitive skin. The lights flickered, and the rotating holo floating above the center of the table blew apart in a burst of light and then reformed. He placed his hand back in his lap, his icy eyes on Athena and the president in silent warning.

Damion chuckled. "I think that means make sure you don't mess up my handsome face. Anything else?"

Athena and Jasper's eyes were on Requiem, who had gone back to looking down at his hands. Athena licked her lips. "No, that's about it. We'll meet in about three hours in the training room down the corridor from the mess hall. You may not want to eat, or if you do, eat light. I know that 47 probably hasn't eaten today. If you want to double-check the *Ares* and give any last-minutes suggestions, you are more than welcome to. You know your Zodiac better than anyone else, especially since it seems that 47 made a lot of modifications we're not familiar with."

"He's the best." Damion stood up and took Requiem's hand.

Requiem let Damion pull him out of the chair, looking a bit surprised at the public display of affection.

"The flight suit you arrived in is already back in your room," Jasper told him. "That would be the wisest thing to wear. It hasn't been cleaned, since it would be strange if they gave you the kindness of clean clothes. The suit's actually been made to look dirtier, as if from days of imprisonment."

"Three hours?" Damion asked at the door. "I guess I better get myself all sweaty then, just to make it real."

"With the clothes on helps," Athena yelled as the door shut behind them.

"You don't have to be there," Damion told Requiem once they were in the lift.

Requiem didn't answer immediately. He kept his head down, the parts of his hair that were still long enough covering his face. "I am aware that I do not need to attend. However, even though I do not know how I will react, I do know that I need to be present."

"And you don't listen to anyone but me still," Damion reiterated.

"Understood," he whispered, squeezing Damion's hand. "Do you wish me to be there?"

Damion sighed. "Not if you can't handle it. I'd understand."

"I do not know if I can or cannot. But I believe it would be worse if I did not know what was going on and how you were faring," Requiem replied after a moment as they stepped off the lift.

"It's an ass-kicking, remember? I'll get bruised and a bit broken before they stuff us in the *Ares*."

"I do not have to like it. I understand the need for it to look legitimate to match your story. I am only saying that I may not be able to prevent myself from wanting to retaliate against your faux attackers," Requiem said as they approached their room again to retrieve Damion's original clothing. "I will attempt to stay away from any terminals or electronics as a cautionary measure."

"Well, I'm sure we hurt a few of their friends when we were being captured, so a bit of it may be payback." Damion pulled Requiem into their room and began kissing him.

The breath that Requiem had taken to reply was caught in his chest as Damion took control of his mouth. His fingers grasped Damion's upper arms tightly, his eyes wide in shock. After a moment, they fluttered closed and he kissed Damion back.

After they were both out of air and Damion's legs were shaky, he said, "I don't want to leave, but I have to. And I don't want to get my ass kicked, but I have to. This is the only thing I don't have to do but *want* to."

Icy eyes still wide and pale skin flushed, Requiem licked his lips and nodded slowly in agreement. He brought his fingers to the tab of his vest, pulled down the zipper, and let the garment fall to the floor in front of the now closed door. "Do with me what you wish and how you wish," he said with a small and unknowingly loving and seductive smile.

"You have the very best ideas." Damion smiled and quickly stripped off his shirt and undid his pants. "I wish I had a way to mark you as mine." He kissed his Core again, trying to burn the taste of Requiem onto his tongue.

Requiem waited until they both needed air before speaking, his words husky and staggered between pants. "The marks you leave on my skin are not enough for you?" he asked with a teasing smile and a tilt of his head. "Or is it because those will fade with time?" His smile wilted a little at the thought, his fingers falling to the fastening of his own pants.

"You're mine forever, right? I want to prove that." Damion latched his teeth onto an already bruised piece of skin.

"How do you know you will want me forever?" Requiem hissed, his fingers freezing in their attempts to push off his pants. He stifled a groan. "Even if you did, how would you prove it beyond what you have done already?"

"I'm thinking about it," Damion mumbled around a mouthful of flesh while he helped Requiem remove the rest of his clothing.

"Which part?" Requiem's body was frozen in position, Damion's teeth holding him there like a cat who had been scruffed. Soft pants escaped through his slightly parted lips, and his glazed eyes were unfocused.

"Marking you forever." Damion pulled his lips away from the nearly bleeding neck so he could kiss Requiem once again. Damion felt impatient and suddenly frantic. He wasn't afraid—no, this wasn't fear that had him scrambling to claim Requiem. This was something different.

Requiem barely had time to suck in a startled breath before Damion was claiming his mouth again. He wrapped his arms around his lover's waist, his body arching into the passionate kiss and the warmth the man's body and mouth provided. "That would mean you want me forever." He tilted his head back to let Damion see his face and his smile and the emotion that glittered in his eyes. "But I still do not know how you would mark me further." He paused, freeing one of his hands to rub at the back of his head where it was shaved, revealing the tattoo on his skin. "Unless…."

"What?" Damion forgot about the marking until his lust-filled brain began to function. "Tattoo?"

"It was merely a suggestion." Dropping his hand back to Damion's waist, Requiem met the man's lips. He pressed the warm line of his naked body along Damion's, rising up on his toes so his lips could claim Damion's hesitant kisses.

"You think you can get one?" Damion's right brow arched.

Requiem sighed and fell back off his toes. "I would not even know the first thing about it. It was an idea, an illogical one, obviously. That is all."

"I didn't say it was illogical. I'm just surprised." Damion kissed Requiem slowly. "Think we could have some fun, then find someone?"

"Find who?" Requiem mumbled as he melted into the kiss, his eyes fluttering for a moment.

Damion pulled Requiem toward the bed, because that was where he had left the lube. "Someone that is decent with a needle."

"You really would like to do so? Tattoo me?" Requiem followed instinctively and somehow gracefully, his body still fully aligned with Damion's.

"If you're up for it, I don't think it's a bad idea." Damion was happy to see they hadn't emptied out the tube completely.

"I am, as you say, up for it if that is what you wish." Requiem stood there, head tilted to the side as he studied Damion, seemingly oblivious to the fact that Damion was checking out their supplies.

"Then I guess we can't take too long." Damion bridged the gap between them and resumed his earlier exploits.

"That does not leave us much time at all. There is no way that we can do what we wish within such a small time frame," Requiem replied before his lips were captured again, his fingers digging into Damion's back. The kiss was slow but still almost feral, conveying their needs, wants, and emotions. Requiem sighed in contentment, his body melting against Damion's, almost becoming putty in his arms.

"We'll make the time." Damion groaned with Requiem's lip between his teeth. He urged Requiem to straddle him while lying slowly back on the bed.

AFTER THEIR heated round of sex Requiem remained where he was, still on his side, back against the headboard. "Is there not a saying that goes something along the lines of 'making that last one count'?"

"You're right." Damion kissed Requiem's cheek. "I have to make sure you don't forget about me."

"I believe it is the other way around," Requiem said with a small, lazy smile. "I do not believe you have the fortitude to go celibate for as long as the mission requires."

"You're worried I'll cheat on you?" Damion wasn't surprised, since he had almost slept with the captain a few times. But even then he couldn't follow through.

"I do not understand what you mean when you say 'cheating.' If it means that you will have sex with other people, I would not be surprised." Requiem shifted onto his back, wincing, probably from the pain in his back and head. "There is a large difference between a few hours or days when I am unconscious for one reason or another, and months where I am simply not there."

"You think I'll cheat." Damion let out another long sigh. "I don't want to."

Requiem was quiet for a moment as he wrapped an arm around Damion's waist. His brow was furrowed slightly as the information went through his head. Finally it smoothed. "I remember now, where the term cheating comes from. But my confusion stems from the fact that, in order to cheat, you first must have a defined relationship. That is something we do not have. It has always been Fighter and Core, now former Core, but still the fact remains. To cheat, you have to have something to cheat on." He gave a small shrug, his eyes closing slowly. "You may not want to, but you may not be able to help yourself either. You are not one to be able to go long without sexual activity."

"You don't want us to be defined?" Damion asked.

"I did not say that. I did not believe you wanted this. You do not seem to be the type of person that likes to be restricted by definitions."

"I don't want to hurt you either." Damion knew it wasn't in him to fool around if he was supposed to be with someone permanently. That was why he normally stayed away from permanence.

"And to force you to do something you do not want to do, to do something against your nature, would hurt you." Requiem sat up.

"This is not something I can tell or ask you to do," Requiem continued. "But I would like to remind you that you were the one who wanted to brand me and said the word 'forever.' I will always be with you in mind, if not body." He slid from the bed and stood on shaky legs. "I am still getting to know what emotions are, Damion. I cannot predict how I will act and feel."

Damion raised an eyebrow. "You mean you're not sure that you won't hate my guts in a few months?"

"I could never hate you, Damion. Ever." Requiem pinned Damion with an icy look over his shoulder before walking to the bathroom to get a wet washcloth.

"Promise?" Damion wasn't sure why those words made him feel better, but they did.

"On my life. So in the end, the decision about labels is up to you."

"You like my tattoo?" Damion asked, turning his arm toward Requiem.

Requiem tilted his head at the odd question, looking at the tattoo that graced Damion's upper arm. His gaze roamed over it for a moment before meeting Damion's eyes. "Yes."

Damion nodded with a grin. "You know, a few days ago you wouldn't admit to liking something so directly, but it's a good sign. How about you get the same thing?"

His eyes fell back to the tattoo, looking at it more carefully now. It was a picture of a full moon, so well done it seemed to glow with light. A black-and-purple butterfly, wings as ornate as if made of lace, was breaking out of the moon like it would a chrysalis. Breaking free. Living free.

"It would be... appropriate," he finally whispered.

"All right, let me find pants and then we'll find someone that is good. If not today, well..." Damion sighed. "Maybe when I come back."

Requiem lowered his eyes as he picked up the flight suit Damion originally arrived in. "You are as good as I am at circumventing questions that you do not want to answer." He handed the garment to Damion before going by the door to gather his own clothing.

"Me?" Damion didn't even try to look innocent as he pulled on the tattered suit. "Nah, I just like leaving options open at times."

"I see." Requiem kept his back to Damion as he pulled on his own pants and then the vest he had abandoned on the floor.

"You okay?" Damion asked as he finished.

"I am acceptable." Requiem turned and let a small smile show as he zipped up the vest and fixed the collar, wincing slightly as he brushed the bite mark on his neck. "We do need to go, though, if we hope to do as much as you wish before time runs out."

"You're not aware that your eyes look tense." Damion pulled Requiem into a tight hug. "How much time?"

He sank into the embrace, hiding his sad eyes in Damion's shoulder. "Approximately two hours and fifteen minutes," he said. "Not enough."

"Yeah, not enough." Damion continued to hold Requiem for a few more minutes.

Requiem hugged Damion back tightly. "You need to go."

Damion released him. "Let's go find a tattoo artist."

"There is one on level five. They have shops and vendors set up on that level. Along with restaurants, bars, studios, and more." Requiem keyed the door open without looking at Damion, but he slid his fingers down the arm to grab his hand.

"When do you have time to find all this shit out?" Damion looked at him with amazement and curiosity.

"When I first jacked into the medical facilities computer and hacked into their schematics." Requiem stopped when Damion didn't follow him. He tilted his head, a questioning look on his face.

"You retained all of that?" Damion moved forward to follow the pale man.

"I have a good memory" was all he replied as he walked them to the lift.

"You will always retain a lot. Still Core-like for a while." Damion felt odd wearing his tattered uniform as he walked through the hallways.

Chapter Fourteen

Requiem

THE GLARES they received spoke great volumes. People on this ship didn't appreciate seeing the Corporation Alpha uniform. Requiem kept his head down, his fingers tightening on Damion's. "I can no longer call myself a Core. While I may still have most of a Core's abilities, a Core is under the Chrysalis Corporation's control and gives full loyalty to the Creators. I am of no use to them anymore, unless I am wiped and plugged."

"What do they call the ones here? The ones that they've turned?" Damion had never asked.

"Broken," the pale man whispered after a moment.

Damion reached out and grabbed Requiem's wrist. "You're not broken."

Requiem came to a stop at the tug but didn't look at Damion. He attempted to ignore the people around them who were trying to subtly eavesdrop. "That is what they call those who used to be Cores here. Broken or Dolls. Broken because many of us cannot work the system once we have our emotions back. It is difficult to have the emotionlessness that it takes to understand the system once you start feeling things you never have before. Dolls because those who can still work the system generally cannot handle the emotions, and therefore jack into the system and never come out again, preferring riding the stream as opposed to dealing with emotions. Those of us who can deal with it all do not have a name. We're too rare. So they call us whatever comes to mind first, Broken or Doll."

"You're Requiem," Damion stated simply. "That's all that matters to me."

Requiem gave his lover a brief smile before lowering his head again. "As long as you give me purpose, I will continue to be so." He kept walking, pulling his wrist gently from Damion's grasp to step into the lift.

"Your purpose is to help me keep focused." Damion sucked at undercover operations because he had a direct personality.

"And here I thought I was better at keeping you unfocused." A smile could be seen from behind Requiem's curtain of hair, brief but genuine. "I will do my best." He pushed the button for the fifth floor.

"Yes, you are," Damion said. "What's the guy's name who can do that tat?"

"Korvin. No last name. No history. Known for his art." Requiem quirked an eyebrow at the slightly glazed look in Damion's eyes. Having a few more seconds, he raised a hand and ran his fingers over Damion's cheek.

"Just thinking about your tongue," Damion answered the unspoken question.

"My tongue? What about my tongue?" Requiem let his hand drop, now very confused.

"I'll explain it later during a really long night when I'm away." Damion stepped out of the lift. "Let's go. We're running out of time."

"As you wish." Requiem was still quite confused, not understanding what the difference would be between explaining now or later.

The lift let them out not into a corridor, but into a large open area that looked almost like a park. Pathways were created out of brick that circled around small trees and flowerbeds. The paths led to a number of shops and other businesses that lined what seemed to be a small street or boardwalk. People bustled about, and children's laughter could be heard.

"He's approximately three hundred and thirty-four feet to the right," Requiem said quietly, moving behind Damion.

Requiem didn't understand the people around them or their faces. He didn't understand the laughter from the children or the carefree look of the adults who moved about, greeted each other, talked, ate, walked, played. He just… didn't understand their emotions.

"Just let me know when we're about there." Damion looked around and spoke low, "This place reminds me of the market back on Mars that me and my brother used to run through getting yelled at by Mom. This place is far cleaner."

They received stares as Requiem led Damion down the faux cobblestone street, past a bookshop, a restaurant, a jewelry store, and a music shop. He paused in front of the tattoo parlor, which had a sign that simply said Tattoo.

"Hell, I guess I could have found it." Damion stepped into the shop. "Hello?"

"Yeah?" A man appeared from the back room. He looked to be in his midthirties, about five foot six with brown hair that reached his shoulders. He was wearing a black tank top and matching cargo pants that tucked into combat boots. He was thin, probably about 140 pounds, but it was all muscle. Every bit of skin showing, except for his face, was covered in art. His brown eyes flicked from Damion to Requiem and back before he crossed his arms over his chest and leaned against the doorframe. "What can I do for ya?"

"You have time for him?" Damion asked.

Again the man's brown eyes flickered to Requiem. He pushed off the wall, walking closer, arms still crossed as he looked over Requiem, his eyes lingering on the ports. "Only if he wants me to have time for him." He looked back to Damion, emotionless but clear in his meaning. He wasn't going to brand Requiem if he was unwilling.

His meaning wasn't quite clear to Requiem, though, until Requiem noticed something out of the corner of his eye. He looked back to the artist, his eyes traveling the intricate designs on the man's arms and what they fairly successfully hid. "You are a Core," he whispered.

"Was," the artist corrected. He put his thumbs in his pockets, leaning slightly to one side. "Now I'm Korvin." Emotion finally trickled onto his face as he looked at Requiem. It showed understanding and pity.

"Where is your Fighter?" Damion asked.

"Damned if I know," Korvin replied with a shrug. "Damned if I care. He sold me to a ring for drug money."

Requiem knew Damion was holding back his frustration because this was something Requiem wanted. "Look, we don't have much time, and I'd like to see this."

"He still hasn't answered my question. I only have time for him if he wants me to have time for him," Korvin replied easily, rocking back and forth on his heels.

Requiem looked to Damion and then back to Korvin. "I… would appreciate it if you did have time for me," he finally whispered.

"This is something you want done? Because I'm not going to do it if you're just following orders," Korvin said brazenly, not even looking at Damion.

"This is something that I want done. Damion did not order me to do this. He rarely orders me to do anything," Requiem replied with a nod of appreciation.

Damion looked at the artist and then his lover. "Why does everyone think I'm a jackass?"

"Because you're a Fighter," Korvin said with a small smirk. "It generally comes with the territory. Especially the male Fighters." He turned, waving a hand for them to follow. "Come on back and tell me what you want."

"We sort of know. Well, he does, I think."

"The same design. It is appropriate. Unless you wish for me to get it modified," Requiem stated as they walked into the room behind Korvin. There was only one table, along with a recliner. A rolling tray was nearby, as well as a counter with ink displayed along it. In the back corner were a drawing table and a holo-transfer.

Korvin waved Requiem to the chair as he grabbed a spray can from the rolling table and sprayed a layer of glove over his hands. "And what design is that?" he asked as he got the laser-tat ready.

Damion unzipped his jumpsuit so he could pull up his shirtsleeve to show off his arm. "I had this put on when I was eighteen. He seems to think it's still fitting."

Korvin's eyes roamed over the dark colors, as if memorizing it. "That it is. Especially if he's escaped the Chrysalis Corporation for good. It symbolizes breaking free." He turned and pulled bottles of ink off the counter.

Requiem eased down in the chair nervously.

"Where do you want it?" Korvin asked.

He looked at Damion for advice.

"Somewhere he can cover up. He's not flashy." Damion pulled his suit back on and zipped it. "How about on his chest?"

"Over his port or beside it? And on which side, right or left?" Korvin asked before turning on his rolling stool to look at Requiem. He mimed Requiem unzipping his vest.

Requiem pulled down the zipper and shrugged the garment off his shoulders to pool on the seat behind him. Korvin froze for a moment, his eyes trailing over the ports on Requiem's chest and arms. Each one was like a disk bubbling slightly blue under the pale skin. Each time a port was accessed by a jack, the thin layer of skin covering the devices was pierced straight through, slowly growing back over the entrance once the jacks were released. However, the more often the ports were accessed, the more skin growth was delayed until they looked like Requiem's— visible holes where each port was implanted. They looked like hungry little electrical mouths, eager and waiting to feed on the system the jacks fed them. It was clear that Requiem's skin had ceased to grow back over them, too damaged by his constant control of the computer system.

He moved to Requiem's side, placed a gentle hand on the pale man's shoulder, and leaned him a little more forward so he could look at the ports on his back. Then he looked at Damion. "Did you order these, or were they personal modifications? Or was it an experiment by the Creators?"

"I didn't order him to add shit." Damion found a chair to sit in, and he let out a loud grunt. "He always had his own agenda."

"You're braver than I am," Korvin said before going back to the tray. "As much as I loved the system and would have liked to meld with it completely, getting more ports, especially as many as that, would have been too damn painful." After shaking an ink bottle, he snapped it into the gun with a hiss from compressed air releasing. "The Creators are sadistic bastards when they implant them."

Requiem's eyes flickered to Damion and then back to Korvin.

"It hurts?" Damion frowned.

Requiem let out a quiet sigh and let his head fall forward, his hair hiding his face.

"Of course it hurts! The Creators slice open your skin, implant the port, connect the nerves to it basically with a soldering gun, and then graft skin over it. And you're awake for the whole thing." Korvin turned, shaking his head. "How could it…." He trailed off, seeing Requiem's bowed head, and then looked at Damion. "He never told you, did he?"

"He never told me a lot." Damion laid his eyes on his lover. "Secretive bastard."

"He may not have been able to tell you." Korvin gave Requiem a conspiratorial look. "The stims have something in them that locks in knowledge that we're not allowed to share. We might try to tell someone, but we just can't speak it, no matter how hard we try."

Requiem nodded slowly in agreement, relieved that this man understood.

"Now, specifically where do you want it on his chest?"

"It's his skin."

"Damion, you were the one who wished to mark me," Requiem said softly. "I agreed to it because I do not mind. It is your decision on where to mark me."

Korvin snorted, looking over the multitude of bruises and red marks on Requiem's chest and neck with a quirked eyebrow. "I think it's a little late for that."

"Those won't last long." Damion grinned. "But on your chest is a good spot."

Korvin sighed, flopping down in his chair and looking at the ceiling as if pleading for help. "And you're the one who said you didn't have a lot of time." He looked back at Damion as if he were dense. "Now, for the last time, or I put the damn thing on his ass, where on his chest do you want it? Specifically, where? Over his port or beside it? And on which side, right or left?"

"By his heart," Damion said with a hint of impatience. "Is that okay, Requiem?"

Requiem gave Damion a faint smile, nodding in acquiescence.

"All right, then. Now we're getting somewhere." There were a few more questions while Korvin used Damion's skin art to make a basic stencil to put on Requiem's chest, but soon all was ready. "You mind sitting where I can see your arm? I have the stencil, but it'll be better if I can look at your art while I do his. I can freehand the majority of it, but I need to be looking at it." Korvin rolled his chair next to Requiem's left side, moving a lever so that the chair tilted back until he was lying at a perfect level for him to work.

Damion uncovered his arm once more.

"Now this isn't like how they used to do tattoos in the old days. It doesn't hurt much anymore, just a slight burning. Not that you would notice." Korvin lifted his eyes to give Requiem a short smile before looking back at the expanse of pale skin that went above the skin-grafted port. He placed the tip of the gun to his skin, and with just another brief glimpse at Damion's arm, he started it up.

Requiem didn't even jump at the sudden heat that burst over his chest. His eyes were locked on Damion as the heat settled into a point, following the tip of the tattoo gun. No one spoke as Korvin worked, occasionally glancing at Damion's arm or sitting up and changing the ink bottles.

"You don't look too fazed." Damion glanced at the clock.

Pausing in the action of shrugging, which earned him a glare from Korvin, Requiem gave Damion a small smile. "It does not hurt. Merely an… annoyance really."

"I'm almost done," Korvin mumbled, seeming to pull himself out of deep concentration to say the words. "So stop looking at the clock. Perhaps five more minutes."

"Apologies." Damion sighed. "Guess I didn't think the time would go so fast."

"Time always goes faster when you do not want it to," Requiem replied sorrowfully. Then he winced slightly as Korvin ran color over the skin graft over his port.

The artist let out a long sigh and sat back, inspecting his work. "All right, done." He stood up, stretched, and then grabbed another spray bottle and sprayed a fine mist over the ink to cool his skin. "That'll help with the healing process."

Damion went to look at his lover's chest. "That's really good work." He gave Korvin a grin. "What do we owe you?"

The artist flapped a hand over his shoulder as he cleaned up. "Nothing. You guys are doing enough for the cause. Don't think that the rest of us Broken haven't heard about the new arrival. Word travels fast, even on a ship this big. Just survive to come back for this one. That's all the payment I need."

Requiem looked down at the artwork that was slightly red around the edges of the ink and within the ivory of the moon. Korvin had changed the coloration of the butterfly from the black and deep purple to black and ice blue, close to the coloration of Requiem's eyes. It was a subtle difference, so that the art was the same as Damion's but individualized by the colors. It was beautiful, looking as if it could come alive at any moment, the lace of the wings flapping in exuberance.

"And you." Korvin turned, pointing at the younger Core. "You can come visit me. While I may be Broken, I still remember what it was like when they first took the chip out of my head and the stims out of my system. I remember the confusion, the emotions that I couldn't name and didn't know how to deal with. Your payment to me will be to learn."

Requiem's eyes flicked to Damion. He was suddenly nervous, but he nodded slowly.

Damion's lips curled into a quick snarl before they smoothed out. "If you want to, I suppose, but remember what I said." He looked up at the clock again. "Come on. We don't have much time, and I want you to look over the *Ares.*"

Requiem nodded again, confused by Damion's expression, and slid from the chair then pulled his vest back on, and zipped it up. He looked to Korvin, whispering a thank-you before following Damion out. He was silent as they moved to the lift, not speaking until they entered it.

"You were not happy that he asked me to come speak with him. May I ask why?" he finally asked.

"I just don't like knowing that, in twenty minutes, I won't be able to protect you from people who may try to take advantage of the fact that you don't know what emotions are," Damion admitted.

Requiem thought about it for a moment, the whirring of the lift a background noise to his thoughts. "You are teaching me what emotions are. I do not know how to prevent what you are concerned about. What do you think might happen?"

"That you'll fall in love." Damion rubbed his eyes. "With someone else."

That shocked Requiem. He brought his head up to look at Damion with searching eyes. He was quiet for a few moments, just looking at his lover before commanding the lift to cease movement. They were between floors, the next floor being the one with the docks attached to it.

"Do you love me?" he finally asked.

Damion's mouth screwed up in an odd way again, and his eyes narrowed as he glared at the floor counter. "I… I think I do."

"You think? How do you know?" Requiem asked quietly, knowing that this was a difficult question and willing to be patient.

"I know because I care more about what happens to you than to me," Damion said.

Requiem tilted his head, his eyes on Damion even if the man wouldn't meet his stare. "Is love also when… you want to be with that person constantly? When you enjoy their company and like it when they touch you? When they look at you, it… makes you warm inside?" They were all honest questions. He was looking for an explanation to what he had been feeling.

"Yeah, sounds about right." Damion gave Requiem a small smile. "It's also kind of scary."

"Why is it scary?" Requiem reached out hesitantly, knowing Damion was vulnerable right now and not knowing if the man wanted to be touched. He ran the back of his fingers lightly over Damion's cheek before dropping his hand. "There is no worry about me falling in love with anyone else. If what you have explained as love is correct, then I am already in love with you. Therefore, I would be unable to love another."

"Even if I'm away for a year?" Damion asked.

"I will leave that up to you. I do not know much about emotions, but this one I have felt for a while. I believe I will continue to feel this way. *But in the end,* I cannot make promises without all the evidence needed to back them up. I do not have much data to work from." He let him have a small smile. "*It* is up to you. Do you believe you will still think you love me a year from now?"

"It's up to both of us, not just me." He shook his head. "I can't see my feelings changing."

"I do not foresee myself ever trusting anyone the way I do you. And therefore, there would be no room for any emotion such as this to grow with another." He tilted his head again, his eyes still on Damion's face. "So we have decided we love each other. What now? What does this mean?"

"That we do our best not to die and not to let our smaller brains do the thinking," Damion said.

"Smaller brain?" Requiem asked.

"Yeah, the penis brain," Damion grumbled.

"There is no brain in that part of the human anatomy. There is only the one." The former Core still didn't get it.

Damion shook his head. "I mean not sleeping around."

"Ah, I understand." Requiem leaned against the wall of the lift. "I told you once that I do not expect you to be able to do so. It is not impossible of course, but judging by your past history and the amount that we have sex, I do not believe you can go long without the activity." He finally lowered his gaze to the floor, trying not to show the hurt he felt in his chest from the thought of Damion being as warm with another as he was with him. "As I have no desire to have sexual relations with anyone but you, I do not foresee a problem for myself."

"See, that's my problem." Damion looked at Requiem with dark, burning eyes. "I'm not a cheat. I always said I'd never be one, but keeping myself unattached was the easiest way to make sure that never happened."

"Then why attach yourself to me?" Requiem still didn't look up, but he unconsciously raised his hand to rub at where Damion had permanently branded him. Right over his pounding heart. He didn't want to trap the man. He wanted the Fighter to make his own choices, but it didn't mean that Requiem had to like them.

"I can't help it." Damion lifted his hands and then let them fall. "I tried and it didn't work, so here we are and it's something I need to deal with.... It would have just been easier to deal with if we were together."

"I can understand that." Requiem finally looked up, seeing the confusion and helplessness in Damion's eyes. He was sure the same was in his own. "I believe you will do your best to stay... loyal to me." He hesitated a moment, licking his lips. "Would it be... would it be wrong of me at this time to ask you to kiss me?" He needed to feel that warmth again.

Damion chuckled. "Not really, come here." He pulled Requiem flush against his body and kissed his lover as hard as he could.

Requiem's body became pliant against Damion, and he let out a long sigh as their lips met. The kiss was filled with desperation, promises, and confessed love in the form of tongues and teeth. He ran his hands underneath Damion's arms and along his back to wrap them around his ribs. Even if Requiem had to stand a little on his toes, they fit perfectly, and if they had been lying down, their legs would have been intertwining. Requiem didn't ever want to leave Damion's arms.

Requiem felt whole and warm in Damion's arms, so he barely noticed Athena's voice over the intercom above their heads.

"In a lift? How cliché can you guys get? Plus you're holding up commerce. Damion, we moved the voluntary beating into a private practice room on the same level as the refectory. You need to be there in forty-five minutes. I don't want to disturb you guys, seriously I don't, but we do have a schedule." Despite the teasing, she truly did sound apologetic.

Requiem sighed and reached out to the wall behind Damion. The intercom let out a squealing howl of protest before dying completely.

"That's not very long. I wish I'd brought lube. Still, we've both got our hands." Damion couldn't help but muse over what exactly they could do with that time, "Any cameras?"

He was still mostly glaring at the intercom, as if Athena was standing there with them to interrupt them again. "Negative. There are no cameras." He turned to Damion, now confused. "Why do you ask?"

Damion chuckled as he tugged at the fastening of Requiem's pants. "I need to fill myself up on you before I leave."

"But... I thought you wanted me to check over the *Ares* before you departed," Requiem said, but he didn't object in any way to Damion unzipping his pants. His own fingers were already pulling down the zipper of Damion's flight suit.

"We'll make time." Damion pressed a kiss against Requiem's lips again. He took Requiem's shaft in hand and slowly stroked.

"You keep saying that and then say we have none," Requiem mumbled before he couldn't speak anymore. He groaned against Damion's lips, losing his balance a little and falling back against the wall of the lift as he pushed the top of the suit off Damion's shoulders.

"I'm going to get on my knees and give you something to remember me by, as well."

"Get down on your knees? I do not understand." Requiem gave Damion a puzzled look before his eyes rolled up as he did something with his hand that caused his legs to nearly go out from under him.

"You'll understand in a minute. Just hold on to something." Damion knelt and guided his lover's soft head to his lips.

"What am I supposed to hol—oh!" Requiem's fingers scrabbled at the wall behind him, unable to find purchase as a hot, wet pressure surrounded him, sending his mind flying in several different directions.

Damion worked quickly, lavishing his tongue up and down the shaft.

Requiem's head thumped against the metal wall, the sound punching through the suckling noises. He eventually had to grab on to Damion's shoulders to keep his knees from collapsing. His eyes were rolled up into his head and he was panting heavily. "D... Damion... cannot... too soon... stop...." His orgasm was approaching too fast, the pressure of the tongue, the scrape of teeth, the suction was too much for him to handle, and he was hanging on by a thread.

Damion didn't stop working on Requiem's taut flesh. He only tightened his grip on the base of his leaking cock. This was something that surely neither of them would forget.

The grip of Damion's fingers prevented him from exploding. It merely heightened the need without giving him the ability to come.

Damion's mouth was near maddening, and Requiem groaned his pleasure and frustration. His body was trembling, his skin slick with sweat, causing his vest to stick to his chest. His fingers tightened almost convulsively on Damion's bare shoulders as ecstasy raced through him. "Damion...." The name was let out in a combination of a pant and a moan.

Damion pulled back so his lover's release wouldn't gag him, and then hurriedly swallowed the salty stuff.

Trembling, Requiem slid down the wall to the floor as his knees finally gave out. He was panting rapidly, his eyes half closed and looking just as a man should after having an amazing orgasm. His pale skin was flushed, pants around his ankles, sweat trickling down his skin. When he finally could, he cracked his eyes open to look at Damion. They were glazed, but lust and love shone through. "What about you?" he finally managed to say.

Damion looked down at his erection. "I am hard as carbine steel. You need to help with that."

"I would be happy to. How do you wish me to do so?" Requiem reached out to grip Damion's shaft then stroked it slowly.

"That's a good start." Damion's chuckle was low. "Now squeeze it a bit more as you move your hand."

Requiem did as requested, watching Damion's face as he alternated between squeezing and stroking faster.

"Now put your mouth on me." Damion's voice was strained with lust.

He didn't hesitate, wanting Damion to feel as good as he'd made Requiem feel. He ran his tongue over the head of the Fighter's cock, a long swipe that placed the taste of precum right on the center of his taste buds. It was an interesting flavor, like nothing he'd ever tasted. Pleasant. Damion's harsh pants brought him back from his inspection, and he took the man fully into his mouth.

"Try not to bite." Damion's words were still shaky. He gripped Requiem's hair, giving small tugs when something felt especially good.

Requiem was very careful with his teeth, not biting, but occasionally using them to scrape gently down the sensitive skin. He used the sounds of Damion's gasps and groans, the tugs on his hair, to judge what felt good so he could repeat and elaborate on it. All Cores were very fast learners, and Requiem used that ability to its fullest now. Eventually, curious, he slid his hand up Damion's inner thigh and ran his palm over his lover's sac.

"Requiem!" Damion's hand tightened in his white hair. "So good! I'm close. Gods!"

The pale man increased the suction of his mouth, pink-tinged cheeks hollowing as he sped up, his tongue running along the thick vein underneath with more pressure. He gently fondled Damion's sac while his other hand gripped his ass.

"Ah!" Damion screamed as his orgasm suddenly burned through his body.

Feeling the tensing of Damion's body and hearing the yell, Requiem took a hint from what Damion had done earlier and pulled back slightly so that he wouldn't choke. He swallowed quickly but still took the time to explore the flavor on his tongue before letting the Fighter slide out of his mouth with a pop. Licking his lips, he leaned back against the wall and looked up at the panting man. Joy surged through his chest to see the expression of pleasure on Damion's face. Pleasure Requiem had given him.

"Damn, you're good."

"That was acceptable to you?" Requiem asked with a small smile, pleased that he had done well. The sounds of Damion's moans, sighs, and cries had excited Requiem once again, but he had pushed it down, knowing they really didn't have time for anything more. They were cutting it close as it was.

Damion grinned as he looked at the ceiling. "Fuck! I should have asked you to blow me like that more often."

"More often? This is the first time you have. I would have done so previously, if you had asked. I will be sure to do so more often in the future." Requiem struggled to stand while impeded by his pants.

Damion continued chuckling. "My hand will never feel that good while I'm away."

"I would hope not," Requiem said with a grin as he was finally able to stand. He tucked himself back into his pants and fastened them before holding out a hand to Damion.

Damion took Requiem's hand and stood slowly. "Time to put ourselves in order."

After releasing Damion's hand, Requiem pulled the flight suit back up and helped Damion zip the thick fabric. He paused with his fingers on the tab before leaning forward and kissing Damion gently. "I feel strange. As if my chest is ripping apart."

"I know." Damion pulled Requiem into a tight hug. "It's what you feel when you lose something."

"But I have not lost you. You are right here. And when you leave, you will still not be lost. I will know where you are. I do not understand."

"We haven't ever been apart before, not really." Damion squeezed his lover once more. "Now we need to get moving."

Nodding, Requiem pulled away and released the lift. "Training room first?"

Damion

"ARE YOU sure you don't want to check out the ship?" Damion wasn't sure about Requiem watching him get the crap beat out of him.

"I will do it after. I do not trust these people, and we do not know if we have harmed them or people that they have known in the past. It might be a ploy to get revenge, and I do not want to take that risk," he explained calmly as the lift stopped and the doors opened.

Athena was waiting for them, practically tapping her foot in impatience.

"What? We late?" Damion tried to look and sound confident and normal even if he didn't feel that way.

"No. But many people are because they had to run to another transport," Athena stated in a sickeningly sweet tone, a fake smile plastered on her face.

"Don't be mad that you weren't able to watch." Damion continued to grin. "Besides, you can work out all that lust for me with your fists."

Athena turned and waved for them to follow. "I will not be involved in beating the snot out of you. I will merely be watching the show."

Silently, Requiem reached out and gripped Damion's hand. Damion squeezed back and followed the captain. "How many guys are waiting for me?"

"Just four. We tried to find people who were objective and wouldn't hold you responsible for all the Corporation's done. It was hard, but we believe we have a good bunch."

"You believe?" Requiem scowled.

Athena merely shrugged.

"Remember they're pirates." Damion shrugged too. "It's just picking the side less evil at the moment."

"Less evil can still get you terminated," Requiem retorted as they moved through the hallways.

"That's why I'll be there. To make sure no one gets killed." Athena glanced over her shoulder at Requiem, piercing him with a knowing gaze. "On either side."

"It's only fists, so I'll be fine." Damion wasn't afraid of pain. He just wasn't used to not defending himself.

They eventually came to a door, which Athena opened. She stood to the side, letting the lovers into a small training room. Four men were in the room, but they went quiet as soon as Damion and Requiem entered. They were standing on the sparring mats in the back, their faces blank. Requiem let go of Damion's hand and went to stand against the wall next to a sim holo exercise machine.

Damion walked toward the men, trying not to see them as threats. "The president is going to get the same treatment, right?"

"Jasper's already gotten his wounds."

The men waited silently, seeming to weigh the Fighter. One nodded in greeting.

Damion gave the guys a smirk. "Who goes first?"

The men looked at each other for a moment, and then one closed his eyes and shrugged a shoulder. Without any warning, and faster than Damion could track, the dark man punched him in the ribs.

Requiem

REQUIEM'S EYES narrowed, and his body started to tremble with the need to do something. It had been a cheap shot. Not the stomach, but the ribs.

Damion stumbled to the side and cursed. If his rib wasn't broken, it was surely cracked. He caught his breath. "Don't you have anyone on this ship who hits like a man? These love taps won't do much."

One of the other men grinned. Of course he was about six foot four and made of what looked like pure muscle. Cracking his knuckles at the challenge, he stepped forward and grabbed Damion's arm before spinning the Fighter around. His arms slid under Damion's armpits and his hands around the back of his neck, effectively trapping him in a full nelson. The first man stepped forward and punched Damion again repeatedly, this time in the stomach.

The other two men looked at each other and shrugged, seeing that there was nothing for them to do. One ambled over to talk to the captain, while the other wandered around the combatants to see better, shouting out pointers.

Requiem was gritting his teeth as he watched, his arms crossed over his chest while anger welled up inside him. Something didn't feel right, and it wasn't because he was watching Damion get beat up.

Athena laughed at something the man beside her said. Requiem took a moment to look and saw the man maneuver the captain so that her back was to the fight.

It was then that Requiem was grabbed roughly, both his arms pinned behind him, and another hand was placed tightly over his mouth. He struggled against that grip, his eyes rolling up to see the fourth man standing over him with a wicked smile. Requiem looked back to Damion in time to see one of the other men punch the Fighter in the face and then turn to kick him viciously in the side.

Requiem screamed in alarm through the hand covering his mouth, struggling even more against the man holding him. He kicked back and heard the man grunt.

"Stay still, Broken!" the man hissed in his ear. "I really don't want to hurt you, but I will if you don't stop."

But he didn't stop, straining toward the holo-unit next to him. His eyes flicked to Athena again, but the damned woman was walking out the door, her eyes focused on her wrist unit.

Damion finally had enough and kicked out at the man in front of him, succeeding in connecting with his opponent. However, Requiem knew that it had cost Damion too much of his quickly fading energy, watching as Damion panted, spitting out a mouthful of blood. The attackers had already gotten too many unguarded hits in on Damion before they had both realized that this was an actual attack.

"Shit," the man holding Requiem cursed.

Requiem used that opportunity to push backward, slamming the man into the wall so his hand slipped from Requiem's mouth momentarily. "Damion! Fight!" he yelled before he was silenced once again.

"Stupid Core!" The man wrenched his arms up higher until Requiem's shoulders were straining. Seeing the holo-equipment so close, he lurched to the side, throwing his captor off balance so they both slammed into the device. Even touching it with his bare feet, desperation driving him, Requiem tapped into the system.

It seemed Damion wasn't against anything if it involved saving his own life. Even if that meant biting the arm that was choking him. The pirate yelped in pain, his arm loosening slightly, just enough for Damion to slip free. But then the other man finally stood and rushed the Fighter with a growl.

Requiem used his feeble tap into the system and his body as a conductor to shock the man holding him. The pirate let out a scream and released Requiem's arms as he collapsed to the ground. Requiem lunged for a better contact on the holo-unit and ripped off the control panel, plunging his fingers into the system.

But his attacker recovered too quickly and grabbed him around the waist, lifting him up and throwing him roughly to the unpadded ground. "You little shit! I told you I didn't want to hurt you!" the man growled, slamming Requiem's head into the tiled floor.

Damion

DAMION WAS trying to scramble away from both men who already had a head start in the fight. He was able to get to his hands and knees and looked to his left just as the bigger man stomped toward him. When the brute reached down, instead of lashing out with his fists, Damion extended his longer leg and his heel caught the man's thick jaw. As the man reeled back, Damion kicked at his knees. An audible pop and scream of pain followed. By that time the man who had broken his ribs was rushing toward him. Damion got up and braced himself with his arms up and legs planted as firmly as possible.

The man Damion had just kicked appeared to be unconscious. The other attempted to tackle Damion, seemingly intent on knocking them both to the ground.

Requiem

IT TOOK Requiem a minute to see straight as the man pinning him to the ground screamed encouragement to his compatriot. He felt helpless, his arms and legs held down by a man who outweighed him, his head swirling. He needed to get to the holo-unit. Growling in frustration, he bucked his body frantically, trying to get free.

His captor turned his attention back to Requiem, scowling at him. "You just can't do what you're told, can you?" He slapped Requiem across the face.

Taking advantage of the loosened grip on him, he swung up, punching the man in the temple, which caused him to fly off Requiem. Ignoring his dizziness, Requiem crawled to the unit, plunged his fingers around the wires, and immediately tapped into the security system. Klaxons went on in the room and in the hallway as Requiem was dragged by his ankles away from the wires again. But the damage had been done.

Athena had needed to deal with the one man trying to keep her away from the training room. She took out her pistol and shot the man above Damion first—a clean shot through the traitor's head—and then raised it to shoot the one holding Requiem.

She narrowed her eyes. "What the fuck do you think you'll be able to do when you're hiding behind him?"

"Barter," the man said. He had Requiem in a headlock, up on his toes to keep himself from choking.

Requiem's vision was blurry and he had blood in his mouth, but he'd had worse. But the holo was too far away for him to reach. Damion must have still been busy with the other man, trying to finish the task he had begun.

"You let me go," the man demanded. "Give me a ship and let me fly free or I snap his neck."

Requiem sighed in annoyance, keeping his double vision on the two forms of Athena.

"You've been on my ship long enough to know what I think about dealing with people who double-cross me. I would shoot that ship out of the air before it got five feet. Want to stop bullshitting and tell me why?"

"Because he's a traitor to the human race!" the man said, thrusting his chin in Damion's direction. "Millions have died at his hands, or hands like his, and he shouldn't be allowed to live. The Cores are innocent, they don't know what they're doing, but yet this one continued to follow that traitor. I wasn't going to kill him, but if you don't let me go, I'm going to have to."

"You did this to kill Damion?" The captain's eyebrow arched. "This was something that you planned alone?"

"Who else would? Everyone else is about forgiveness for those you've chosen to come onboard the ship. But I haven't heard him apologize. I haven't heard him be sad for what he's done. So yeah, we planned it. We would have been fine if the doll hadn't fucked it up."

Requiem's captor squeezed his neck even tighter as he spoke, adding bursts of white to Requiem's vision. He struggled to get air into his lungs. What was it with people choking him?

"If you wanted to kill him, then you should have discussed it with me first." Athena glanced over at Damion, and Requiem's gaze followed.

The Fighter was holding his ribs and glaring at the man hurting his lover, but he cursed at the captain. "I didn't come here of my own free will! Will you shut up and do something before he kills him?"

"And what would you have done? All you've done is coddle them!" the man accused Athena. "Would you have killed him?" He scoffed. "I don't think so."

"You want me to shoot him?" The captain pointed the gun at Damion.

"What?" the injured man was obviously thrown by her offer.

Requiem had an inkling of what Athena was doing and was willing to play along. It helped that he didn't like the fact that a gun was pointed at his lover. Despite the arm on his windpipe, he struggled harder against his captor.

"Stop that!" the pirate growled, shaking Requiem while still keeping himself covered. "You won't shoot him! Why would you shoot him when he's so important to your mission?"

"He's not. The Core is." She gave Damion a smirk. "He's expendable."

"You double-crossing bitch, you—" Damion was cut off as the gun went off and he dropped to the ground.

Requiem screamed. It was more of a gurgle than anything, but it was realistic, especially as he struggled even harder, kicking back at the pirate behind him. He had seen Damion fall, knew he wasn't dead, knew Athena had purposefully missed. But the momentary image of Athena shooting Damion was still there.

"Fucking shit! You actually did it!" his captor said with half a laugh, loosening his grip on Requiem.

Taking the advantage, Requiem slipped out of the loosened grasp and collapsed to the ground, gasping for breath. Athena didn't skip a beat. The moment Requiem was down and away from the idiot, she first shot the man in the center mass and then between surprised eyes as he fell. Brain matter, bone, and blood exploded out of the back of his head, peppering the floor and wall behind him. Whether it was gunpowder bullets of the past or high-power energy bullets of their age, both did the same amount of damage. Both were equally deadly… and messy.

"Son of a bitch!" Damion yelled as he struggled to get up. Even if he wasn't shot, he had to be sore as fuck. "Requiem!" He stumbled toward Requiem.

Requiem attempted to roll onto his back, but the man's body had fallen across his legs and warm blood had already soaked through his pants. Pushing himself on his arms, he kicked the body away and finally got his legs free.

"I am acceptable. Do not worry," he told his lover in a broken voice, his throat hurting from the grip that had been on it. "Are you well?"

He sat up, blinking as he tried to bring Damion back into focus. His head was pounding, and blood dripped into his right eye from a cut received from the hard floor.

"No," Damion answered as he pulled Requiem into his lap, pressing his sleeve against Requiem's bloody eye. "You need medical."

"I do not require medical any more than you do. You are worse off than I am," Requiem replied, pushing Damion's hand away from his face. His head was pounding, but he knew Damion must feel much worse.

Damion's head snapped up to look at Athena, all his anger burning in his dark eyes. "You said this wouldn't happen!"

"I didn't think it would! I underestimated the people that I'd chosen." Athena seemed furious and betrayed as she walked over to the one unconscious and one dead man on the mats.

Security came in then, looked around the room without batting their eyes, and started collecting the bodies. They handcuffed the unconscious man and dragged him roughly out of the room.

Athena knelt down next to Damion and Requiem. "Please accept my apology. I didn't mean for this to happen." Her voice and expression seemed sincere, her shoulders slumping.

"Just get us to medical! Screw your timeline. He needs to be seen."

"Damion. I am fine. I will go to medical after you have departed. I still need to do a check on the *Ares*." Requiem sat up, trying to pull himself out of Damion's arms to prove that he was fine. His head pounded and swirled slightly, but he hid it well.

Athena pulled Requiem's chin toward her, making him look at her. She inspected his eyes before doing a visual check of Damion. "He has a concussion, and you have broken ribs and possible internal bleeding. As much as I want you to look legitimate, I also want you to be able to fly, and I don't think you can do that right now. Lizzy has a way where she heals wounds to look a week or so old rather than healing completely. You both need to get to medical."

As if called, two nurses came in with stretchers.

"We don't have time for both of us. Just take him," Damion argued as they manhandled him into one.

"Hawk, shut your whiny hole," Athena said.

Requiem nearly vomited from the dizziness and pain that came with moving his head. "No tank. Please, no tank," he mumbled.

"Can't you give him something?" the Fighter screamed.

Requiem sighed, thinking that Damion was the one who should be sedated. "Damion, I am fine. Merely a headache. You are the one with the broken bones."

"It hurts to breathe, talk, and move, and that's the way it's supposed to be," Damion grumbled.

"And no, we can't," one of the nurses added. "Head wounds are too touchy to combine with meds."

They were already being rolled down the hallway at a fast clip that made the urge to vomit even stronger for Requiem. He closed his eyes and held it down. If he threw up, it would only aggravate Damion even more. "It is minor, Damion. I will be acceptable soon enough. I plead with you not to worry about me and concentrate on your own injuries."

"You were supposed to look severely injured. Not actually be that injured," Athena mumbled as she followed the gurneys. "And 47 wasn't supposed to get hurt at all. I'm very sorry for miscalculating my own crew. You can rest assured that I'll be investigating it further and that 47 will be protected while you're gone."

"If there are Gods out there, then Loki is cursing my life." Damion rubbed his sore jaw, the pain no doubt getting worse as the adrenaline wore off.

Athena snorted. "How? By giving you your Core and the challenges to keep him? If you want to give back the gift the Gods gave you, then I'll be happy to take what you don't want." She paused for a moment and started smacking Requiem's cheek. "Hey! Wake up, Snow. No falling asleep now!"

Requiem blinked blearily, having been disturbed from his slipping into sleep. "Snow? Who is Snow?" he mumbled.

"You are. You're pale enough to be, and your eyes are the color of glaciers. Keep awake with me for a while longer until we get your head fixed up."

"You fall asleep and you won't be able to see me off," Damion warned.

"Not going anywhere until I run diagnostics on the *Ares*," Requiem slurred, his vision blurred. His one eye was crusted with drying blood.

"So that just means that neither of you are going anywhere until you're both fixed. Glad we got that out of our systems." Athena rolled her eyes as they moved out of the lifts and double-timed it down the hall.

"Did I agree to that?" Damion wasn't even looking at her. He kept his eyes on Requiem. "You going to build me another ship?"

"You may not have agreed to it, but that's what's going to happen," Athena said as the door to medical slid open. "Another ship is not needed. Once Req—47 is back on his feet, he can check it over."

Requiem didn't reply, trying his hardest to keep his eyes open, but the bright lights from the ceiling pierced into his brain, causing it to throb more.

"I swear, I see you two more than anyone else on the ship," Lizzy said as she rushed over. She had a flashlight in her hand and was immediately shining it in Requiem's eyes. He closed them swiftly and tried to push her away with weak hands.

"Stop that," she grumbled at him, but she shut it off a moment later. "Severe concussion, possible frontal skull fracture. So a scan," she told one of her assistants as she moved to Damion. "Well, isn't your pretty face a mess. Should leave you some scars to break it up." She shined the light in Damion's eyes now as a scanner was set up over him as well.

"Why is it all the women that want to sleep with me also want to mess me up?" Damion tried to smirk but failed. "Where will they take him?"

Lizzy snorted. "Maybe you did hit your head if you think I want to sleep with you." She felt gently along his jaw and then his ribs. "Five broken ribs and a fractured jaw. Possibly more fractured ribs. Won't know until after the scan. Easiest thing would be to put you both in the tank."

"No!" Requiem yelled, but he couldn't even try to sit up to get away.

"Can you not put him in there? He'll just get more hurt like last time, and you'll be lucky if this time he doesn't scuttle the ship." Damion tried to sit up.

"Will you stay down? Gods, you're already lucky you didn't puncture a lung!" Lizzy snapped as she roughly pushed Damion back into a prone position. She sighed, looking over at the panicked man. "Yeah, I'm sure I can figure something out besides putting him in the tank. It'll just take longer to heal." She turned from them both, giving orders to her nurses and orderlies.

Chapter Fifteen

Requiem

DAMION WAS shortly stripped down to his waist and then scans were completed of his ribs and face. Requiem was wheeled under another scanner that wrapped around his head. Now that he knew he wouldn't have to go back into the tank, Requiem had calmed down and was fighting off sleepiness, having to be gently shaken awake every few minutes.

Damion didn't fight them pulling off his uniform so they could dunk him into the thick healing water. While Requiem himself had an issue with the tanks, he also knew Damion didn't like tanks much himself. Damion had explained once that he had learned about the healing liquid in infantry. It was a way for them to patch up soldiers and get them back to fighting that much sooner.

The pounding in Requiem's head started to fade. Not completely, but it was a bit more bearable so he could open his eyes and keep them that way. He felt someone working on his scalp, right below the hairline on the right side of his forehead where the pirate had repeatedly bashed his head into the metal floor. It stung a little as the nurse pushed the pieces of skin back together and sealed it. He kept his concentration on Damion's form floating in the tank until he saw the president walk into the medical facility, talking with Athena in hushed tones.

The president looked like he'd been put through the wringer himself. He was wearing the same clothes they had seen him in when they were captured, except torn and dirtier with some bloodstains. He had a black eye and a split lip and probably more below his clothing from the way he held himself. Requiem's attention shifted as the scanner moved from his head and he was gently helped into a sitting position. His head still hurt, but his eyesight wasn't blurry anymore and he didn't have blood dripping into his eye.

One of the Brokens, a female they had passed a few times in the halls, came up to Requiem with a small smile. She had on an assistant's jacket, but she seemed a bit out of place in the infirmary. "Hello."

Requiem's eyes flashed to Damion and then back to the woman in front of him, sliding his body back a little on the gurney. Everyone else in the medical facility was cleaning up or watching Damion's vitals. He whispered a quiet "Hello" back to her, not quite sure what she wanted.

"I'm like you." Her smile stayed on as she didn't move to either touch him or help him. "I have been watching you."

"Why?" he inquired after a moment, slipping off the gurney, being cautious. She may have been a former Core, but he didn't know her and didn't trust her. Carefully, his head suddenly spinning, he made his way over to the tank. After one quick look at Damion, he leaned against the cool, thick glass and slid his way to the floor to sit.

"I'm… interested." She followed him over. "I want to talk with you."

Requiem looked at her for a moment. "Why are you interested? Are there not many other former Cores on this vessel? Why are you so interested in me?" he questioned, searching for a motive she might have to harm him or Damion.

"You care for your Fighter. You are also very powerful, and the rumors about you are interesting."

Requiem looked behind him to check on Damion. The Fighter seemed to be napping, or perhaps he was put to sleep to ease the pain of rapid healing. He turned back around to look at the other Core, tilting his head slightly. "I am interesting because… I care for my Fighter?" He thought about it for a moment and shrugged. "I do not perceive myself as powerful. I have strived to advance myself further. I do not know what the rumors are about me, but rumors are rumors, and whether there is truth involved in them is something that needs to be investigated further."

"I heard you had a lot of ports. Why?" She tilted her own head.

"Multiplying the number of ports you jack into assists with accessing the system deeper. The more intricate your understanding of the system, the more information you can download. Once you understand the intricacies of the system, you are able to remotely access without jacking in." Requiem was still a bit wary. He had not provided this information in the past because he didn't want the Creators to have the knowledge. It was not something every Core could do. For some it would merely overload them and shut the Core down, killing them.

"You're interesting." The female Core looked toward Damion. "But why the loyalty to him? Really, the Fighters only use us."

"Not all Fighters," Requiem whispered, turning again to look up at Damion, finding the man's eyes open now. Dark brown, almost black eyes met glacier blue, and Requiem smiled. Relief poured through him to see the Fighter awake. "I do not need to explain it to you. You would not understand."

Damion rapped on the glass, signaling he wanted out, and Requiem was happy to see a few of the attendants rushing over.

"May I come speak to you more about this at a later time?"

Requiem barely glanced at the woman—girl, really. "What is your designation? Your name?" he questioned instead as they began to slowly pull the Fighter out of the tank.

"Phoenix," she told him before turning away.

Requiem stayed where he was, watching the female Core walk away. He was glad he had never given her an answer. He wasn't sure if he wanted to talk to her again.

"Fuck if that shit doesn't always feel weird," Damion complained as he came out. "And I still hurt."

"Well, we couldn't heal you completely. They're supposed to look a few days old," Lizzy mumbled as a nurse handed Damion a towel.

"Got it, got it." Damion dried off and accepted his ruined flight suit. "We have to go now?"

"We pushed back launch time by about two hours," Athena called up to the platform. "That'll give you time to heal up a little more, and I know you wanted 47 to look over the *Ares*. But no more than that."

The president was standing next to her, frowning slightly, his mind obviously on other things.

Wincing as his head protested being moved too much, Requiem used the tank to get to his feet, ignoring the slight dizziness that followed.

"What's wrong?" Damion asked the president as he stepped down to where Requiem was shaky on his feet, letting Requiem lean against him for stability.

Sighing, Lizzy followed Damion, still not done with him. She stopped him from pulling the rest of his suit up as he hit the bottom of the stairs. "Arms up," she demanded before beginning to wrap thick gauze tightly around his ribs. "Can't have you undoing all the good the tank did."

Jasper looked up at Damion and shook his head. "I'm merely going over scenarios and hoping we have enough time to intercept the *Zeus*. If we encounter resistance, we will both be unable to defend ourselves. I don't foresee that happening, but it wasn't something I had to think about before I discovered we had traitors in our midst."

"We will be doing a full sweep of the ship to weed everyone out and make sure we don't have anyone else with that type of animosity," Athena said, anger flaring in her eyes. "I need to be able to trust my crew."

Requiem had a mock-up of the system running through his head at the possibilities of finding those types of people. "Such as the person who sabotaged the *Olympus*," he stated quietly.

"You better make damn sure we don't get attacked." Damion looked at Athena while ignoring what Lizzy was doing to him. "And have a plan B in case we do."

"There's always a plan B," Athena stated. "We'll be watching. If you're attacked, we'll launch our own attack. You'll fight on the side of the Corporation, and we'll get out of there as fast as possible. This will prove that we're not on the same side. Also, once you get in range of the *Zeus*'s sensors, you're going to key your own distress signal. That'll bring them to you."

Requiem listened while he gingerly touched the sealed wound on his head and leaned back against the coolness of the glass tank.

"That will have to do." Damion sighed again. "You done, Doctor of Pain?"

"As much as I can be, Captain Pain in the Ass," Lizzy replied after giving one last tug to the support bandage. Then she helped him pull the upper part of his flight suit back onto his arms and shoulders.

Requiem pushed away from the tank, testing his steps until he could walk normally, despite the slight wavering of his vision. He moved next to Damion, taking in his form and assessing his injuries before taking the man's hand in his own and squeezing.

Damion put an arm around Requiem's shoulders. "How you doing? You sure you're up to looking over the ship?"

Requiem leaned into the warmth of Damion, being careful not to press too hard against Damion's ribs. "I do not need to be in peak physical condition to jack in," he replied quietly, keeping his eyes down when he felt Athena and Jasper watching him. "I do not want the *Ares* to launch until I have done my own diagnostics check over it. I designed and modified the vessel. There is a large chance that I will be able to see something that their technicians missed."

"Will the Creators have enough information from the ship to try to duplicate your Pulse?" Damion asked.

"Not after I am done with it. Also, they do not have a Core capable of powering the Impulse Barrier, and they would not even if they duplicated my port alignments. I experimented for two years before I perfected the alignments in a way to be able to delve into the system. Adding my research on top of that, which I never shared, I do not believe they will be able to duplicate it for years." Requiem paused. "But nothing is impossible."

"Well doesn't that make me feel all warm and fuzzy," Athena mumbled. "All right you two, get out of here. You have about two hours to work on the *Ares*. I'll have security checking in on you to make sure there's no other people who decide to continue the revolt. Are you two good to walk?"

"We'll walk, but don't time us." Damion took a step forward. "We'll head straight for the ship."

Requiem felt Damion's body tense and wrapped his arm around the man's waist to help him walk.

As if an afterthought, Lizzy walked over with a bottle that she shoved in Damion's pocket before sticking him in the neck with a hypo-needle. "That'll help with the pain. No need to thank me," she stated as she walked away. "No strenuous activities for either of you. And 47, I want you back in here after Hawk departs for more treatment on your skull."

Damion nodded. "Heard her, Requiem? Right back here and they won't put you in the tank."

He let out a soft sigh. "As you order." They wouldn't be able to put him in the tank if they couldn't find him either.

"Don't get all stubborn on me now." Damion shook his head. "You look bad."

"You are the one with multiple broken bones, not I," Requiem reminded him as they moved toward the door.

"And you're the one who has a fractured skull that's still healing, so both of you shut up," Lizzy shouted from the back office. "Both idiots, I swear."

"Hey, this idiot is trying to help your side here, so be nice," Damion snapped. "And Requiem's Impulse Barrier could have been used to kill a lot more of your pirate friends. Just make sure Requiem is safe while I'm gone."

"Just say that a little louder. I don't think my whole crew heard it," Athena hissed as she and Jasper followed them out into the hall. "Fuckin' Zeus, Hawk, you trying to make your love toy a target?"

"The Impulse Barrier does not kill, merely immobilizes," Requiem stated. He paused for a moment, squeezing his eyes shut and then reopening them to try to clear the fuzziness. "Correction. It does not kill non-Cores. If a Core is too integrated into the system, it can shut them down."

"It's not like anyone on board could get the plans out of him anyway," Damion grumbled. "Shit. What a day."

"You say that a lot," Requiem stated quietly, looking up at him with a small smile.

"They think they can get it out of him," Athena said. "Don't you want to spare him more pain, you stupid lug?"

"Athena, calm," Jasper said in his soothing tone. "There's nothing that can be done now. I'm sure Fighter Hawk will use more discretion in the future."

Damion only glanced back at the politician. Then he did a rare thing and kept his mouth shut all the way to their ship.

Athena and Jasper split off from them about halfway to the bays, heading back to the office to rework some plans now that things were delayed. Requiem kept his arm around Damion's waist, their steps perfectly in line the whole way. They both stayed silent and kept each other walking, Damion with his labored breaths and Requiem with his fuzzy vision.

As soon as Requiem saw the *Ares,* though, he let out a long, pained breath. Even through his distorted eyes, he saw the shape his ship was in. It was battered with dents, deep gouges, and scorch marks along nearly every inch of it. As soon as they were close enough, he let go of Damion and walked the last few feet of the catwalk alone. He pressed his hands on the cool metal. It wasn't powered up, but he could still feel the power within the craft, teasing his senses like an old friend—a sick old friend who made its unhappiness known. He had to push down the instinct to fix the craft completely. He could only soothe it enough to fly and have some defense mechanisms.

"She's torn up pretty damn good." Damion frowned at his—*their*—ship. "I'm telling you, we need another ship after this, something new. You know... for when I come back."

Requiem looked back at Damion, feeling as if Damion had just told him they would have to take his leg. "New... ship?"

"I don't think I can bring the *Ares* back here, I mean." Damion rubbed the back of his neck. Well, he tried and then stopped to hold his ribs. "When I get back, the president is going to 'promote' me and I'll be reporting you dead, so I'm not sure if they'll fix her up or just scrap her."

He blinked at Damion for a few moments, close to crying. He turned back to the ship, his head tilted back as if looking her over. "Don't let them scrap her. Have them incinerate her. I would prefer them not pull her apart to look for my secrets. Secrets they will not even understand." His fingers curled against the metal as if he could grip it.

Damion eased his body to kneel down next to Requiem. "All right, I'll do my best." He put a hand on Requiem's and gave it a gentle squeeze. "I didn't plan any of this."

"I know. None of this was planned. Not by you and me," Requiem whispered back, resting his cheek against Damion's hand. "But for now, I need to jack in to run diagnostics and see if I can do some preliminary work destroying what I have done."

"Get rid of it all so no one, not even those creeps, can use her against us later." Damion gave Requiem's shoulder another squeeze. "I'll just... sit here and watch."

Requiem nodded and stood, unzipping his vest before pulling down the ladder. "I do not know how long it will take. You will probably be more comfortable in your flight chair." He started to climb the ladder, having to pause for a moment to let dizziness subside before continuing up.

"Yeah, but I really don't want to move at this exact moment." Damion shrugged. "Just don't get lost in there."

When he reached the top, Requiem lifted the hatch before looking back down at Damion. He had a moment of vertigo before he could open his eyes again. He rubbed his face to try to stave off the fuzziness. "Are you acceptable? Perhaps you should have stayed in the... in the tank longer."

"I'm supposed to show up like this, remember? You, on the other hand, should be resting." He winced as he shook his head.

"I would not be able to rest." Requiem lowered himself into the *Ares,* taking a moment to look around. The interior smelled like burned wiring and metal. He let out a long sigh. "Are you going to be able to—" He paused, his eyes falling on his own chair. Ignoring the pounding of his head, he dropped to his knees and looked at the wiring entrance. It had all been replaced. Badly, but replaced all the same.

"To what?" Damion asked, sounding unhappy. "Hey, you okay?"

"My jacks. They are new. I mean… they are made to look old, but the originals… they were cut." He saw where the wiring was carefully spliced together. He didn't know why he was… upset… yes, upset with the sight of his wiring being augmented by someone other than himself. The thought of anyone but himself working on the *Ares* put a bad taste in his mouth.

"They screw it up?"

"Not precisely. It is not obvious unless you know what to look for," Requiem replied as he ran his fingers over the wires. "Normally it would not be unacceptable work. However, for me, it is." He paused, standing slowly. "Why were they cut?"

"You were dying, and they were in the way," Damion said.

"I see. They didn't release when the power dropped. Once I went into cardiac arrest, they should have detached. There must have been a glitch in the system," Requiem replied quietly after a moment. "I should have told you my code to release them."

He let the vest fall from his shoulders and unbuttoned his pants. He wouldn't be able to jack into the system with his clothes in the way. He had a moment of longing for his flight suit.

"Wait, you had an override code and never told me? Why the fuck not?"

"It is the code I use to jack in and out of the system. I did not think it would be important for you to know. I apologize for that mistake," Requiem said wearily as he pushed his pants down his hips, leaving him in just his boxers. He slid into the seat, finally feeling as if he was complete.

Well?" Requiem heard the sound of Damion's boots on the ladder as he very slowly climbed down. "What is it?"

Sighing in annoyance at himself, Requiem got up from his seat and moved back toward the main controls, where Damion usually sat. After he typed in the power-up sequence, a low hum rose throughout the craft as the power came on within the ship. He went back to his chair.

"2-8-8-2-4-6-2-2-5-9," he said as he lay down in the crevice that fit his form perfectly. "Damion, please be careful. You may have to look injured, but you do not need to suffer any more than you already have."

"I need to keep an eye on you." Damion forced out a chuckle despite his eyes being pinched with pain. "Why all the numbers?"

"It spells out 'attainable' in numerals," Requiem stated as he slid from his chair again and went to help Damion into the *Ares*. He shivered slightly at the coolness of the metal flooring on his bare feet. It caused goose bumps to flare up all over his skin. He ignored this, placing his hands on Damion's hips as the man grunted in pain. "You should sit."

"Dear sweet Jupiter, it does look like shit in here." Damion hadn't been back since they arrived and probably hadn't been paying attention when they were taken prisoners. "You just plug in while I check out my controls."

"As you order," Requiem replied with a smile, after subtly helping Damion sit down in the chair. He moved back to his own seat and once again slipped into its comforting embrace. After flipping up the panel, he took a deep breath and punched in his code. He gasped as the cool metal of the jacks injected into his ports. He barely noticed the long moan that came after it as his mind moved into the bright world of the system. It had been too long, and it felt like seeing a best friend for the first time in years. The system embraced him, comforting him as he moved through it, the outside world disappearing as another formed in Requiem's mind's eye.

Inside his mind, there were darkness and green flashes of current that only a Core could translate. Occasionally there would be a break in the transmissions, green-and-blue sparks showing him the damage quickly so he could set to work fixing it immediately if he needed to. When he saw that, he would pause to see if it was something he should fix right then or leave alone for now if it wasn't a primary program issue. Once he went through that, he began to disable the Impulse Barrier piece by piece. His fingers twitched where they were splayed next to him in the chair. While he wasn't using his fingers to affect the system, it was instinctual to try and do so. It was his thought and baseline electrical energy within his body, boosted by the *Ares* itself, that let him fix and control the system. The fact that he had more ports in his body than any other Core he met allowed him to have a firmer hand and more control on the ship.

About an hour and thirty-nine minutes later, Requiem gasped loudly, his body arching as he came back into his own mind. He blinked rapidly, and it took a few moments for his eyes to focus back on the real world. Sweat coated his body as he tried to get moisture back into his eyes after having them open for so long.

"Took you long enough." Damion was twisted around looking at him. "How is she?"

"It would have been longer if I had not set a timer," Requiem replied, panting as he continued to separate himself from the system that didn't want to let go of him. "The *Ares* is only working at 46 percent capacity. You are down to one engine, life support, communications, and the forward guns. I have completely disabled the Impulse Barrier and erased its programming."

"Good," the Fighter said, but his smile didn't reflect the word. "You look worse."

"I am acceptable." Requiem wiped the sweat from his face, not even feeling the pull of the cords connected to his ports. "In need of a shower, but acceptable. How are you feeling?" He didn't move from his reclined chair or extract the cables from his ports. It was comforting to be where he was.

"Sore as shit." Damion rolled his eyes. "Come on. Time to get this show started."

Requiem wanted to protest that he was comfortable and didn't want to move, but he knew it wouldn't go over well. Without retracting the cables so that he could stay connected to the warm embrace of the system a little longer, he sat up, looking at the floor with bleary eyes. "Where are my clothes?"

"You took them off." Damion handed them to him. "Here."

He rubbed his face again before taking the clothes from Damion. "Could not jack in with them on." He placed his clothes on the table before flipping the panel open and punching in his code. He gasped again, his eyes going wide, his fingers going white, and his body bowing as the cables unsnapped from his ports and retracted.

"I'd rather not let everyone see you in your birthday suit either." Damion slowly climbed out of the ship.

"My birthday suit?" Requiem questioned as he pulled on his pants.

Damion grunted as his feet hit the deck. "Naked like the day you were born."

"I see." Requiem threw his vest on but didn't zip it up before he climbed the ladder out of the ship. "It would bother you? To have others see me bare?"

"Yes, more than they already have," Damion said.

Requiem landed on the deck and swayed as his vision swirled. He kept a hand on the outer ladder as he waited for it to stop. "Why?" he eventually asked, his eyes closed.

"I guess I'm the jealous type." Damion put a hand on his shoulder. "You okay?"

"I will admit to being a little dizzy. Nothing to worry about." Requiem cracked his eyes open to look up at Damion with a small smile. He laid his cheek against Damion's hand, rubbing against it slightly. "Why would you be jealous? You know I am yours."

"Because jealousy is in everyone, and I don't want to share." Damion smiled. "Never good at it."

"I do not want to be shared," Requiem replied with a frown and then lowered his eyes, as if he had stepped over his boundary. "Unless you wished me to be. As I have said, I am yours to do with as you wish. But… it would not make me happy."

"No sharing." Damion cut his hand through the air. "Period."

"I am pleased to follow that order." Requiem lifted his head to favor Damion with another bright smile.

"I'm pleased," Damion said, but this happy moment was cut short by Athena and the president's arrival.

Requiem's smile faded, and he let go of the ladder just to slide behind Damion, hiding himself. He subtly grasped Damion's hand, lacing their fingers together as he placed his forehead against Damion's back between his shoulder blades. He let out a long sigh.

"Are you ready?" Jasper inquired softly, his eyes flicking behind Damion to glimpse Requiem.

"As ready as I'll ever be," he said with a sour smile. "What about you, President?"

"Let's get this over with," Jasper replied as he limped down the dock to the Fighter, Core, and the *Ares*.

"Come on, 47. It's time for them to go," Athena stated gently. "I'll show you to the shuttle where you'll be able to monitor and communicate with Hawk."

Requiem clung tightly to Damion's hand, suddenly terrified to let him go.

"Get going," Damion said in a low, gravelly voice, but he was unable to look his lover in the eye. "You make sure to take care of yourself. Remember what I told you."

"As… as you order," Requiem whispered, the words catching in his throat. He kept his head bowed to hide the burning tears in his eyes. Shaking slightly, he let his hand slip from Damion's and walked around the Fighter. He could feel the man trying to avoid looking at him, so he continued to keep his head down.

Damion gave Athena a hard stare. "You're going to swear to take care of him?"

"As carefully as you would," she promised quietly. Athena reached out to wrap her arms around Requiem's shoulders as he came near her, but he sidled out of her reach, turning around to look at Damion. His eyes were glassy with unshed tears, and his hands clenched into fists at his sides. "If he lets me, that is," Athena said dryly as she looked at Requiem.

"He's stubborn." Damion's expression was warm, if not a bit pained. "But he's also very smart."

"The smart ones are always the biggest pains in the ass," Athena quipped.

Requiem's body was shivering from the effort of holding himself in place. All he wanted to do was run to his lover, cling to him, and make him promise not to leave him. He knew he couldn't do that, but the fact that he wanted to confused him. Was this what love was? The want to curl into a small ball and bawl his eyes out to keep Damion from leaving? To bring him back? Did it go hand in hand with his want to see Damion smile, to hold him, to feel his warmth and have sex with him? This was definitely a big con to the emotion.

"I guess we should go," Damion said as he looked at the president crawling into his ship. But he wasn't moving.

"Damion…," Requiem whispered, his voice cracking as he stepped forward. His eyes did not leave Damion's form.

Athena gripped Requiem's arm tightly, but not in a way to hurt him, gently pulling him back. Her eyes were full of pity. "You should go, Hawk. Procrastinating is only making things worse for both of you."

"Yeah, yeah." Damion gave Requiem a small wave. "I'll be hearing you soon." He pointed at his ear, but that was all he said as he turned back toward the *Ares*.

Requiem watched his lover gingerly climb the ladder and drop into the *Ares*. He continued to watch as the ship powered up and the docking clamps were removed. He didn't even look away as Athena's hand dropped from his arm so that she could protect her eyes from the wind stirred by the engines. He used that moment, while Athena was blinded, to slip away, leaving the docks.

Chapter Sixteen

Requiem

REQUIEM DIDN'T see, hear, or feel anything—except cold. He felt lost, like a ship without a rudder in the middle of the ocean, something he only understood from an Earth history program. One arm was around his own waist while the other was pressed against his chest, right over his heart where he had been branded. He moved through the hallways without purpose, without direction. He distantly knew that he had to get to his shuttle, had to keep an ear on Damion. But it wasn't the same. Hearing Damion's voice would never be the same as feeling him next to Requiem, feeling his warmth. So he walked, the blurriness of his vision not even a factor.

When he felt the brush of warm fingers against the cold skin of his arm, Requiem's eyes widened, and he quickly moved away from the touch. Losing his balance, he hit against the wall, his back slamming into it, and he slid to the floor as his head swirled. His eyes landed on Phoenix, and seeing who she was, his expression closed down. "What do you want?" he finally asked. His voice was harsh, slightly cracking with the pain he could hide in his expression but not his voice.

She squatted down next to him, and her eyes assessed him. "You were supposed to rest after your Fighter left."

"I am acceptable. Please do not concern yourself with me," Requiem stated as he leaned away from her. He was actually supposed to go back to medical, but there was no way he was going there. Now that Damion wasn't there to protect him anymore, Lizzy might attempt to find out what made him tick. Using a nearby doorway, he pulled himself to his feet, fighting nausea and the swirling in his pounding head.

"If you do not rest, you will pass out and then someone will find you." Phoenix stood and continued to follow him. "Or you may injure yourself further."

"It does not concern you or anyone else. Either way, it does not matter. And now I request that you please leave me alone." Requiem tried to speed up, to get away from the girl, but nearly tripped over his own bare feet. He turned a corner and spotted a lift. He headed toward it, keeping a hand on the wall to help balance himself.

The girl kept up with him easily since she was not impeded by injuries. "You are not thinking logically."

"No, I am not. In fact, I am trying not to think at all. Logically or illogically. Why do you insist on following me?" Requiem pushed the button to call the lift. All he wanted was to be left alone.

She waited a few feet away. "Because you're putting yourself in danger."

"Because I want to be left alone? Because I want you to go away? I do not follow your thought process," Requiem mumbled, leaning against the wall next to the lift doors.

Phoenix shook her head. "Because you look as if your body is about to fail, and you will pass out on a ship where you are a target."

The door opened and Requiem slipped in, hoping fruitlessly that she wouldn't follow him. "Why do you concern yourself with me? You are not associated with me. I do not understand." He leaned back against the wall and slid to the ground, his knees to his chest, his throbbing forehead resting on them.

"You are interesting," she said simply as she stepped into the lift with him and pressed a button.

"I do not believe I am." Requiem's voice was muffled by his knees. It was everything he could do to keep himself together. He felt like something was missing, taken from his chest, and something else was building in it. Something uncomfortable that crept up his throat. "What is the correct process to follow in order to get you to leave me alone?"

The girl tilted her head to the side. "Let me take you somewhere safe to pass out."

"Your assumption that I am going to pass out is misguided," Requiem replied, knowing as he said it that Phoenix was right, but not wanting to admit it.

Before Damion, he took care of himself—as much as he could, anyway. And he was content to go back to that process. But... he didn't know if he could. It had been so long, and Damion.... He swallowed a thick lump in his throat as he felt his eyes burn. He squeezed them tighter to hold off the tears. If only he could be alone. He felt if he was alone, he could release this pressure building inside himself. "If it will assist in my purpose, then I will agree to what you ask," he finally told the girl.

"What is your purpose?" she asked.

"To be alone," Requiem repeated as if it were obvious, which it was. His frustration was evident in his voice before he could stifle it. "What is our destination?"

"Korvin's den," she said but didn't move to help him.

Requiem stiffened. "Why there?" Despite Damion not having said anything to the contrary, he knew Damion didn't want him spending time with the other former Core. Perhaps it was because of the jealousy emotion he had been speaking of.

The girl's shoulders lifted in a shrug. "He will make sure after you lose consciousness that you are unharmed."

"What is your basis for concluding that I will lose consciousness?" Requiem inquired as he finally raised his pounding head. The blurriness was getting a bit worse, but he ignored it as he pushed to his feet.

"Your gait is off 70 percent and you're heavily leaning to the right, meaning you are having bouts of severe syncope." She still didn't offer help.

"Your experimentations run toward medical?" Requiem asked as the doors opened. It was an easy assumption. All Cores had their experiments and research. He looked toward the open doors and the promenade beyond as if exiting was the hardest thing in the world. His vision was spinning and a bit gray around the edges. He was so tired.

"The human body is extremely fragile," Phoenix answered. "As Cores we were altered to be better than average humans. It seemed essential to know how we were different." Her left hand slowly extended. "I could assist."

"Interesting. And logical," Requiem murmured and attempted to focus his eyes on the extended hand. He knew he was being illogical and stubborn, as Damion would say. His eyes flicked from the hand up to Phoenix's face and back. "I would accept your assistance."

"Then you should take my hand and I will make sure you do not fall on your face." She had the barest smile while she stood there patiently waiting.

After another moment's hesitation, he took the offered hand. "So I do not concern you further, I will make sure to fall backward if it does happen."

"It is more logical to lean backward, since most humans carry most of their fat in their buttocks." She pulled Requiem forward and let him lean into her when his balance was off.

Requiem attempted to keep their physical contact to a minimum. He wasn't used to human contact except for.... His throat clogged up again, and he wiped the back of his hand over his eyes to hide the tears threatening to explode. He just wanted to lie down and hope that when he woke up, Damion would be back. He felt out of his element, alone, and if he wanted to admit it, scared. His vision was getting worse, his exhaustion pulling at him the more they walked.

When they made it to Korvin's, the artist did not appear startled by their presence.

Phoenix told the man, "I have someone who is in need of your back cot."

Korvin stepped out from behind his workstation. "Here I thought he'd last a day before having to be helped."

Phoenix had a small smile when she spoke. "I believe his limits are overestimated."

Despite his misgivings, Requiem was leaning heavily against Phoenix, his body trembling with exhaustion and pain—both physical and emotional. He blinked, trying to focus his eyes, but it was unsuccessful. "I need to get to the shuttle," he mumbled to himself and thought about leaving the artist's shop. "And I believe that she would not have left me alone until I agreed to come here. I have come, and now I should depart." He pushed away from Phoenix, fully intending to walk out the door. But he only made it as far as the frame before his legs gave out on him and he slid to the floor. He stared at the wooden slats, unable to comprehend what had just happened.

"You won't make it anywhere unless one of us carries you," Korvin warned, and then he did just that. "Just rest in the back here for a few minutes."

Requiem didn't say anything and kept his face turned away from Korvin, his body stiff. "I apologize for being a burden. Thank you for your assistance," he finally whispered.

"It's fine." Korvin set him down and then put his hands on his hips. "What is this shuttle about?"

Requiem swayed slightly, blinking to try to stay conscious. "It is where I will be able to communicate with...." He swallowed thickly, blinking the tears from his eyes again. "To communicate with my Fighter."

"Ah," Korvin said as if he understood everything. "Just sit here and rest. I'll get you some water."

"Thank you. I will rest for a few moments and then take my leave," Requiem replied as he leaned back against the wall, trying to keep his eyes open.

Korvin turned to talk to Phoenix, but they spoke too softly for Requiem to hear them. The girl left quietly, and Korvin went to get that glass of water.

He really did need to get to the shuttle. He was familiar with the systems already but wanted to get started on a chair similar to the one on the *Ares,* except with a few modifications. He would have to find the tools he needed, but that wouldn't be a problem. Maybe it would keep his mind off the fact that Damion was gone…. Damion was gone…. The reality finally smacked full bore into Requiem's face and he couldn't contain it anymore. Despite his best efforts, a tear leaked from his vacant eyes and trailed down his cheek, only to be followed by another.

"You look like shit. Do you need medical?" Korvin pulled up a chair and sat next to Requiem. "Here's the water."

"I do not need medical attention. I am acceptable," Requiem stated in a shaky voice, taking the water with an even shakier hand. He sipped at it gingerly, trying not to spill it on himself after he swiped at his leaking eyes with the back of his hand. It didn't help—the tears just kept coming.

"It's okay to be sad, to miss him." Korvin folded his hands together. "Most Cores are happy when their Fighters leave or are killed, but in your case it's better just to let it out."

"Let what out?" Requiem took his red-rimmed eyes from the wall across from him to look at Korvin.

"Just cry, let it out." Korvin gave Requiem a rueful smile. "This is the hard part about feeling, and it's a fucking bitch to deal with. That is why some go mad."

"I think I may be doing so as well." Requiem put the back of his hand to his mouth as the end of his words ended in a hiccupping sob. And then he couldn't control it anymore. It was as if a dam had broken and he couldn't find the valve to shut it off. The tears spilled from his eyes and his chest hurt. He was unable to catch a breath. He buried his face in his hands and involuntarily bent over so his arms rested on his knees as he sobbed.

One to usually shy away from any human contact, Requiem barely even noticed when Korvin placed a warm hand on his shoulder or that the man took his cup. He was lost in a world of his own pain, anguish, fear, and loneliness. He felt lost and directionless, even if he wasn't truly. He had a direction, he had a purpose—and that was watching over Damion. But for the moment, nothing made sense. Requiem's north star was gone, and he felt as if his compass was as well. The only thing he could feel was pain. Pain from his heart, his stomach, and his pounding head, which had only gotten worse from his sobs. And eventually what both Korvin and Phoenix predicted came true. Even with his eyes closed, the grayness in his vision closed in, turning black, and Requiem knew no more as his injuries and exhaustion took over.

Chapter Seventeen

Damion

IT WAS approximately three hours to where Damion and Jasper's path would intersect with the *Zeus*. After Requiem's adjustments, the *Ares* moved at a fairly good clip even with one engine down. There was silence within the ship, the only sound being the occasional beep of instruments and the hum of the one remaining engine. Jasper sat in Requiem's chair, the only other seat besides Damion's own. He had turned it around on its axis so he could see out beyond Damion into space.

"Athena will make sure your Broken is safe. She'll protect him as her own," the president said to finally break the silence. His voice was still the normal calm and placid tone, but slightly tinged in pain from his own injuries.

"Were you born with that gift to blow smoke up people's ass?" Damion grumbled. "She will make sure he's safe as long as she needs him."

"No, I wasn't born with it. But it did come naturally. It's served me well since my son was taken from me." Jasper leaned back in Requiem's chair. Damion noticed Jasper was taller than Requiem, so the chair wasn't completely comfortable, but it served its purpose. "You truly think she'll harm him? When she's proven continuously that she has a soft spot for Cores, which is only strengthened by the evidence of the number she has on her ship?"

"Look, everyone gets their panties in a twist, but I don't usually fucking trust anyone." Damion took in a deep breath. "Now it's not a matter of if I think she'll hurt him or kill him. I just don't trust that if it's between Requiem and her ship, she'd still protect him. I trust him and no one else. No offense, President. It's all about protecting your own, and I can't protect him if I am a galactic year away."

"Please, call me Jasper for now. I never liked being called president," Jasper replied, staring out at the moon they were passing by. "You're right if you think she'll choose her ship over your Broken. But then again, she'd choose her ship over herself. She feels responsible for every single person on her ship. Sacrificing one life to save all the others is not a question to her." He paused for a moment. "You do not believe your Broken can take care of himself?"

"He will fight to the death to stay alive." Damion had a dark grin on his face. "I just don't want to put him in that position again. You think you'll find your son?"

"Again? It's happened before?" Jasper let out a long sigh, his eyes switching to stare at the hatch. "I hope so. And I continue to hope even when others have told me not to."

Damion turned to look at the older man. "Your wife on the pirate side as well?"

"My wife died a year after Jaz was born. There was a global epidemic on Saturn that struck one out of every thousand people. She was one of those who contracted it." Jasper's voice was rough and held no political authority, only heartache. "Right after that, since I was just getting into politics and had the opportunity, I moved Jaz and me to Earth. He was taken a few years later."

"Will you even recognize him if you do see him?" Damion asked, a bit doubtful that the child would look the same.

"I've had an aging composition done several times over the years. They are 99 percent accurate." The president arched his back and reached into his back pocket. He pulled out a small holo-frame and handed it to Damion. The first picture was of a young boy smiling with the unabashed glee and innocence that all children had. "The first one was captured just before he was taken. The rest of them are compositions up until his current age." He leaned back in the chair.

Damion paled as he looked at the picture, his eyes widening the longer he looked at the composite. "Depends... I mean maybe."

Jasper never noticed, too intent on staring at the ceiling and not hearing the catch in Damion's voice. "Maybe? So you don't know? I find pictures very important for recording memories."

"If he was turned into a Core, like you think, he probably wouldn't even remember you or his real name... right?" Damion felt his very sore jaw ache a bit more. "What would you do? Try to steal him?"

"More than likely, he would not. They took him late in life for a Core, so they would have done a complete wipe. I would like to think that some part of him would recognize me, but I doubt it." Jasper's tone was sorrowful, and he closed his eyes, swallowing thickly. "As for what I would try to do... I've been trying to figure that out for the longest time. More than likely, I would take him. Have the chip removed, wean him off the stims, and try to build back the life we had. I know he would never be the same sweet boy that I knew him to be. But he's still my son."

He paused. "Why do you ask? Wouldn't you do the same if 47 suddenly didn't recognize you? If he was abruptly taken from you and you found him and knew you had to take him back? To free him?"

"He was wiped once while we were on *Zeus*." Damion felt an old deep anger resurface. "It felt like I had lost him."

"You didn't actually lose him. You could still see him, touch him, speak to him," Jasper said. "What did you do?"

Damion chuckled. "Let's say it's a technique that shouldn't be used with family members."

Damion would have to take another long look at 108 before he jumped to conclusions. How could 108 be this Jaz? How could the president or Athena's other operatives not uncover it in all these years?

"What do you... oh...." Jasper cleared his throat as he sat up, looking at the holo in Damion's hand before reaching out for it. "Yes, I don't suppose it would be." He paused for another moment as he took the holo, a sad look in his eyes before he turned it off and put it back in his pocket. "I've never seen a closer connection between Core and Fighter before," Jasper said, and it was obvious to Damion that Jasper was trying to get the topic off his son.

"Really? I guess I've just never seen the Cores as anything but humans. It's gotten me in deep shit too," Damion said as he leaned forward. "We should be able to start sending out our signal."

"You're avoiding the topic. That's fine. I understand. I'm probably not your favorite person right now," Jasper stated quietly. "We're still an hour from the cross zone, but now would be good. Would give the illusion that we've been trying to get in contact for a while."

"The Commander is going to try to throw me in the brig." Damion sighed as he initiated the distress signal. "What is this promotion? Will I ever get to fly again?"

"The Commander will not throw you in the brig," the president replied in a voice that didn't leave any room for argument. "You'll be promoted to captain, which gives you full access to the *Zeus*. Nothing will be closed to you. And if it is, you have every right to find out what's behind the closed doors. You'll have to act like you have a personal vendetta against the rebels for killing your Core." He paused again, listening to the distant sound of the signal. "Would you want to fly again? You would need a new Core to do so. The only ones who fly with your skill are Alphas. All others are considered cannon fodder. I could red flag you to be able to be chosen by a new Core if you wish."

Damion winced and hoped Requiem wasn't hearing them. "Never mind. I'm going to be a shitty captain, but my dad will be happy."

"I guess taking a new Core, however temporarily, is not an option? It might actually be a good cover for seemingly getting over losing 47." Jasper shrugged. "I think you'll do well in the position. You were always a rising star. The Commander merely stifled your ability."

Damion was not certain how the Commander had stifled him. Requiem had been a paradox of a Core. A coveted pariah. The Commander had given them only a few opportunities to fly. The trouble was, in the short time he piloted the *Ares* with Requiem they showed how efficient they were as a team. His once simple dream of being a pilot, living in the big ship, being respected by both his Alphas and family was all gone. There had been no long years together. No true great battles. Only confusion, espionage, pain, betrayal, and change.

"If I take a new Core, what will I do with him?" Damion shook his head. "I mean, when we finally do get to go back, I couldn't just leave him behind either, and it would complicate things between me and Requiem. I am going to miss flying, and I'm not sure if I'm up to all you think I am, but I have never backed down from a challenge in my life."

"We are in the business of liberating Cores, Hawk. If possible, you would bring him with you when you leave, and Lizzy would remove his chip." Jasper's gray eyes flicked over Damion's form as Damion made some adjustments to their trajectory. "You really do care for Requiem, don't you? I didn't truly believe it at first, perhaps because I've seen so many Cores abused by their Fighters. I thought that perhaps it was an act you played to keep him loyal and complacent. But it isn't, is it? You care for him, perhaps love him."

"I'm truly fucked. I probably am in love, but I never fancied myself as the monogamous type. Then throw in that I won't even see him for months or more, and when I do, he won't be the same Core or man I left." Damion winced and held his side.

"He will still be the same person. With more emotions, yes. Hopefully less naive. But for lack of a better word, the core of him will still be the same person." Jasper watched him carefully. "Or are you afraid that he'll change into someone more independent? Someone who won't have to rely on you as much as he does?"

"He's never really needed me since he made it years on his own before I came along. But yeah, he might change his mind." Damion cursed. "My ribs are hurting again. You won't be on the *Zeus* the entire time with me?"

"Yes, he survived for years of being forced to choose Fighters he didn't want, experimented on, beaten, and I'm sure raped. Sounds like he took really good care of himself," Jasper replied in a flat tone and then sighed, switching subjects. "The shot that Lizzy gave you must have worn off by now. I'm sorry to say I don't have any more. And no, I will only be there for perhaps a day or so before I have to go back to politics. I'm sure they've already begun an uprising and are trying to put someone in my place."

"Great, then I'll be left with the Commander," Damion grumbled. "Maybe flying again would be a good idea. Only so I don't kill him too fast."

"What about as a trainer for those up-and-coming Alpha Fighters? You would need your own Core, of course, but it would give you an opportunity to make sure those new Fighters treated their Cores humanely. In the end, it's up to you. You'll have to try to gain the Commander's trust in some small way. We both know that he won't ever trust you completely. But just enough to get him off your back."

"If I want him to trust me, I'll need to treat the Cores like shit. Or I could help him get promoted or laid." Damion made a disgusted face.

Jasper clenched his teeth. "The Commander has no trouble getting sex. He's the one who samples the Cores first. Those he sells, that is."

The president glared out at space for a few moments, his normally calm face flashing with hatred. "In retrospect, it's probably not wise for you to take a Core. Especially if you're going to be in communication with 47. He's different than other Cores. His loyalty was to you first, and then to the Creators. Another Core would report all suspicious activity, and you know for a fact that the Creators would be suspicious of you."

"Instead of flying, I'll be spying." Damion wasn't angry, just lost. He was always so sure of things, but Requiem had his mind muddled and he was going to be doing work he had no idea how to do. He needed to investigate his hunch about 108 being the president's son. What a mess. "I hope when they pick us up, they give me a shot."

"More than likely we'll immediately be taken to medical and then give our reports. You don't have to lie about anything you saw on the Titan, so don't worry about it. I'll corroborate that no matter how much they tortured you, you didn't give anything up, and instead just continuously mocked and cursed your interrogators. You don't even have to lie about how 47 died. Just about the part where we brought him back. You can even say we made sure he was dead and that the chip wouldn't do any damage or track him by shooting him in the back of the head. Any number of things." Jasper paused to shift in his chair, wincing at the movement. "I believe you'll do fine. If I didn't, you wouldn't be here."

"Right, well at least the Commander will be happy to hear Requiem's dead." Damion thought about it. "Maybe if I sound happy, he'll trust me."

"After you got in so much trouble and fought so hard to protect him? That would be out of character. No, act normal, as if you really would if he had died. Even say that you killed some of ours in revenge. But more out of anger that you lost your ample supply of sex, as opposed to your lover. Emotional disconnection might be good."

Damion raised his hand and touched the side of his jaw. "That creepy woman should have given me more drugs." He hissed as a headache began. He was determined to just act like himself because it was what he was best at. And he was really pissed about the loss of his sexual outlet, even though, of course, that wasn't all Requiem was to him.

"Who the fuck do they have on the comm systems today?" Damion cursed. "I swear when I get to be captain, I will have them scanning for distress signals for days straight. They probably have some stupid back birth son of a bi—"

"Unmarked Fighter, verify your ship's identification code," a voice demanded out of the comm.

"I... I'm." Damion stared at his comm for a moment until his brain caught up to his mouth. "My Core's dead, I don't know the damn codes. This is Fighter *Ares* from flagship *Zeus*."

"Well now's your chance to find out who it is," the president said, amused.

There was a short pause on the other end of the comm. "This is *Zeus*. We thought you were dead, *Ares*. There's been no signal for five days. What is your name and class for verification? What is your status?"

"Alpha Damion Hawk, and I was getting my ass kicked by pirates the last five days. I also have the president with me, so immediate help is needed." He turned and cussed as his ribs pulled. "Don't you have some emergency line per a certain secret code?"

"You have the president with you! When the *Olympus* came back without him, we thought that he had been assassinated." There was a brief pause, and voices could be heard in the background. "Four Fighters are coming to retrieve you. ETA approximately twenty-three minutes. Welcome home, Alpha *Ares*. Good to hear you survived."

"Fuck, if I knew it would just take that, I would have said it first," Damion grumbled. "You knew that would happen?"

"It's not the first time I've been on a disabled ship. But it's the first time I wasn't sure whether or not they would blow us to space dust to get rid of me. It's a positive sign that they didn't," Jasper replied as he lay back down in Requiem's chair.

"Positive sign? What? You were risking us getting blown to hell?" Damion's voice went up an octave.

"It was more of a risk if you traveled by yourself," Jasper pointed out in an unconcerned tone. "And don't yell, you'll strain your ribs and lungs."

"Thanks for the advice." Damion clenched his teeth, really wishing he could be around one person who didn't hold things back.

"Then don't make it worse. Rest. We still have about a half an hour before your friends get here. The real test will be after that." Jasper closed his eyes, as if he were going to live by example.

Damion thought about complaining but stopped with the knowledge that soon he was going to be asked a lot of questions and he needed to come up with the answers. Taking Jasper's advice, he leaned back in his seat and put his feet up on the console, trying to get comfortable while they waited for their pick up. He knew that it was likely the last time he would be able to rest for a long time. Life was about to become even more interesting—and dangerous.

Friday, October 28, 455 MC
2133 GMT
In the battered Ares, approaching the Zeus

ARIANA is a full-time working single mother with a love of chai tea lattes. When Ariana is not working or raising two amazing children, she is plotting with her co-author. Ariana has been in the medical field for eighteen years and has a love of travel. She daydreams most of the plots of the T.A. novels—daily, hourly, nonstop, which drives TC nuts at times.

TC is a full-time cat mom with a background in theatrical carpentry. TC has traveled outside the USA to multiple countries & 47 states within the US. The main headliner in regards to editing and keeping their writing in order as well as trying to untangle all of A's random ideas. T.C. lives in Florida with her amazing parents & beloved kitties. She's been battling Sjogren's Disease while drinking coffee and kicking ass. She is always happy to speak to those who are also battling Sjogren's Disease or those who have questions about the second most common autoimmune disease in the world. For those that have questions, need advice, or just need to talk to someone with the disease, you can contact T.C. at pirate. carpenter@gmail.com

The duo has been writing unprofessionally for ~~nearly~~ over two decades together and hopes to share their beloved characters and stories with the world.

Website: chrysaliscorporation.net
Facebook: www.facebook.com/chrysaliscorp
Twitter: T.A. Venedicktov
Email: 29hogtiedmuses@gmail.com

T.A. VENEDICKTOV

CHRYSALIS CORPORATION

Chrysalis Corporation: Book One

Together, they can change the rules of the galaxy and the definition of humanity.

When Damion Hawk is offered an opportunity to escape the destitute life of a miner on Mars and become an elite Alpha Fighter pilot, he jumps at the chance. Within the Chrysalis Corporation, Damion must learn to work with his Core—a man with computerized implants, no human emotions—and no rights. But unlike other Fighters, Damion can't treat Core 47 as a tool. He sees 47 as more than a machine, and he'll take deadly risks to help 47 find the humanity inside him.

Fighters and Cores are designed to work together and enhance each other's strengths in defense of their employer. Damion and 47 will need each other's support as suspicions about the all-powerful Chrysalis Corporation arise. Someone wants Damion and 47 gone, and they need to find out who and why while hiding 47's growing emotions and the love forming between them. If they can succeed, they might save not only themselves, but all Cores enslaved by the Corporation.

www.dsppublications.com

CPSIA information can be obtained
at www.ICGtesting.com
Printed in the USA
JSHW021024270920
8258JS00005B/77

9 781644 056271